DEADLAND 2
IMMORTAL

T0344645

PAUL MANNERING

PERMUTED
PRESS

A PERMUTED PRESS BOOK

ISBN: 978-1-68261-555-3

Deadland 2:
Immortal
© 2018 by Paul Mannering
All Rights Reserved

Cover art by Christian Bentulan

PERMUTED
PRESS

Permuted Press, LLC
New York • Nashville
permutedpress.com

Published in the United States of America

PART I

PART 1

CHAPTER 1

It started raining a month ago, the first downpour sending tiny rivulets through the red dust of the Australian Outback. The trickles merged into streams, which ran to flooded creeks, which became thundering rivers. The growing torrent washed away everything in its path. Dead trees, trapped boulders, carefully built fences and barricades, all now lay strewn along creek beds still stained ocher with the desert silt.

When the rain stopped the heat of the desert sun sent the water soaking into the earth. Humid mists rose through the trees and scrub as a man, his clothes smeared dark with dirt and filth, staggered towards a groaning chorus of alarm. The trees that stood around the high-water mark now wore tutu-skirts of grass and branches torn from the ground-up soil. The man passed through the trees and blinked with near blind eyes at the long depression beyond.

The flood had torn the bottom out of the creek bed, gouging the hard clay until the low banks now stood ten feet high. A water-filled pit ran for nearly a hundred feet to where an ancient bedrock boulder lay as it had for a million years, making a natural barrier above the new stream. In the hole behind the rock a crowd had gathered. They had fallen, one by one, down the slick clay sides of the stream. Now they moved like sheep, bumping into each other, moving in a slow tide from one end of the hole to the other. Each walker was a desiccated and torn corpse walking in constant, mindless confusion.

The man hesitated at the edge. Moaning, he shuffled back and forth, the calls of the others luring him closer, the strange geometry of the hole keeping him back.

With the clumsy imprecision of the dead, the man worked his way through a turn that put his back to the pit. The maneuver took some time, and the angry moans of the trapped zombies behind him never ceased. The sun had moved in the sky by the time he returned to the road that was no more than a sunbaked strip overgrown with the shifting desert sands. It disappeared into the dust that led from the ruins of the coastal cities far to the south to peter out among the salt brush and ghost gum trees of the northern interior.

The dead man walked with no destination in mind. Hunger drove his feet, and the rustle of bushes, the stirring of dust, and the flight of small animals caught his attention. Where his gaze fell, his feet followed as surely as the rest of him. Over time, others walked with him, the shuffling movement of his walk reminding them of something they could no longer recall or understand. Hunger was the only constant now.

The house stood in the dappled shade of the Queensland rainforest. It had been built from rough, hand-sawed gum tree planks, the cracks and gaps between the lumber slabs packed with wattle and mud daub. A roof of freshly cut wooden shingles kept the recent rains at bay. Next to the house a cow stood in the shade of a bark-roofed stall, chewing her cud, her swollen udder twitching as she flicked flies away with her tail.

The feet of the walking dead didn't bleed even though several of his toes were gone. They'd been torn off as the dead flesh of his feet broke down on the long walk along hundreds of miles of broken highways and rough ground. The cow lowed as the shambling zombie approached. The noise cut through the dead man's senses and he moaned in pain. Turning towards the cow, he raised his hands and all confusion left him. He needed to kill the source of that sound.

Else stood naked, up to her hips in a natural spring-fed pool. Silt stirred up with every step she took, giving the water the color and consistency of chicken soup. She lifted her hands and let the liquid trickle down over her swollen belly, watching fascinated as the baby cradled in her womb writhed and kicked in response to the cool touch.

She felt confident that she could give birth unaided; women had been doing that for more years than she could imagine. Every book she read on the subject made it seem like a natural thing. Pregnancy took nine months, the medical texts said, and it had been 254 days since the Courier died. She counted from that day, having no other day to count from.

"Soon," she murmured, stroking her distended stomach. "Soon we will meet and I will teach you everything."

Mona Lisa screamed and Else's head jerked up, every sense alert for danger. She moved to the edge of the small pool; gathering her clothes from the edge she dressed in moments, pulling a loose dress over her head and checking her rifle with practiced ease. Slipping a razor-sharp machete on a belt over her shoulder, she ducked into the trees that led to her small house in the bush.

The Courier had called the undead *evols*, an old acronym made of the words "Extremely Violent Lucid Organism." They never travel alone. They follow each other with the same lack of purpose that has guided all their actions since the destruction of the source of the virus that created them, a genetically engineered organism called Adam. The dead man tearing at Mona Lisa was joined by others emerging from the tree line. They came forward, drawn by the cow's painful bellows, the smell of freshly spilled blood, and the thrashing of the dying animal.

The dead swarmed over the carcass. Blackened teeth tore at the warm meat. Fingers clawed and gouged. Their mouths opened wide and they gulped down the succulent feast.

Else took a count of their numbers, twelve of them, seven males and five females, their dry, grey skin hanging in paper-thin strips. Bones, stained the color of lead, poked through the rips and holes. Cow's blood oozed from torn throats, and chunks of chewed meat fell from the empty space below one woman's rib cage. All but one of them appeared long dead. The fresh walker fought savagely for the best access to the feeding. Shoving the others aside, he burrowed inside the dripping carcass and gorged on the soft tissues inside.

Else raised her rifle, flicked the safety off, and took a bead down the sights. She squeezed the trigger and the first zombie's head exploded. The corpse tottered and fell. Else moved as soon as the weapon fired. The weight of her pregnant belly barely slowed her down, and she ignored the sudden urge to urinate. The evols grunted in confusion at the sound of the shot, their senses still overwhelmed by their feeding frenzy. The second zombie fell to a bullet that tore through her eye and sprayed her blackened brain matter over the others, who slowly began to respond to this new threat.

Else worked the bolt on the rifle, firing in a steady rhythm until six corpses lay still on the ground. With the dead almost upon her, she slung the gun over her shoulder before drawing her machete and stepping forward. She noticed the dead always moved aimlessly until they fed. Now their Adam virus–infected brains were energized with fresh nutrients and their pace and reflexes quickened to almost match her own.

The first zombie to reach her was a woman. Stained remnants of a business skirt and blouse hung from her in ragged strips. Something had ripped chunks of her hair out by the roots. It might have snagged on branches during her long journey from her George Street office building in Sydney to the wild rain forests of northern Queensland.

The machete flashed; the office woman's throat oozed black

fluid and her head slowly slid sideways off her neck. Else moved on. The next one sprang at her, teeth bared and fingers spread wide. She twisted away from his first attack, swinging the blade down to cut through the vertebrae and send the corpse quivering to the ground.

"Twenty-four articulated bones, not one long one," she said aloud and spun to face the next evol. A woman who had been disemboweled long ago lunged into range. The virus took control of the brain, and as long as the central nervous system remained intact, the dead remained animated.

"Destroy the brain, and they stay down." Else often spoke out loud to the unborn child in her womb. The books said it helped with development. She found it eased her loneliness.

With a wild swing the machete blade tore the top off another woman's skull at the bridge of her nose.

The dead moved to surround her, responding to some predatory instinct, working together to bring down their prey. Else turned to face them. She hacked off a reaching arm and ducked under the other hand that swept at her face. The machete slashed. A head rocked back, attached only by a thin sliver of skin. It fell like a hood against a dead man's back.

Else bared her teeth as clawed fingers grabbed at her dress and hair. She yanked herself free and stepped back, swinging the machete at the hungry dead. Raising the blade to her shoulder like a baseball bat she readied herself for the next attack.

A sudden spasm ripped through her belly and her knees buckled. Gasping in pain, the machete tip dropped and buried itself in the ground. "Not now," Else whispered through the rippling spasm. "Just a Braxton Hicks, not a real con—*unnngghhh*." Her stomach felt like it was tearing open. The remaining zombies snarled and crowded forward. Else sank to one knee and thrust the machete upwards. The evol's skull, more bone than flesh, cracked against the blade. With a savage howl Else shoved harder; the bone burst and the machete jutted out through the top of his skull. The zombie's eyes crossed and it slumped to the ground, dragging the blade out of Else's hands. She staggered to her feet, the ungainly weight of her abdomen pulling her off balance. Unslinging the rifle, she loaded a single round from the ammo belt she wore into the chamber. Shoving the muzzle into the hole where the dead woman's nose used to be, Else pulled the trigger. The head came apart and the zombie dropped, knocking the rifle barrel down.

"Fuckers!" Else hissed. With her hand flat like a knife, she punched a man in the throat. Using her fingers, she burrowed through the gel of his putrescence and grabbed the bones of his neck. With a snarl she ripped his head off. Gripping the heavy skull like a bowling ball, she clubbed the next evol into the ground, striking him again and again until both skulls shattered and the man on the ground twitched and lay still.

Her breath came in panting gasps as Else twisted, her feet sliding on the gore-slicked mud. Nothing moved now except the flies that crawled over Mona Lisa's remains. Else wondered how she was going to get rid of the body. She might have to find a vehicle, or a horse, maybe two horses to drag it down to the river. The crocodiles would take it from there.

She returned to the house in the trees. She had repaired it, patched the walls and the roof. Strengthened the door and fixed the fences. There were only two rooms when she found it, now it had three, a library and storeroom making up the extension.

The door had started sticking since the rains came. She put her shoulder against it and shoved, almost overbalancing as it popped open and she half-fell inside. Another contraction rippled through her and she felt wetness flood down her thighs.

Fear gripped Else. Maybe something was wrong. The pain she was feeling seemed worse than the books suggested. Leaning back against the door she breathed through the spasm, clenching and unclenching her fists. Sliding the bolts home, she secured the door.

The interior walls of the house were covered in hanging tools. Handmade shelves held collected tins of food, and a sheaf of rifles were stacked together in one corner.

The bed had been here when Else arrived, a skeletonized body lying on it. She had wrapped the bones in a blanket and carried them to the river.

She focused her gaze on her books. They were stacked high in every available space of the three-room hut. Books on every subject, two nonfiction books for every novel. She had read them all and until recently her main scavenging trips had been to find new reading material. The baby would learn to read too.

Else slid the heavy wooden bar across the door and moved carefully across the room to set the rifle down with the other weapons. She would clean it just as soon—

Another contraction rippled through her and she panted with the force of it. Gripping the edge of the water-stained sink stand, she stood almost doubled over and tried to collect her thoughts. *Breathe. Just breathe, the way the books taught you. Get the clean cloths ready, the ones to wrap the baby in. And the sharp knife. To cut the umbilical cord. Just keep breathing.* Memories of the Courier came to her mind. She needed him now, more than ever. Everything else she had come through. She had found a way. Learned through trial and error and reading books. But not this. This she didn't want to go through alone. She laid out the soft muslin and blanket for the baby. She found the sharp knife and put the pot of water on the fire to boil. Finally she pulled her loose dress up over her head and stood naked and shivering in the sudden chill of the late afternoon.

Distant thunder rolled and a stronger contraction tore through her. "Fuck," Else moaned and staggered against the bed. The fire kept the interior of the house warm, and she lifted the pot of boiling water from its hook and poked the knife blade into the hot liquid. The contractions were coming steadily now, less than a minute apart.

Crawling, she reached the bed. Resting her face against the soft blankets that draped over it, she panted, riding out the contractions. She remained kneeling against the bed covers, her knees on the floor, as the sun went down and the air grew cold with an approaching storm. The wind came first, buffeting the trees and the small house. The monsoon rain hit a minute later, a wall of water that had terrified Else when it first poured out of the sky. She reminded herself that the hut was waterproof and strong. The wind went round it and the rain slid down the wooden shingles. There were no trees close enough to blow down on the house.

Else panted and breathed, relaxing when she could. Still kneeling beside the low bed, her head and shoulders supported by the bedding. It just felt right to be in that position. A great sense of pressure filled her lower abdomen; the pain was unlike anything she had experienced before. With each contraction she moaned and pushed downwards with her entire body. The sense of pressure and pain grew. The thunder crashed and lightning split the sky directly overhead. Else groaned and an answering groan sounded outside. She lifted her head and stared at the door.

Not now. Come back tomorrow. Tonight, I'm busy giving birth. Else bit down on the blanket, tears welling in her eyes as an evol shuffled against the door.

"Breathe," she whispered. "The door is strong, you are strong, and the baby is strong." The door shuddered under a heavy blow. "Fuck off," Else muttered, closing her eyes and pushing hard. She had to do this, for the baby. Nothing else mattered right now. The dead would not have her child.

The storm drove the dead into a frenzy. Each roar of thunder and eye-searing flash of lightning overwhelmed their senses. Else knew they had no filters, no protection from the stimulus of their sensitive ears and eyes. Being dead destroyed a lot of the brain. Being infected and dead meant what was left drove you to walk, feed, and infect others.

Sweat ran down Else's face. Every muscle clenched and she bore down with a long, low moan. Something slipped deep inside her. With a wet slithering sound a wet lump emerged from between her legs. Reaching down, Else cupped a hand around the tiny head and shoulders. With a final push the baby sluiced out of her and into her hands.

Laughing through a sudden upwelling of tears, Else lifted the tiny form up to her chest. A quick scan satisfied her that everything was correct. The baby, a boy she realized with heart-clenching delight, wriggled in her hands and began to cry with a shrill mewling sound. The evols outside crashed against the door and the walls. Else ignored them and laid her son down on the bed. Taking the knife from the hot water, she cut the umbilical cord where it joined the baby's abdomen and tied the oozing stump off with a piece of string. Smiling down at the tiny, yet perfect human, she wrapped him tightly in a muslin sheet and small blanket she had prepared.

The contractions continued, but the thrill of seeing her son for the first time left her immune to this lesser pain. "It's just the placenta, the final stage of labor," she spoke to him the way she always had, explaining everything as if he had asked a question. Gathering the baby up, she held him to her breast. Getting him into position for real was harder than she thought. He mewled and nuzzled but didn't latch on.

"You have to suck, baby. It's what makes the milk come."

The scratching at the door continued. Fingers pressed under the door and around the slight gap where the bar held it closed. The sounds of a grunting argument came through the wood and then the fingers withdrew. A moment later a loud crash shook the hut. The door shuddered and cracked. Silence for a moment and then another impact. This one burst the door from its hinges and sent it flying against the far wall.

Evols crowded through the space, snarling and snapping at each other as they pushed their way inside. The first two dropped to their knees and smeared their fingers and faces in the fresh blood and fluids pooled on the wooden floor, slurping and sucking the nutrient-rich goo off the boards. The others stumbled around, confused by the empty room.

CHAPTER 2

Else clutched the crying baby to her naked chest and hurried through the trees. A hatch in the back wall of the hut meant she always had a second exit, as the place had no windows. There had been no time to dress, and the wind-driven rain had her shivering as she splashed through puddles with numb feet. The thunder crashed and the lightning came close on its heels. Every flash blinded her night vision, and the branches and deadfall slashed at her bare skin. She could hear the river over the approaching storm. The rushing chatter of the rising flood was loud enough to keep her bearing in the right direction. Else broke through the trees, the ground underfoot turned to sucking mud. She struggled through it, balancing the baby in one arm and trying to keep him out of the rain and wind.

A hand lashed out of the darkness and she fell back, twisting the baby away from the evol and dragging herself away through the mud. In the next flash she saw the wide space of river mud was littered with struggling corpses.

Grabbing a branch from the muck, she leaned on it and probed the ground ahead. The wind tore at her hair and the mud scraped up to her knees. Leaning forward, she pulled her feet one at a time out of the mire. The evols trapped in the mud reached out to her, groaning in desperate need. Else ignored them.

The boat was tied up out there, on the other side of the mudflats.

She'd gotten turned around somewhere along the way and come out too far downstream. Her usual route took her through the trees to the edge of the river. There was no going back now—the moans of zombies had brought others to the edge of the trees. In the brief flash of the lightning's glow she could see the dark shapes of others coming up behind her.

Using the stick and moving carefully between the thrashing zombies, Else made her way across the mud. The baby, cradled in one arm, had managed to latch onto her breast and she felt the strong tugging sensation of his first suckling.

"I'm glad you can think about food at a time like this," she murmured to him.

An evol reared up out of the mud. Else jerked the stick back and stabbed it through the throat with the broken end. Twisting it, she forced the stake deep into the dead man's neck and bore down on the branch until the zombie shuddered and lay still. Pulling her stick free she waded on. The packed mud near the river was firmer, and in the lightning flashes she could see the wide, slick smears where crocodiles had slid into the water.

Turning up stream, Else could see the trees where the boat would be tied. She had checked it that morning and even the recent flooding hadn't torn it free from its moorings. They made good time along the mud bank. The baby had gone quiet, cradled against Else's chest; he seemed to be sleeping. Adrenaline kept her going. Adrenaline and an instinctive need to protect the tiny person she carried.

She strode on using the stick to help keep her moving when the ground underfoot jerked. Expecting another evol, Else reared back with the stick raised ready to strike.

A deep, hissing gurgle came from the ground. A large croc twisted and snapped at the end of the stick, biting through it like a breadstick.

Else crouched slightly, legs bent, ready to spring away. The croc turned, its massive head splitting open to reveal a long, pale, triangular mouth rimmed with sharp teeth. With the baby tucked in her arm and the remains of the stick clutched in her other hand like a club, Else hissed and bared her teeth at the croc. Mouth wide, it rushed at her.

Else jumped, landing lightly on the beast's back and sprinting three steps towards its tail. The croc spun and twisted, his heavy tail thrashing with enough force to crush bone. Else jumped again, her feet splashing in the water and she almost fell. The baby mewled and began to wail. The woman turned and faced the croc again as it charged. She threw herself sideways and stabbed down with the short stick. The tip pierced his eye and Else was thrown clear. She went under the water and immediately surfaced again, pushing the shrieking baby up to keep his head above the surface.

The croc went berserk on the mud bank. Writhing and turning, he slapped the mud with his tail. As Else scrambled out, the twelve-foot-long monster slid into the dark water. Leaping to her feet, Else ran along the bank towards the shelter of the trees. The baby cried louder, the water soaking through the blanket now chilling him.

"Shhh baby, it's going to be okay," Else said through chattering teeth. The rain eased a little as they reached the trees. She found the path that led to the boat and hurried along it, both arms cradling the tiny baby to her shoulder.

The boat was little more than a skiff, a flat-bottomed aluminum dinghy that Else had packed with emergency supplies. A shotgun, ammunition, a first aid kit, tinned food, bottled water, a spare machete, and blankets. All tied together under a canvas tarpaulin. She untied the tarp and pulled out the blanket. Stripping the baby, she swaddled him in a fresh, dry cotton blanket and gently set him down in the middle of the skiff. Covering him with the tarp quieted him and the movement of the boat on the high water rocked him to silence. Drawing the machete, she took hold of the mooring rope and hacked it from the tree.

The water next to the skiff erupted as the crocodile, with the stick still buried in his eye, ambushed Else from the water. She swung at it with the machete, burying the heavy blade between the beast's nostrils. The croc flailed and the skiff danced sideways in the wake of his heaving tail.

"No!" Else screamed and leapt to right the boat before it was swamped.

The croc pressed the attack, head slamming from side to side as his jaws snapped at the woman. The stink of blood and the pain in his muzzle sent the croc into a biting frenzy. Desperate to save the baby, Else shoved the skiff out into the river current as the croc lunged at her again. She threw her legs wide to avoid the slamming jaws and scrambled backwards as the massive head slapped down between her thighs.

Something pulled her up short as she struggled to her feet. A sudden tearing pain flaring between her legs. The croc jerked his head back and Else screamed as the placenta came gushing out of her. The croc snapped its jaws, tossing the umbilical cord he had seized and the attached afterbirth down his throat. Dizzy with pain and loss of blood, Else lifted the machete high over her head with both hands and slammed it down, point first, into the croc's skull. It died without a sound.

The skiff spun in the water and was immediately carried out of reach. Else dived, cutting through the water in a fast and desperate stroke, the machete clutched in one hand. She'd taught herself to swim in gentle creeks and still water holes. The flooded river didn't care how well she swam in still water. It threw her down the riverbed, keeping the skiff and her baby in sight, but too far to reach. The flood rapids buffeted Else and trees swept past her in the darkness. She grabbed hold of a floating log as the last of her strength drained away. "Baby..." she croaked into the black sky.

CHAPTER 3

Something wet pressed against Else's face. Her hand punched out and grabbed soft flesh as she jerked awake. She opened her eyes and blinked in the dim light. The Aboriginal man she'd grabbed by the throat made a choking noise and dragged at her hand.

She sat up, tossing the blanket that covered her aside and realizing she couldn't see her baby. Her grip remained vise-like on the guy's trachea. "Where is my baby?" she hissed.

"Hurgh," the man said, his hand desperately waving towards the open door of the tent they were in. The tent flap pulled back and a woman, as dark skinned as the man, ducked inside. A baby was cradled in her arms, waving its tiny naked arms and legs. Else sprang to her feet, letting the man go. He fell to his side coughing and gasping. Else threw herself at the woman and snatched the tiny child from her. She examined every inch of the child and then thrust her back at the woman.

"Found you by the river," the woman said, her voice and expression calm in the face of Else's anger. "Her momma died last night and she's hungry now. Best you feed her, aye? I dried up a long time ago." The woman chuckled, a deep, warm belly sound. "Get up you lazy fella," she scolded the man in the tent. The old woman turned and walked outside again. Else snarled and followed her.

"Where is my baby?" She shouted in the woman's face.

"No baby, just you, missus," the woman said, jigging the little one on her shoulder gently.

"Where is my baby?!"

"This can be your baby now." The old man had come out of the tent and now stood emaciated and hunched behind Else's shoulder. "Gotta look after the living."

"My baby is still alive," Else snarled, her glare shifting from one to the other. "He's out there somewhere. If you don't know where he is, then get the fuck out of my way."

The woman shrugged, "How far you think you're gonna get?" she called as Else strode out across the small encampment.

"I'll keep going until I find him!" Else shouted back. The camp consisted of a cluster of ragged tents, some small fires, and a couple of bone-thin dogs that panted in the shade of a mangrove tree. Dark faces watched her from the tents, all young children and grandparents.

The old woman shook her head. "She's crazy. Them dead fellas will get her," she said to the old man.

"Crocs'll get her first I reckon," he replied, squinting in the bright light of the early afternoon.

"They didn't get her last night, and they were around plenty." The old woman sighed and cuffed him on the shoulder. "Go on then, go help her."

He caught up with Else as she picked her way along the river-bank, through the strewn rubble of tree branches and mud thrown up by the storm of the previous night.

"Hey girl," he wheezed. "You come back with me. We'll get you some water, some food, and some shoes, aye?"

Else hesitated. He was alive out there, she could feel it. Like a deep tugging in her breast and womb. She would know when her baby died. She felt certain of that.

"I gotta find my baby," she said to the dark flowing river.

"We'll find your baby, missy. But you can't go running off like this. You'll die, and we know what that means."

"Yeah," Else said, turning to follow the man back to the camp. "It means others have to die first."

The residents of the camp, from the old man Billy and his wife Sally to the young children with big white smiles and laughing eyes, all wore carefully mended castoffs.

With some help, Else slipped on pants and a shirt that buttoned up the front. "Nothing new anymore," she murmured, pressing her feet into some battered old boots and tying the laces. She took the tiny, squalling girl from Sally and fed her till the baby fell asleep. Afterwards Sally lifted the tiny thing to her shoulder and burped her gently.

"River goes down to the sea." Billy crouched in the dirt and sketched with a gnarled finger. "We be here." He traced a thick snake on the ground. "The sea is here. If your baby's in a boat, then he's gonna keep on going. All the way out to the beach. If he's lucky he's gonna catch up on a log, or run aground. Otherwise, he's gonna go out to sea. No coming back from out to sea."

"He's not out to sea," Else said. "I feel him still. In here," she pressed a hand to her stomach, still swollen and soft.

"Takes a long time for a child to leave you," Sally said softly.

Else scanned the horizon, always watching for the approach of evols. She saw a solitary man, hair plastered grey and skin painted white, with long bloody marks across his chest and arms, standing on the edge of the distant trees. He had one foot pulled up and resting against the side of his knee, making a 4 shape.

"Who's that?" Else asked.

"Jirra. He lost his woman yesterday. She bled out when the baby came. If you gonna feed his baby, mebbe he'll show you the way to the end of the river," Billy said.

"Tell him we need to go. Right now," Else said, glancing around the scattered faces.

"When he's done burying Bindi, then you go."

"The dead can wait," Else said and walked off towards the trees.

Jirra watched her come, this white woman with the long blonde hair. Her breasts and belly heavy, her skin as pale as the ghost of his Bindi. He had sung to his woman as he covered her body on the high platform. Sung to her and told her he would be back when the birds and the sky had taken her flesh. He would be back to lay her bones to rest and remember her spirit.

He had given no thought to their daughter. The grief of losing Bindi blinded him to everything else. He watched the white woman come, seeing the strength in her legs and the determination in her eyes.

Else took a good look at the man standing on one leg as she approached. He had the tightly curled black hair of the other people. His skin under the ash-white paint was dark brown and his eyes shone almost black. He stood, calm and relaxed, one hand curled around a long spear. He wore a ragged pair of shorts and his feet were bare.

"I'm Else and you need to come with me, right now," she said by way of greeting.

"Jirra," he replied. "Where do you think we need to go?"

"My baby boy is alive. But he's out there, down the river somewhere. You need to help me find him."

"Babies die quick without their mothers. Yours is dead," Jirra said. Else's fists clenched. It would not happen. She had already lost someone. Never again.

She narrowed her eyes. "Only your woman is dead. Your baby girl is still alive. I'll keep her alive. You help me find my baby and we both have someone to raise and to love us."

Jirra considered her offer for a moment. "If your boy is dead, then my baby girl is gonna die too. You won't wanna take care of her anymore."

Else stepped forward, her face twisting in anger. "If you don't come with me, I will kill you myself. Right now."

Jirra's calm face regarded Else for a moment, then he walked past her and headed over to the camp.

The sun beat down, evaporating the receding floodwaters into a thick, choking humidity that blocked a body's sweating mechanism and left Else feeling like she was suffocating. She carried the tiny girl-child in a cloth sling against her chest. The baby's father, Jirra, walked ahead, his long legs picking the way through the flood-strewn jetsam like a mudflat feeding bird.

Else carried a full water bag and some food in a wrapped parcel slung over her shoulder. She carried a machete in her hand, ready and watchful for evols, crocodiles, and snakes.

"How long till dark?" Else said to Jirra's back.

"Three hours, maybe four," Jirra said without pausing to look at the sky. He carried a bundle of spears and a woomera spear thrower.

"Where'd you come from, lady?" Jirra asked.

"Sydney."

"Long way from here, aye?" he said.

"Long way. I took a long time to come here. I've been traveling my whole life."

"That's what life is," Jirra said. "A whole lot of traveling."

Else didn't try to explain. She knew she was different from other people. Even Jirra with his near-black skin and his wide face had been born and grown up through the years. He wasn't Tankbread, a vat-grown human clone destined to feed the dead. Else followed Jirra because she needed to find her baby. That small and helpless creature was her legacy. The thing that made her normal, gave her a chance to live a proper life. To be human.

Jirra gathered sticks and speared a couple of fish in the shallows of the river without breaking stride. In the last moments of daylight he crouched at the edge of the riverside trees and made a small fire. Else washed the baby and her damp wrap in river water and then fed her again while the swaddling cloth dried. Jirra sat in a silhouette on the other side of the fire, sharpening the heads on his spears and then scraping a whetstone along the machete's gleaming edge. The fish he had speared now hissed and spat over the small fire.

"You kill many?" Jirra said without lifting his eyes or hand from the blade.

"I kill the ones I have to," Else replied. She wanted to tell him that she almost killed them all. That a man carried her across the world and back again. A man who then gave his life to save them all. But he would ask her what was his name? *What name should we whisper when we remember this hero?* And she wouldn't know what to say.

"We move around," Jirra said. "Like the old people did. Since the end our people are better off. No more alcohol. No more reason to try and be like the white man. Now we remember the old ways again. We sing the old songs. We go on walkabout and we live like the old people did."

"How long did the old people live this way?" Else asked.

"Since the Dreamtime. Since the first people. We have always been here. This is our land." Jirra turned the fish over the fire.

"Now it's the land of the dead," Else said and scanned the darkness again.

"Fish is cooked," Jirra replied.

They ate quickly, sucking the white meat from the fine bones and licking the juice from their fingers.

Jirra buried the remains and covered the fire with sand. Else stood up and led the way into the darkness. The little girl grizzled in the cloth sling around Else's torso.

Jirra started to sing, a soft dirge-like lullaby. The baby stilled and they walked on in the darkness. Only the moonlight and the smear of stars overhead lit their way.

"What do you call her?" Else said.

"Lowanna."

"Does it mean anything?"

"It means girl," Jirra's voice came from behind her. "We just call her girl."

"Lowanna," Else whispered and carried the bundle cradled in her arms a little higher. "Your name is Lowanna."

She tried not to think about her boy. He didn't have a name yet. She would give him one when they found him. She would give him a good name. One that would mean something. A name people would always remember. When she found him she would give him a name.

"How much further?" Else said, her pace quickening over the sandy mud.

"A while yet."

"We have to hurry." She thought she heard something, a baby's cry sounding out there in the mud-brown water.

"Baby!" Else called and started to run. Jirra loped after her, hearing only the cry of a seabird.

"Baby!" Else cried again. The river widened here and she could smell the tang of salt on the air. Leaping over driftwood, she sprinted along the water's edge. A glint of dull metal caught her eye. The moon was bright enough to reflect more than the dull water. As Lowanna grizzled and writhed in the sling, Else dropped to her knees by the overturned skiff. The edge of the boat had pressed into the mud. Else dug at it with desperate hands. Jirra reached her and began to scoop the soft ground away with his digging stick.

"My boat. This is my boat. I can hear him crying. I can hear him!" Else panted as she dug. She snatched the digging stick from Jirra and crawled along the edge, digging frantically.

"There's others here," Jirra said, reading the ground with the eye of a master tracker. "Dead men walked here. Live fellas too. They got boots on and they fought pretty hard with some dead fellas."

"Help me lift it now!" Else snapped from the sand. Her fingers scrabbled under the edge of the boat and strained to pull it free of the mud.

"Wait, missus!" Jirra leapt forward, knocking Else on to her side as the skiff came free. A bloody hand lashed out and snatched Jirra's ankle.

"Shit!" Jirra hissed at the sky. He fell back, one leg caught. Else sprang forward, tipping the boat the right way up to grab her baby. A female evol snarled from the wet sand as Jirra smashed at her head with the butt of his spear. The dead girl growled and tore at his ankle with her teeth.

"Fucking bitch!" Jirra snarled.

"Where's my baby?" Else wailed. She swung the machete down on the dead woman's head, severing it from the neck.

"No…no…no!" Jirra whined. Scrambling backwards, he clambered to his feet on one and foot stared down at the blood oozing from his bitten leg.

"Baby!?" Else screamed. The boat was empty. The baby and all her carefully stored supplies were gone. Only the two paddles remained, tied in position.

"Shit…shit…shit." Jirra sagged and toppled into the boat. "I'm dead, missus," he said. The smoky-yellow whites of his eyes were wide and rolling.

"I need to find my baby," Else said, ignoring Jirra for the moment.

"Fuck your baby," Jirra growled. "This dead cunt fucking ate him!"

"No! Where are the supplies? He was wrapped in a blanket.

Where is the blanket?" Else climbed into the skiff and ran her hands over the empty space, not trusting what her eyes were telling her.

"See now," Jirra said, a grim smile splitting his face. "All that noise and we bring them to us. They come to take us home. Welcome us…"

Else looked up. A group of ten evols had stumbled out of the darkness of the tree line and were now making their way towards them. "Where is my baby!" she howled at them. The line of approaching dead groaned and writhed in response.

"Push the boat out; we can make for the water. They can't get us out there." Jirra pulled himself back into a sitting position at the rear of the skiff.

Else stepped out of the boat and pushed back on it. The skiff slid in the wet sand until the edge of the current tugged at it.

"Come on, get in, aye?" Jirra panted.

"Not without my baby." Else scooped Lowanna out of the sling and carefully put her in the bottom of the skiff. "I'll be back when I find him."

"You're fucking crazy!" Jirra shouted at her.

Else walked up the beach. The machete felt good in her hand. A solid piece of killing steel. She scanned the dead faces in front of her. With over twenty-five million zombies in Australia the chances were slim, but she looked each one in the eye, and still all of them were strangers.

"Let's get this done," she said to the advancing line. The first one reached for her, his blind eyes scarred by the scouring of wind-blown sand.

Else swung her blade. It tore through the dead man's head, splitting him between his gaping jaws. She moved on as he fell, spinning and using her momentum to tear the next rotting head from its shoulders. There were those among them that had not been dead for so long. Their clothes were cleaner. Their dead flesh showed little signs of the ravages of the elements. They were all hungry. They came down on Else with savage snarls and raking claw-like hands. She hacked an arm off, then blocked a grasping hand and shoved the tip of the machete into a gaping maw that bled black.

An evol caught her hair, dragging her head back. Else dropped to one knee and slammed the machete up and over her shoulder. The end of it buried in a zombie's chest. He looked down, releasing her and tugging at the steel now sticking out of him. Else jerked the blade free and took his head. The dead pressed closer, mindless of each other and everything except for their need to tear at the warm, wet meat they could almost taste. Dark drool oozed from the mouths of the fresher ones. The older dead had little moisture left in their bodies.

Else rolled to her feet, kicking at a zombie who tried to bite her leg. Her booted foot crushed his nose and smeared it into a black paste across his rotting cheek. A girl with lobotomy eyes gaped at Else. The little control she had over her dead limbs made them thrash aimlessly. Else smashed her face into the sand. The back of the girl's head was a gaping crater, half of her brain already gone.

In the moment it took Else to straighten up, a man with black and broken teeth bit into her sleeve, narrowly missing her skin under the loose shirt. With the machete blocked in her right fist, Else punched her fingers into the eyes above the biting mouth. The grey orbs burst, sending stinking pus spraying out. The man moaned, his head thrashing, tearing the cloth away from her arm. Else snarled and shoved the zombie's head back.

Dropping the machete, she kicked upwards, catching the back of the heavy blade on her booted foot and sending it flying up to within reach of her other hand. With three hard blows she hacked the evol's skull into chunks. Panting, she circled slowly. The sand was thick with black slime and broken bodies. Nothing moved. Else took stock—the fresh corpses were all dressed the same. Frowning, she searched them. They carried odd possessions: seashells and bullets, keys and colored tags. They all had the same tattoos on their arms that Else recognized as an anchor with a lightning cloud above it.

Hacking an arm off, she carried it back to the boat.

"Jirra," she said. "You know what this means?"

Jirra opened his eyes. His breath came in shallow pants. "I can't see..." he whispered. Else leaned over and let the black blood drip down Jirra's chest as she held it close to his clouded eyes.

"Sea People..." Jirra whispered. "Sea People. They come in boats. Sometimes they trade. Mostly they take."

"Could they have taken my son?" Else tossed the severed arm into the water.

"Coulda." Jirra tried to shrug.

"Where do I find the Sea People?"

Jirra moaned, his eyes rolling. Else slapped him hard across the face. "Where, Jirra? Where are they?"

"Big boat...like a cloud on the water...out there on the sea."

Else stood up and stared out into the darkness. She could hear the hiss of the waves. The books told her the sea went all around the world. She wondered if there was any place free of evols.

Gathering Jirra's dropped spears, she laid them in the boat next to him and the wailing baby. Else pushed the boat out and climbed in. Dropping the machete in the bottom of the boat, she took up a paddle and steered the boat into the current. The river grabbed them, driving them towards the sea.

"Help me paddle!" Else yelled over her shoulder. Jirra stirred and fumbled for an oar. He started singing again, a low and chilling sound that made Else's skin crawl. As he sang, he paddled, dipping the oar into the dark water and pulling them straight.

"Gotta hit the waves head on," Jirra said. "We get turned around, we all gonna drown."

Else gritted her teeth. Lowanna cried and wriggled between her feet. The land was ending on either side of her. She felt a sickening sense of the world opening up and she was falling into the darkness.

"Keep her straight!" Jirra yelled.

Else dug her paddle deep, pulling against the water as it foamed. The stink of river mud and salt clogged her nostrils. *The sea goes on forever*, a small voice in the back of her mind said. *It goes on forever and you will never find your way back to land.* "My baby is out there," Else said to the heaving waves. The nose of the boat rose up and crested. Else's paddle swept through open air and she overbalanced. Slamming her hand into the floor of the boat, she braced herself as the bow dropped and hit the water.

"Paddle!" Jirra yelled. Else pulled herself up. Scrambling with her oar, she swept it through the water and they surged up the face of the next wave. Else was ready when they broke through this one. The entire skiff was airborne for a moment and then with a sickening fall they dropped. Lowanna howled as the shuddering blow of the wave hit the bottom of the boat.

"One more!" Jirra shouted and they rode the sickening slope up the third wave. Cold water burst over the bow. Else tasted mud, not salt. The river had pushed itself out into the vast sea like a cold steel dagger stabbing deep into a warm body.

They paddled on, pulling themselves through the water. The waves slid under the skiff now, lifting the small craft and rocking them in a longer motion.

"How far to the ship?" Else glanced over her shoulder. Jirra had slumped forward, his paddle trailing in the water. "Jirra?" Else twisted in her seat.

"Unngh…" Jirra moaned and his head twisted. His dark skin had gone as grey as the white ash of mourning he smeared himself with. Else dived for the machete. The dying man lunged at her in the same moment. She jammed her right arm under his jaw and scrabbled for the knife handle, his teeth snapping at her, black saliva dripping over his bloodless lips.

Else lifted the machete. Jirra's hands clamped on her arm and he pushed her back. Else hissed and swung at the zombie's head with the machete, striking him a glancing blow. He grunted and his teeth sank into her forearm.

The effect was immediate. The zombie's eyes went wide and he pulled back. His back arched, contractions popping his joints as every muscle in his body clenched. Else pulled herself up into a sitting position and watched as his skin swelled and split. Strips of flesh peeled off his bones. Black blood gushed from every pore and spots of dark liquid welled in his eyes. Jirra whimpered, a desperate and agonized sound as the antiviral plasma in Else's blood destroyed the Adam virus that coursed through his dying body.

Else took his head off with a wild swing of the machete. The dark-haired ball splashed into the water and sank out of sight. She dropped the blade and heaved the rest of his corpse over the side. Lowanna still howled, her angry cries not eased by the rocking of the boat. Else stared down at the tiny, blanket-wrapped form. The baby girl's parents were dead, but she needed the same constant care of any newborn.

Else wondered how she could do that. If her boy died, there would be bloodshed. There would be no time for taking care of this little girl. There would only be time for killing until the very end.

Reaching down, Else scooped up the wriggling bundle. Stroking the tiny head, Else studied the baby's features. She smelled wet. Else's body ached to hold her own baby again. There was nothing she could do for Lowanna. The sea would take her as quickly as it took her father.

CHAPTER 4

E lse shivered in spite of the heat of the sun. The coastline was now a faded smear on the horizon at her back. Ahead there was only open water. A rolling carpet of jade green hiding horrors she could only imagine. She focused on paddling. First one side of the boat, then the other. Her oar dipped and stirred the water.

Lowanna had nursed at Else's breast until she slept. Now the baby lay wrapped in a blanket, protected from the sun in the slight shade under the bench seat. Else didn't know why she hadn't simply dropped the girl over the side with her father.

The bite wound on Else's arm had been bound with a torn strip of cloth and already it itched from the rapid healing of her cells. Lowanna's life was her responsibility now and by keeping her alive, Else would have to take care of this baby and her own son when she found him. That, she told herself, were the rules.

She paddled until her arms ached and her head throbbed. The water bag that Jirra carried was almost empty. Else didn't dare drink anymore. The salt in the air and on her skin dried her out. Her tongue seemed to swell and clog her mouth.

The heat of the day grew more intense, the glare off the water made her close her eyes and paddle. It would be so easy to lean over the side and slip into the warm water. Let the sea ease her passing and to float off into darkness. Else jerked awake and resumed paddling.

My son, she reminded herself. *He is out here. Someone has taken him and I have to get him back.*

At first she thought it might be a rocky island, a long white blush on the horizon. Hard to see through the glare and the haze. Else focused on it, pushing herself towards this object. Willing it to come closer. The sun set behind her and a slight breeze came up, pushing the skiff closer. The white rock shifted and changed. Becoming clearer, more defined, and taking on the shape of a large metal ship. The massive white boat wallowed in the water, like a sow with a litter of piglets made up of smaller boats lined up, nose first, against her side.

Else pushed on. The ship was nearly three hundred meters long and towered over her tiny boat. She constantly scanned the rails and decks for signs of life or movement. Seabirds circled and landed on high perches. Soon she could hear the chatter of their scolding and smell the ammonia of their shit.

It was a cruise liner, Else decided. One of the white ships she had read about in a moldering magazine. They once took people on journeys around the islands of the South Pacific. Now it was a home to birds and, she hoped, the Sea People Jirra had told her about.

Mostly Else avoided other survivors. They wanted her to do things their way. Or they wanted to do things to her without her permission. That meant they ended up dead, and she didn't like killing people unless they were already dead.

Paddling closer, Else let the skiff drift the last ten meters to the outer ring of small boats. They varied from rubber Zodiacs with outboard motors to an old fishing boat with masts for trawler lines and nets, sticking up like big insect antennae from its back. Along the rail of the ship a heavy rope net had been rolled up and tied off. Else could see no way to climb up the smooth metal sides.

Turning the skiff, she made her way to the front. A massive anchor chain as thick as her thigh rose out of the water and vanished into the ship through the hawsehole portal high on its shoulder. Lowanna grizzled and mewled. Else lifted her gently and tucked the baby inside the cloth sling. Here, against her breast, Lowanna started to suckle and Else felt the now constant pang of the loss of her own child more deeply than ever.

With Lowanna secure against her chest and the machete sheathed and hanging across the other shoulder, Else tied the skiff to the anchor chain. Stepping out of the boat, she pulled herself onto the thick chain and climbed hand over hand until she hung above the water.

The baby's weight was nothing compared to the ache and sudden cramp that burned in her arms and shoulders. Gritting her teeth, Else moved a hand up to the next link. Feeling the sharp grit of rust digging into her palms, she moved on. One hand at a time she slowly made her way up the chain, the stink of guano getting stronger the closer she got to the deck of the ship.

Reaching the end of the chain, Else swung her legs up and hooked the back of one heel through the wide portal. Straining, she twisted her upper body and pulled herself the last few feet and finally got a hand on the edge of the deck. Standing on the chain, she peeped over the side and took stock.

Birds nested in the sheltered corners of the open decks, and someone had set up rainwater-catching tarpaulins in the open spaces. Fishing nets hung in wide sheets from rope lines strung across the deck, and Else could see that the metal plates of the deck had been swept clear of guano.

Satisfied that there were no signs of movement other than the birds, Else pulled herself up and climbed over the rail. Her booted feet silent on the deck, she moved to the lengthening shadow of the nearest wall. Keeping her back close to the rust-stained steel, she crept along the deck. Her senses tingled and the machete made a comforting weight in her hand. Lowanna lay still and warm against her chest. Else reached the end of the wall; ahead of her the bow of the boat tapered off into a point. More nets hung from rope lines and mysterious containers were stacked in a haphazard fashion across this section of the deck.

Crouching down Else studied the landscape, looking for signs of evols. Finally satisfied, she started to move across the front of the ship when a movement caught her eye. A flash as something small darted between the stacked crates and coiled ropes.

Machete held ready, Else left the wall and moved into the maze of boxes, when she heard the soft laugh of a child. Curious, she moved closer to the sound. Coming around a corner she stopped. Ahead, crouched down in the flat-footed way of small children and totally absorbed in something on the deck, was a young girl.

Else hesitated. The child was dressed in faded clothes. Her long sun-bleached hair seemed cared for, though it was twisted into rope-like plaits and had a number of shells and small metal ornaments woven into it. The pallor of her skin in the twilight looked warm and alive.

"Look at you, pretty birdy. Look at you, little birdy..." the girl crooned and reached out to stroke something at her feet.

Else could hear it now, the thin cries of a young seabird, either taken or fallen from one of the high nests. The girl straightened up, her thin legs tanned and smooth.

"Pretty birdy..." she cooed again and Else saw the nearly ready-to-fly fledgling huddled on the deck. The girl raised her bare foot and stomped down on the baby bird, crushing its back and making it squeal, a sharp anguished sound. The girl stomped her foot again and again, giggling as she crushed the life out of the chick.

Else watched as the child grinned at the smear of mashed flesh and feathers, then scraped her foot along the deck, wiping it clean. Lowanna stirred and started to grizzle. The child spun around and stared at Else with wide green eyes. Her expression was a mixture of guilt and angry surprise. A dark bruise running from her eye and down across her tanned cheek colored her face even darker.

"Go away!" the child shouted and bolted through the nets and containers towards the high structure of the ship's interior.

Else followed, ducking and weaving past the ropes and nets. She reached the door just as the girl was heaving it open. Overbalancing, Else slammed her shoulder into the wall and grabbed the girl by the back of the neck. The child screamed as Else swept the machete up to the girl's face. "Shut up!" she growled. "Shut up or I will cut your fucking head off."

The trembling girl went silent. Else felt a warm wetness spreading over her leg as the terrified child wet herself.

"Who else is on this ship?" Else snarled over the girl's shoulder. The girl whimpered and said nothing.

"Tell me," Else warned.

"Ev-everybody," the girl whispered.

"Show me," Else said, aware that Lowanna was crying lustily now and even the noise of the roosting birds wasn't enough to cover it.

The girl reached out and gingerly twisted the door handle. Else stepped back, the tip of the machete hovering over the girl's shoulder. The child pulled hard and the door creaked open wide enough for them to slip inside. A puff of stale air that stank in a thousand different ways wafted out over them.

"The ones inside, alive or dead?" Else asked.

"Alive," the girl replied and stepped into the dark. Else followed her. The girl stopped and looked back. "You have to close the door," she explained. Else reached back and pulled the door shut. They stood now in the pitch dark of a narrow corridor.

The child seemed at ease here. "I'm going to get in trouble for sneaking on deck," she said. "But not half as much as you're going to cop it," her voice carrying a malicious smirk in the darkness. A click, and a jury-rigged line of electric lights banished the shadows.

"Where is everyone?" Else said.

"Below decks and the up-highs are up there," the girl waved at the ceiling. "Captain and crew mostly. They live good up-high. One day they'll take me and I'll live above too."

"How old are you?" Else asked.

"Dunno. Almost old enough for boobs, I reckon." The girl stared at the wriggling lump on Else's body. "That baby yours?"

"Kinda," Else said, not in the mood for further explanations. "Show me where your people are."

The girl walked ahead, leading Else down a flight of stairs. Turning at the landing the girl skipped down the next flight. Else followed her; close enough to cut her down if necessary, but not too close. The walls here were painted in garish graffiti. Stick figures marched in crooked lines and tiny crosses floated above their heads. Scraps of faded cloth and plastic hung from the ceiling and walls. Older art had been covered with new layers in some places. In others the paint had been scratched away and rough letters, spelling out names, were etched into the metal. The girl stopped at a door set in the painted wall.

"You can still run away," she said with a sly smile.

Else lifted the machete and pressed the point to the girl's cheek. "I can still cut you too," she smiled back.

The girl twisted away and opened the door. The smell was stronger now. A miasma of shit dissolving in piss, the stench of sweat, sex, and cooking smells all combining into the stink of people living in tight conditions for a long time.

In the vast empty metal chamber beyond lay a tent city. Each small area was marked off with grey and stained hanging sheets. People talked, laughed, swore, and coughed in the gloom. The electric lights stopped at the bottom of the stairs. Guttering oil lamps hung sporadically throughout the open space, straining to burn in the foul air.

Else blinked at the huddled mass of faces that turned to stare at her with open curiosity. The girl walked confidently along the narrow path between the clustered families and tugged on the arm of a man standing half-hidden in the gloom. He leaned over and looked down the girl's pointing arm to where Else stood, wary and alert, scanning the strange crowd from the doorway.

The girl returned, the man in tow. He wore a patched shirt, the red check pattern on it faded to a bloodless pink. His thick beard and roughly cut hair framed cold blue eyes that stared at Else as he calculated the value of the woman at a glance. The girl held his hand as they approached.

"Where the hell did you come from?" he said by way of greeting.

"The land," Else said. Still watching the peering faces, looking for any sign of her baby in the crowd.

"Why'd you wanna come out here?" the man asked.

"Looking for my baby. He got taken. A friend said the Sea People might have taken him." Else casually lifted the machete and rested the back of the blade on her shoulder. "I'm here to take him back."

The bearded man regarded her for a long moment and Else stared back at him.

"They call me Hob," he said.

"Else," Else replied. "Where's my baby?"

"She's already got one," the girl said from her place by Hob's waist.

Else bared her teeth at the girl and tightened her grip on the machete handle.

"Shut it, Sarah," Hob said, one hand raising to cuff the girl. She shrank back and gave Else a dark look.

"This is Lowanna, she isn't mine. Her parents are both dead. My boy is only a couple of days old. He was in a little boat. The flood washed it up by where the river goes out to sea. When we found the boat, evols came and Jirra said they dressed like Sea People. We killed a lot of them, but Jirra didn't make it. He was Lowanna's father. Her mother died after she was born, a few days ago. So I'm looking after her now and I'll ask you one more time. Where the fuck is my son?"

Hob shrugged. "We got laws here. Laws keep things straight. You get a share of water. You get a share of food. You bring back salvage, you get a bigger share. We got another law. Law of salvage. You find it off ship, it's yours. A gun, a tin of peaches, or a kid. All the same under salvage law." Hob raised his voice as he recited the law, and the watching crowd murmured their agreement.

"I'm not staying here. I just want my son." Else shifted Lowanna in the sling to a more comfortable position on her hip. "If you don't give him back, you'll be the first to die."

Hob grinned and slowly turned his back on Else. "We got a dispute over salvage!" he shouted to the crowd. They grumbled and shifted in anticipation. "We got a law for that too!" he roared. The crowd agreed noisily.

"When two parties are at odds and no agreement can be reached, let them decide it between themselves. One fight. One winner. End of story!" Hob was talking to them and Else. She could see the way they responded, the way his words roused them from the stupor of living in such close and desperate misery.

These people wanted to see someone else suffer. They wanted blood on the walls, broken bones and shattered teeth. They wanted their frustration and fear to be crushed. They wanted a victory and damn the cost. No glory could be too small or remote. Else aimed to disappoint them.

The gathered throng came alive. They leapt and crawled over each other, scampering up the walls on ropes and onto ledges with the practiced ease of monkeys, or people shut in a confined space for far too long.

"Are we gonna settle this in the Hole!?" Hob shouted. The crowd took up the call.

"Hole! Hole! Hole!" they roared.

"Where is my baby!?" Else pushed back at people who pressed against her, the stink of them turning her empty stomach.

"The kid is salvage. You gotta fight for him!" Hob sneered.

"I'll kill you!" Else shouted to be heard above the crowd.

"Not me, love! You fight the one who claimed salvage!" Hob addressed the excited crowd: "This woman came from on land! Came here saying we took her salvage!" Hob feigned indignant surprise and the crowd dutifully booed and hissed.

"Rowanna!" Hob yelled to the ceiling. A woman came through the press of people. She ignored the hands that patted her shoulders and back. She took no notice of the shouts of support and the instructions on how to kill the stranger. She held a tiny bundle that nursed against her swollen breast. She stared at Else with dead eyes.

"Rowanna, do you want to give up the salvage you rightly claimed as your own?"

The crowd went still, listening for an answer to Hob's question.

"They took my Alex," Rowanna said. "I prayed to the Captain that he would be spared. Captain gave me salvage. I thank the Captain for that. I'm never giving up my baby. He's Captain's gift to me."

Hob turned to Else, grinning a showman's smile. "How about you, girly? You gonna crawl back into the mangrove swamp and dust? You gonna walk outta here and go back to dodging evols?"

"I'm leaving," Else said, never once taking her eyes off the tiny figure in Rowanna's arms. "And I'm taking my son with me."

"We have a contender!" Hob bellowed.

Else charge forward. The mob grabbed her, holding her arms and lifting her into the air. They carried her through the dark corridors of the ship. She would have fought them all. Cut them down and waded through the river of their blood, but two men hung off each arm, keeping her still.

The Hole was deep in the belly of the ship, a dark and empty chamber of steel walls and doors. The gloom retreated from the sputtering light of oil lamps as the crowd pushed into the room. A fence of woven wire had been erected around an open space. The wire strands had been braided into cables with shards of glass and jagged metal jutting out to form vicious barbs. Hob stepped up to the fence and twanged a taut line.

"It ain't Thunderdome!" he told the crowd and they howled in delight. "It's the cage match to end all fucking cage matches. It's the judge, the jury, and the fucking executioner! You come in here, you'd better believe in your cause!"

The crowd stamped and cheered, clapping their hands as they were swept up in the excitement of the show and the suffering to come.

Hob waved the noise down to a guttural growl. "We got a salvage dispute. We got two women set to tear each other apart for the right to claim a puke-stain as their own. Another mouth to feed, who fucking needs it?!"

The crowd roared in approval and Hob waited till they subsided to continue. "Salvage is salvage, we don't dispute that. The last one standing gets to claim the kid and the Captain's reward! Even King-fucking-Solomon couldn't give you a deal like that!"

The crowd cheered again and Else was forced to the edge of the wire. Hands lifted the screaming Lowanna from her sling and Else twisted in the rough grip of a dozen hands, glaring at a young woman who took Lowanna in her arms and cradled the baby gently.

"Gotta hand over the knife. You'll get it back," Hob said. "If you win," he added with a grin.

Else growled as the machete was taken from her. The lowest wire rope was lifted and she slipped into the square ring. She stood for a moment, taking stock of the surroundings. A movement high above the spectators' heads caught her attention. A small camera mounted on the wall turned and stared back at her.

Rowanna came in from the other side. She had stripped down to a ragged pair of long shorts and a filthy bra, stained with grime and sweat. Her hands were empty and any remaining expression had drained from her face.

"Get it on!" Hob yelled, banging on a steel corner post with the back of Else's machete. Else stepped sideways, feeling the floor under her feet and watching her opponent. Rowanna didn't move for a moment and then took a hesitant step forward. Then two more. She was now within five feet and Else closed the gap in two long strides. Her fist slammed into Rowanna's nose. Blood gushed, sending Rowanna stumbling backwards.

Shaking her head, the woman blocked Else's next punch by grabbing the fist with both hands and biting down on Else's knuckles. Else raised her other fist and slammed it down on top of the woman's head. Rowanna dropped to one knee.

Else drew her foot back to kick at the woman's head. Rowanna sprang upwards, her entire body driving into Else's swollen belly and knocking the wind out of her. The body blow pushed Else back against the wire. She felt her flesh tear, and a sharp stabbing pain blossomed in her shoulder.

With an enraged howl Else clapped her hands hard against Rowanna's ears. The woman screamed and pulled back, her ragged nails slashing at Else, tearing her shirt and raking her skin.

Else pulled herself off the sharp wire. Feeling blood pour down her back, she ripped her shirt off and twirled it into a thick cord. With a snap she flicked it at Rowanna's shrieking face. The woman lurched backwards, one hand slapped to her eye as blood and fluid spilled down her face.

Else stepped up and punched her opponent in the cheek,

crushing the bloody eyeball that hung by a strand of tendon against her face. Rowanna's scream became shriller.

Else lashed out with a snap kick. As straight and hard as a blade, the edge of her boot crushed Rowanna's throat, reducing her screams to a choking gurgle. Lost in the red fury, Else leapt on the woman and buried her thumbs in her eye sockets. Rowanna convulsed, her feet beating a desperate tattoo on the bloodstained floor.

Else howled and felt the thin wall of bone at the back of the woman's eye sockets collapse under the driving pressure of her thumbs. She pushed them into Rowanna's living brain until the woman shuddered and lay still.

Every muscle of Else's body ached. The room spun around her and she could hear her baby crying. She staggered to her feet and felt the floor tilt crazily.

"Baby…" she said, reaching out towards a sudden flare of darkness that swallowed her whole.

CHAPTER 5

Shifting murmurs of half-heard phrases always filled Else's sleep. The voices came from before she could understand words. From the time when her senses floated in a warm liquid womb and the world was only half-perceived. Like a dream, she remembered the soft shapes of men and woman dressed in white, inserting long needles into her liquid world. She moaned as once again a sliver of steel slid into her arm.

"She's waking up," a male voice announced. Else opened her eyes and then sat bolt upright, flailing in panic. She gasped in pain as the fresh stitches in her back pulled taut.

"Relax, no one here will harm you," the man said, his voice slurring. Else slid sideways off the bed. Hampered by the plastic tubes buried in her arm, she half-fell to the cold floor.

"Where's my baby?" Else demanded. She tugged at the lines in her arm, wincing at the sharp pain this caused.

"He is fine. Sleeping in fact, just as you were."

"Who are you? What are you putting in me?" Else gained her feet and stood unsteadily in some kind of cotton shift dress, glaring at the man in the off-white coat on the other side of the narrow bed.

"My name is Doctor Clay. I'm giving you saline, some essential nutrients, and blood. O negative blood. Your type has proven difficult to match with anything other than a universal donor type."

"Take these needles out. Do it now!"

"As you wish." Doctor Clay moved around the bed and slowly reached out. "Hold still…" He slid the first IV line out and instructed Else to press a finger on the spot while he removed the second needle. Else looked around the room, a clinic of some kind with only two beds in it and the other one was empty. Cabinets lined the walls and everything shone in either stainless steel or sterile white.

"I'll see if I can find something to dress that with." The doctor moved stiffly. Else waited until he was clear of the bed and then started looking for the baby. Every cell ached to hold her son again. But there was no sign of him.

"Everything okay?" the doctor asked.

"Where is my baby!?" Else lunged at the white shape, her head spinning in a slow yaw of dizziness.

"You will see him again soon."

Else frowned; this all felt wrong. The way he moved, the slight slur in his voice. She hesitated, a sudden flare of awareness igniting her nerves and making her skin ripple in disgust. Doctor Clay stood staring at her.

"You're dead," she said. Doctor Clay blinked slowly. Else let her eyes search the room for a weapon.

"There's no need to panic," Clay said. "You are in no danger."

"You are. You're in so much fucking danger right now, if you had any sense you'd be screaming." Else took a step forward, her bruised hands curling into fists.

"Things are different here. You will learn that." Doctor Clay's voice remained calm, but he took a step backwards for each one that Else advanced.

"I've spent my entire life destroying things like you," Else said. "Things that thought they were right and just and doing the best for everybody. But they were wrong. You're always wrong. You don't know what is right for me, for my baby. Not for any of us!"

Doctor Clay backed into the wall. He reached for the door handle and Else slammed a hand down on his wrist.

"No," she said. "I'll destroy you all. No exceptions. Ever."

Else's hand drew back and the doctor's eyes went wide. He opened his mouth to speak. Else punched at his throat. The dead doctor blocked the punch and Else's knuckles tore open on the metal band of his wristwatch. Clay's nostrils flared. His eyes clouded and Else jerked her arm back from his twitching nose.

"You should not assume we are all mindless. Many of us manage to function quite successfully postmortem." Doctor Clay lunged at Else. She stepped aside and threw a surgical tray at him.

Clay knocked it aside and came on, his face twisting into a savage expression of hunger.

"We are the new dominant species." Clay's gums were as white as his teeth.

"You feed on the living. You do nothing but destroy!" Else flinched back as the dead doctor slashed at her face with an open hand.

"We are the answer to your destruction of the natural world. We are the Earth's revenge." The doctor strode towards Else, his fingers curled like claws. "I'm going to eat my way in through your belly," Clay said. "Then I'm going to gorge myself on your heart. And once I've sucked every last shred of meat from your warm bones, then I'm going to eat your kid."

Else stopped backing away. A cold certainty settled over her shoulders. "There's no way you will touch him. No way in hell," she growled.

"You are nothing but animals, to be kept in cages and bred for food," Clay sneered, but he stopped walking to speak. Else could see his brain firing, slow and steady. She took the opportunity to look around; anything could be a weapon. She'd killed evols with guns, knives, swords, baseball bats, rocks, and once, a sheep skull.

Stepping sideways, she tore open a high wooden cabinet. A pile of soft bandages and cotton balls spilled out onto the floor.

She twisted aside as Clay smashed his fist into the cabinet door next to her head.

"I've been more than patient with you!" he barked, black saliva spitting from his mouth.

Else ripped a foot-long chunk of wood from the shattered cupboard door. Spinning it in her hand, she held it like a stake and stabbed down. The shard of wood plunged into Clay's shoulder. It caught on his collarbone and Else twisted it with one hand. With the other she punched Clay in the jaw, snapping his teeth together with a loud crack.

Howling, Clay grabbed Else by the throat and threw her back across the room. She hit the empty bed and tumbled over it on to the floor.

"Adrenaline is limited. Human endurance is finite. We are the superior species," Clay said and almost stumbled as he advanced.

"What's the matter, Doctor?" Else sneered. "Can't walk and talk at the same time?"

"I'm gonna eat your fucking tits!" Clay shouted, shards of broken teeth spraying out of his mouth in hard crumbs.

The doctor swung a fast, hard punch. Else blocked it with her right arm and smashed her fist into his face. They traded blows, nearly every strike being knocked aside and countered with another punch. Clay lashed out with a booted foot, kicking Else hard in the side and throwing her back against a metal table that collapsed under her weight. She lay there, feeling her strength draining through the freshly opened wounds in her back. Clay's face was set with a grim focus. He would never stop. The flesh could tear from his fists and he would beat her down with the cold bones of his dead knuckles. She thought she could hear the baby screaming somewhere in the dark. Alone and afraid, he cried out for her to come and save him.

Clay staggered over her. His face was a pulped mess of shattered teeth and grey flesh, oozing black ichor. He paused a moment, assessing how best to start feeding on her prone form. Else reached out and snatched up a metal leg from the broken table. Kicking upwards, she shattered Clay's knee and swept his feet from under him. Springing up into a sitting position, she rammed the jagged end of the aluminum pipe under his chin as Clay collapsed forward. The pipe pierced the doctor's jaw and his falling weight drove it up through his brain. Doctor Clay finally died as he slid down to be at eye level with Else.

"I've never counted how many of you motherfuckers I've destroyed," she whispered into his face. "Because you don't matter to me. Not a fucking damn."

Pushing the corpse aside, she crawled over to the bed and pulled herself up.

There were no other clothes in the clinic that Else could see. The homemade cotton shift she wore was soaked with blood, sweat, and black gore.

Pulling the aluminum pole out of Clay's skull, she cracked open the door and peeked. A young soldier type stood guard at the end of a narrow hallway. He carried an automatic rifle and wore black pants, boots, and shirt. Else watched him for a long moment. He did not move and didn't appear to breathe.

Satisfied that he was an evol, Else opened the door wider and slipped out of the clinic. *They shouldn't be like this*, she thought to herself. Adam was destroyed. The evols lost their minds. Here though, on this ship, they managed to keep it together. They had survived the destruction of the Adam organism and were still walking and talking.

Else moved quickly on silent feet. The guard turned at the last moment. She swung the metal pole up, like a golf swing. The sharp tip tore his body open from navel to chin. A belly full of stinking guts and grey slime spilled out on the floor. The soldier grunted. Raising his weapon, he fumbled to drag the slide back. Else twirled the pole and stabbed him through the eye, pinning his head to the wall. His legs kicked, arms jerking and slapping against the wall. Else grabbed the rifle as it fell from his dead hands.

"What the fuck is going on here?" Else said to the dead soldier as he shuddered and went still. With practiced ease Else checked the weapon. It was well maintained, and the magazine was full. The soldier carried no other ammunition. Else clicked the rifle over to single shot and tried the door at the end of the hallway. It opened a crack and she waited a few seconds, listening hard for any sound.

Else guessed the ship had once been a special place. The walls of the room beyond the door were decorated with framed pictures. Gold and glass glittered everywhere. The passage of the years had done little to dull the brightness and the wealth. She wondered what it would have been like to walk through the lounges and the bars when they were filled with people. Did they try to escape the horror of the end and find themselves trapped here? The crowd of people living in squalor far below decks seemed afraid to leave the ship for more than scavenging missions. But what kept them here? Was this a real sanctuary or just a better prison?

She crossed a restaurant where the chairs and tables had been broken down for firewood. The kitchen ahead of her stood silent and dusty. Any food left in there had been stripped out long ago. Even the knives were gone.

Else looked for a way out, her back burning in lines of fire where the stitched cuts were raised in weeping red welts. She reached over her back and pulled the cotton away from her wounds, hissing slightly when the fabric caught on the tender skin.

Lowanna must still be held somewhere below decks too. Else couldn't leave without either of the babies; she felt she owed Jirra that much. Wincing, Else stood up and peered through the frosted glass to an outside deck area. It was daytime, the sun-cast shadows flickering across the window. Else ducked down; the silhouettes were too small to be people, alive or dead. She opened the door and the stench of stagnant water and nesting birds assaulted her nose.

The outside deck, thick with guano and shed feathers, surrounded a filthy pool. The pool water was a dark brown color. Seabirds roosted around the pool; some sat on makeshift nests while others squabbled and flew off on urgent errands from the rails. The air reverberated with their squalling cries and the flash of their grey and white wings.

Else stepped out of the restaurant and into the edge of the flock. They exploded skyward, a blizzard of birds taking flight. She clutched the automatic rifle against her chest and blundered blindly through the storm. Wings buffeted her and she slapped at the twisting bodies with her free hand. Crusted shit and shed feathers crunched underfoot. Else pushed on, thinking there had to be something beyond the storm of flapping wings. She found a rail and followed it.

At the end of the rail she found another covered area and a large set of glass doors. Else ran the last steps and the door opened in front of her.

"What are you doing up here? You're scaring my birds!" a man, filthy and bearded, yelled at her. His long hair and beard had been braided with bits of plastic and metal. He wore faded jeans and a shirt, stained with guano, sweat, and dirt. "You can't be stirring them up like that! They'll abandon the nests, and they might not come back!"

Else spat a feather out of her mouth and raised the rifle. He grabbed the barrel, pushing it aside as he dragged her inside, slamming the door against the cacophony of birds.

"You don't come up here. You know what the Cap'n'll do if you fuckers come up out of the hold," he said.

"I'm not from down there. I came from the land," Else replied, her grip still locked on the rifle.

"Shit?" the guy said, his eyebrows rising in surprise.

"The Sea People, they took my baby. I've come to get him back." Else pulled free of his grip and hefted the gun.

"How old is he, this kid of yours?" the bearded man frowned.

"Just born. Two nights ago. I think. Maybe three." Else felt a sick realization that she might have lost a night to unconsciousness.

The man rubbed his face and sighed. "You should go home, girl. Go back to your people and forget about him. Your boy's gone."

"No!" the word burst from Else in a near scream.

"Keep your damn voice down," the man snarled.

"Not dead. I can feel him. He is still alive. I hear him." Else felt the rare sting of tears in her eyes.

"Yeah? Well he won't have long. The crew'll make short work of him." The bearded man spat on the stained carpet. "Did you come here on a boat?"

Else nodded.

"Alright, I can get you back there, but you gotta get away from here quick."

"Not without my baby. Or Lowanna."

"Now who the hell is Lowanna?"

"Jirra's child. She's only a few days old too."

"Sweet fucking Christ. Did you bring a full beer tanker on board with you as well?"

Else looked at him in confusion. "I don't know what that means," she said.

"It means you gotta get the hell out. Go back and live your life. Forget this place." The man walked away and Else followed.

"My baby is all I have. I'm not leaving without him."

"Well then you're fu—"

The man went silent. Else heard a door open somewhere above

them. They stood in frozen silence for a second and then the man jerked Else under the shelter of a balcony. His hand went to his lips in a shushing gesture.

Else heard another door open and then the sound of a baby's cry. She would have cried out, but her companion pressed his hand to her face, shaking his head. Above them the door closed and the silence returned.

"You can't save him," he whispered.

Else pulled his hand away from her mouth. "Why not?" she replied.

"There's too many of them. They run this ship."

"What about the dead? Why are the dead here?"

The man shook his head. "What are you talking about? The dead *are* the ones who run the damn ship."

It was Else's turn to shake her head. "No. We killed him. We destroyed the Adam, the one that controlled all the evols. He's gone. They are just mindless zombies now."

"I wouldn't know shit about that," the man said. "Here they stay smart by eating fresh meat."

"That's not enough," Else retorted. "There's no more Tankbread."

The bearded man gave a grim smile, "The dead are smart. They gave a bunch of folks a safe place to live. A place to live without fear of being eaten. There's a price, though. Always a price. Every time one of those folks in the hold squirts out a baby, they gotta toss a coin. Heads, they give it up to the Captain and him and his crew eats the babies. Keeps their brains working. Keeps them smart and almost human."

Else felt cold winds roar through her mind. Newborns, bodies loaded with stem cells. The same combination of biological perfection as Tankbread. So even without the Adam the dead still functioned.

"Oh no…" Else whispered.

"Yeah, so you can forget your kid. You just brought Sunday lunch for these bastards."

Else stepped away from the wall, the gun steady in her hands. She stared up at the balcony. Babies were up there. Probably hers and Lowanna too. "How many of them?" she asked.

"Don't be stupid, girl. Just walk away."

"I said, how many of them?"

The man sighed. "There's maybe twenty. They choose folks sometimes, special ones. There's a few who choose to die and come back as one of them, you know. They give them poison so they die as easy as going to sleep. Makes them come back smarter."

Else nodded. She knew how it worked. She'd learned all she could about evols in the last nine months. "It is said that if you know your enemies and know yourself, you will not be imperiled in a hundred battles."

"Are you crazy?" the man asked.

"A man called Sun Tzu, lived a long time ago. He wrote a book about how to win wars. I've read it," Else replied.

"Well there ain't a lot of use for that samurai shit here, sister. Best you come with me and we get you back on your boat and on your way."

"What's your name?" Else asked.

"Uhh...Eric...Eric Valman." He looked a little embarrassed. "No one's asked for my name in a long time."

"My name is Else. I traveled with a man once. He never gave me his name. I didn't know to ask until it was too late. I always ask now." Else stepped out of the shadow cast by the setting sun.

"I'm not leaving without my baby. He doesn't have a name yet. I need to get to know him so I can give him the right name."

Eric sighed. "Do you know why I'm up here and not down in the shit with those other dumb arses?"

Else shook her head and Eric continued. "It's because I know how to survive. I know not to get noticed. I know how to get by without making a fuss. You, missy, are making a fuss. You are going to get us killed or tossed down the hold with the rest of them."

"I'm going up there. I'm going to kill every one of them. I'm getting my babies back. Then I'm going to leave." Else turned her back and started for the stairs.

Eric grabbed her arm. "Not that way. You'll get yourself killed, and then bring the crew down on the rest of us. By which I mean me. I won't stand for that. Sooner kill you myself."

"Why not just kill the evols?" Else wrenched her arm free.

"Why'd you wanna come in here and start messing things up? We can survive just fine without you screwing with the quorum."

"Status quo," Else corrected.

"Whatever. Follow me." Eric led her through a door and down stairs. The ceiling was hung with empty tin cans; when Else's head brushed against them they jangled softly.

"Mind yer head," Eric said and a moment later a match flared. The small light touched against the wick of an oil lamp and the space glowed. Else breathed again; the darkness always felt so suffocating.

Eric unlocked a steel door and they went into a cramped space filled with boxes of canned food and cases of bottled water. He pushed the door shut and locked it from the inside as soon as Else passed through.

"Excuse the mess," he said, sweeping empty tins off the table and onto the floor. "Take a seat."

"You live alone here?"

"Always have, I was one of the first aboard. When people started trying to escape by boat, it was chaos. They were still allowing ticket holders to get on the ship; I got a ticket. Twenty-four hours later and I would've been one of them that were crushed in the dock stampede. Lot of people died that day. The crew and some navy boys started shooting people on the gangplank. It was a slaughter. I didn't muck about, got myself a secure spot and started gathering supplies. Whole ship was in an uproar before they cast off, but no one paid any attention to me. Even got myself a crew uniform to help blend in. By the time the infection started in the crew, I was locked up good and tight.

"They were smart ones, but not as smart as me. They started out by snatching babies and then they got the people to make more. Sacrifice the kids and live in sanctuary. No one knew what was happening back on shore, but no one sure as hell wanted to go back. So here they stayed. Now they go out salvaging and fishing, but they're shit scared of the land. Better the devil you know, I suppose."

Silence fell over the small room. Else stared steadily at Eric until he blushed. "You hungry?"

She nodded. "The last thing I ate was grilled fish. Jirra cooked it. That was at least two days ago."

Eric busied himself among the stacked cartons of tinned food. "I don't get visitors. I don't encourage them. I prefer being on my own. No need for other people; they just get you killed or die themselves." Cans of various colors and ingredients were set down on the table. "Spam, beans, and fruit salad for dessert," he announced. "As it's a special occasion, I'll even heat it up."

Else sank down to the floor and curled up on her side in a fetal position. The gashes on her back stung where her dressed wounds rubbed. She cradled the rifle in her arms and closed her eyes as Eric ignited a small camp burner. He poured tins of salted meat and kidney beans into a battered pot, and then set it over the flame.

Else snapped awake, a defensive hand lashing out at Eric who was crouched over her.

"Easy!" he scuttled backwards, one hand raised in a passive gesture. "Don't try to move too much. I can change those dressings. I have a few bandages."

The fire in her back had eased; the deep cuts were already healing. In a few days she wouldn't even have scars.

"I dreamed of my baby...I heard him crying," Else muttered.

"He's not here."

"Water?" Else asked, her voice a dry rasp.

"Here, drink slowly." Eric took a battered plastic cup from the table and water trickled into Else's mouth. She swallowed, feeling her insides soak up the moisture like a sponge.

"Where is my baby?" Else said again, sitting up straight and pushing away the musty smelling blanket that had covered her.

"Up top, remember? But you can't be worrying about him now." Eric stood up and ladled beans and Spam onto a plate. "Here, you said you were hungry."

Else set the rifle aside and took the plate and spoon. She shoveled food into her mouth, barely tasting it as she answered her body's need for nutrients.

"How did you come to have two newborns?" Eric asked while watching her eat.

"He was born in darkness. A storm of thunder and rain. I've not seen him in the light," Else said softly.

"And the baby girl?"

Else ignored the question. "He looks like his father," she continued, feeling a bolt of sorrow shoot through her.

"It's an evolutionary trait. Our primitive fathers were less likely to kill a newborn that looked like them," Eric said.

"He is dead. My baby's father I mean." Else put her plate aside and stood up, feeling the floor dip and sway.

"Steady." Eric took Else's arm until her color returned.

"Eric, I need to find my baby. I heard him, in a room on one of the upper decks."

"He's very new."

"Yes. But he is strong and he will learn everything. Just like I did," Else replied.

Eric gathered up the plates and cutlery. "You don't know if it was yours. The holders have a lot of babies down there in the dark. Not much else to do, I guess," Eric said, the trace of a blush rising above his beard.

"I need to leave now," Else said.

"Where will you go? D'you have people out there?" Eric fussed with empty cans while taking sidelong glances at his visitor.

"No one except my baby. I'm going to find him and then we are going home. We will be fine. I've been on my own for a long while. I built a house in the bush," Else added a little defensively.

"How will you take care of him on your own?" Eric asked.

"I've read books about it."

"People seem to have forgotten how to care about the young around here." Eric sighed. "I couldn't live on shore," he shuddered. "I'd be afraid of some crazed dead person attacking me."

"They are spreading," Else said. "Why are their evols on board this ship? Why haven't you destroyed them all?"

Eric glanced at the door. "You wouldn't understand. They aren't like those rotting, disease carrying, mindless things on land."

"They are now," Else said.

"You are a strange one, Else," Eric smiled. "Doctor Clay would love you."

"Why?" Else tensed.

"Clay's a smart evol. He likes to experiment with people. Conduct tests and stuff like that."

"Is he your friend?" Else asked.

Eric laughed and immediately stifled it with a hand pressed against his mouth. "Oh hell no," he said through the compress of his thick fingers.

"I killed Doctor Clay. I rammed a piece of metal through his brain. Then I killed another evol and took his gun." Else wondered why she felt the need to explain. It felt strange that no one here was killing every walking dead person they could find.

Eric stopped pushing empty tins around and gave Else his full attention. "You killed Doctor Clay?"

"Yes. He was already dead, though."

"Well yeah, but…damn girl. You are going to bring the shit-storm down on all of us."

"Good," Else said.

"Good for you maybe; you can fuck off back to where you came from. The rest of us have to put up with whatever punishment the Captain decrees."

"So do something about it," Else replied.

"We survive here by accepting the things we cannot change," Eric insisted.

"Who says you can't change it?"

"We live in peace here. We are protected. We have a safe place to live."

"But not a safe place to raise children." Else straightened up as Eric flinched.

"We all have to make sacrifices," he muttered.

"The children? All the children?"

"Only the newborns, and they only take some of them. Maybe half. There are plenty of those. Not much else to do below decks, remember." Eric tried to laugh and failed.

"Do you know what they do with them?" Else asked. Eric couldn't meet her eye.

"They protect us, they let us live here."

"They let those people live in the dark. They let them live only so they can produce more children for the dead to feed on. Why don't you fight back?" Else slammed a fist into her open palm. "Destroy every last fucking one of them!"

"It's not possible. You aren't one of us. You can't understand," Eric said.

"Oh and you are? Hiding out up here? Some bird-loving hermit

56

living on tinned food and forgetting his own name." Else stepped forward, getting in Eric's personal space until he cringed backwards.

"Just how…How do you think you are going to do anything?"

Else shrugged. "Fighting these things is all I have ever known. They have taken everything from me. I'm going to take it back."

Eric stared at the floor and then nodded. "Okay, I want to show you something. But you have to keep quiet and don't go running off."

"Sure."

"Another thing, that rifle. Leave it with me. If the crew sees you with a gun, they will tear you apart. Without it, they won't look at you twice."

"I'll be back for it. Don't try to keep it," Else said.

"Wouldn't dream of it," Eric said. He exhaled with an exaggerated sigh as she laid the gun down on the small table.

He closed and locked the door to his home behind them. Slipping under the hanging cans, they went back to the deck where the seabirds roosted. Else watched the birds circling and shrieking while Eric unlocked another door. "In here, quick," he said.

Behind the door was a shed that had once held pool cleaning chemicals and equipment. Now it was packed with an intricate-looking chemistry set of rubber tubes and glass beakers. Pots, pans, and scorched dishes were stacked on the floor. The air reeked of the acrid smell of chemicals.

"What is this?" Else asked.

"My lab," Eric said with a tone of pride. "I've been experimenting with making explosives based on a mixture of nitric acid, glycerin, and lye."

Else nodded; her voracious reading appetite over the months included a range of science textbooks. "You get the nitric acid from guano, the glycerin from fish?"

Eric nodded, brightening at the discovery of a fellow academic to talk about his projects with. "Yup, birds, fish, the occasional seal or dolphin. Depends on what I can scrounge from the fishermen."

"You burn wood for the lye?" Else asked, picking up a scorched pot in one hand.

"Yes—scrounged timber panels, anything I can hook that floats in." Eric opened an old refrigerator. "This is the result."

In an old bottle crate, nesting in padded sockets of cloth stuffed with bird feathers and foam cushion pieces, were bottles of oily looking fluid.

"Boom," Else whispered, peering closely.

"Yeah…enough to blow this ship to pieces. I dunno why I bothered with it. Maybe cuz I figure they'll come for me one day."

"Or because you know that what is happening here is wrong, and you want to bring an end to it," Else said straightening up.

Eric closed the fridge door. "Hell…I don't owe those people in the hold anything."

"Except your life. How long do you think you would have survived up here without them?"

The man's brows furrowed. "I remember the Panic. I remember what people did to survive. I sure as hell remember what some of us had to do to friends, family members, and people we cared about."

"Then why have you stopped fighting? Do you call this victory? You and all the rest, you're just slaves."

"Fight? Fight for what? A chance to get chewed on? A chance to die on land instead of here? Fuck that. You can take your holier-than-thou attitude and jump overboard, lady."

Else scowled. "I'm getting my baby back. You do what works for you." She yanked the shed door open and stepped out into the full glare of the afternoon sun. "You wouldn't have made all that explosive without hoping you might, one day, have the chance to use it for something important." She walked off through the scolding birds settling on their nests for the night.

The sea rose and fell with a rhythmic pulse against the rusting steel of the old cruise liner. Else stood at the rail, watching the swell and shivered. This could never be a sanctuary. People, it seemed, clung to irrational ideas. Always afraid to let go in case they found themselves alone. *I know all about being alone,* she thought and then wiped at her eyes.

The flickering light of a fish-oil lamp brought her up short. The only way to escape was over the side or back the way she came.

"I've been told to come and find you, girly." Hob's sneer carried in his voice. The priest wants to see you. But I reckon he might have to wait a bit. You and I, we have some unfinished business.

Hob came closer until Else could see the slender form of Sarah watching from the safety of his shadow.

"Rowanna was a good breeder," Hob said. "Looks like you are going to have to take her place." Hob grinned at Else, who wrinkled her nose at him.

"You stink," Else announced. Sarah gasped and put a hand to her mouth.

"Smart mouth on you, bitch," Hob sneered. He moved so fast Else didn't have a chance to block the backhanded slap that cracked across her cheek. The force of the blow spun her face-first into the rough surface of the wall.

Hob stepped forward. "Hold the light, Sarah." He pulled Else off the wall, tilting her head back by the hair. "You can do what you are told, or I can beat you down," he snarled in her ear.

"I had a baby a few days ago. I'm not going to get pregnant. Not for a while. It's just not possible."

"Well," Hob breathed his foul breath in her face, "we'll just have us some practice then."

"No, I don't want you to touch me like that," Else said.

"Like I give a fuck what you want, bitch." Hob slammed Else's head against the wall so hard she saw stars.

"I killed Rowanna because you made me do it," Else muttered through the haze of pain. "I destroyed that thing called Doctor Clay too." Somewhere off in the distance she heard Sarah whimper in terror. "Do you really want me to kill you too?" she added.

Hob's fist pulled back like a cocked gun ready to shoot Else in the face. She twisted her body, lifting her chin, looking him in the eyes and daring him to strike.

"Hob!" A voice shouted down the deck, "Bring her to the church." Hob dropped his hand immediately.

"I'll be back for you," Else promised, stepping clear of Hob's fists.

"You've been chosen," Sarah's eyes were wide.

"Chosen to become one of them?" Else gestured towards the upper decks.

Hob spat on the deck. "Not if the church wants you. You are hardly deserving. But ours is not to reason why." Hob walked past them along the deck, stopping at a door, which he indicated with a flourish. "In here. You go first, I'll be right behind you."

Else hesitated. "Sarah, if you could get off this ship and live on land and never have children taken away again, would you like that?"

"Come on." Hob pounded on the open door with a flat hand. Sarah shrank back from Else as if she were a monster born of nightmares.

Else went through the door and followed Hob's instructions at her back; turn left, go down those stairs, along the corridor and then down another flight of stairs. He walked behind her, ready to stop her should she try and escape. They walked in the glow of electric lights until the murals painted on the walls morphed into themes of angels and flaming swords. Tiny stick figures were bathed in the yellow glow of crayon. Near the ceiling a crude painting of a figure with a blue hat spread his arms wide, bringing everyone into his embrace.

"There is religion here?" Else wasn't surprised. Religion was an oddly human thing. She had seen it put to good use by Sister Mary and the nuns of Saint Peter's Grace. They were working hard to help people and keep order in a world gone to chaos. She was curious to see what kind of religion was being practiced on the ship.

"Yeah, there's those that worship the Captain and the Almighty and there's those that worship the engines."

"Engines? Do they work?"

"The engineers believe." Hob pushed past Else and twisted a door handle. "After you." She slipped past him and into a dark chamber hung with thick sheets of soft cloth. Her nose twitched; there was a smell here, like burnt flowers. Else stood still, waiting while her eyes widened in the gloom. A silhouette with arms spread wide hung on the far wall. Else stepped closer; it resembled the man, Jesus on the cross, that the nuns worshipped. This figure had been painted to resemble clothes. A white shirt, with gold-striped epaulettes, dark pants, and shoes painted over the wooden feet nailed to the beam. On his head he wore a faded blue cap instead of a crown of thorns. Else looked back as the door closed. Hob was gone.

"Behold the Captain. Through his mercy we shall live forever." The man speaking wore a suit of grey fabric, worn to a dull shine. Around his neck he had a white collar, stained to a nicotine brown with skin grease and sweat. His unshaven and rough-looking face bore stubble the color of cold ashes in a campfire. The eyes sunk deep in the sockets glittered like sparks struck from steel.

Else took a step back. "I've seen this before. On the land, the sisters of Saint Peter's Grace. They had a bigger church, though."

The priest raised his hands and his eyes toward the ceiling. "God is everywhere, child. But only on his blessed ark are his chosen children saved."

Else raised an eyebrow. "Saved?" she asked.

"Indeed, child." The priest warmed to his subject. "And the Lord God said, 'I will destroy man whom I have created from the face of the earth; both man, and beast, and the creeping thing, and the fowls of the air; for it repenteth me that I have made them. And God looked upon the earth, and, behold, it was corrupt; for all flesh had corrupted his way upon the earth.'"

"I have to go and find my baby." Else started for the door. The priest moved in front of her and put his hands on her shoulders. Looking into her face as if searching for something, he said, "Thou shalt not sacrifice unto the Lord thy God any bullock, or sheep for that is an abomination unto the Lord thy God."

"Let me go." Else struggled out of his grip.

"I beseech you therefore, brethren, by the mercies of God, that ye present your bodies a living sacrifice, holy, acceptable unto God! Your child is a gift from God and to God they shall return! This is the sacrifice the Lord asks of us. Through his immortal vessel, the Captain who walks above us we shall find the kingdom of heaven when the waters recede!"

Else tugged on the door handle. The close press of the velvet curtains held a cloying stink that made her nauseous. A tight sense of panic swelled up inside. She flailed against the heavy fabric, trying to find the opening to the corridor.

The priest's hand pressed against her back, his other hand heavy and smooth against the top of her head.

"I absolve you of your sins. You who have given the sacrifice of your newborn child. You are free to enter the kingdom of Heaven."

"No," Else declared. "I won't let you feed my baby to those things."

"You have been chosen. The grace of the Lord is upon thee." The priest's hand felt cool on her skin. Not as chill as the dry flesh of the dead, but somehow soothing. Else turned away from the smothering curtain and slid down the wall to sit on the floor, gasping for air. "I just want my baby back," she managed.

He went down on one knee in front of her. "My name is Jonah.

The Lord speaks through me. He tells me there may be a way to save your child. But you must trust in him."

"I can't."

"You must. You must place your faith and trust in me, the Lord's vessel upon this ark of his covenant. Listen to me and know the truth of his word. You are the innocent lamb, the uncorrupted sword of his merciful justice delivered by the waters unto us. You shall go among the unbelievers and find the corruption in their hearts. Listen for the heresy of their lies and help me deliver them into the Lord's light."

Else tried to make sense of the strange words the man used. "You want me to go and find out who has lied to you?"

"Yes, child. Go among the heathen engineers and the lost fishermen. They plot against our Lord God and seek to bring an end to our sanctuary. But if we leave this ark, the Lord God will cast us out into the desert and we shall wander like the tribes of Israel, forever lost to God's light."

"You sound a little bit nuts, you know that?"

Jonah stood up and pulled Else to her feet. "Go, child. You now do his will."

"Will you help me get my son back?"

"Yes, if you uncover the viper's nest that lurks in the bowels of this ship, then I shall beseech the Almighty Captain for his blessing and the return of your boy-child."

"If you are lying to me, I will nail you to that cross."

Jonah smiled. "Those who do his work are truly blessed." The heavy curtain was drawn aside and Else stumbled out of the close, dark chapel. The tainted air of the narrow corridor seemed fresh by comparison.

Hob looked up from where he sat waiting on the stairs. "You get some of the Lord's grace in ya?" He smirked when he spoke.

"Fuck you," Else replied.

"Well, darlin', let me explain how things work around here. The believers, they're the priest's people. They think this here is an ark. The Ark. They are waiting for Jesus to come back and fly them all to heaven. The ones who do all work of keeping us alive, they're the fishermen. They live on the deck and go out in the boats, bring in fish and seaweed and other supplies. They run us and the crew ashore when we need some fresh population too."

"Fresh population?"

"Sure, folks get sick and die or they get killed. We need to keep making babies. So we go ashore, snatch up some kids. Too old for Them That Walk Above Us to get what they need. So we bring 'em down here, keep them alive and when they are old enough, we make babies with them. Keeps the gene pool fresh and makes a change from banging away at the same old twat."

"Why don't their people come? Come and take them back?"

"Aw hell, there's fuck all left out there. Most of them are happy to find a safe place where they get fed and are safe from the walking dead."

"Sarah, she isn't your daughter?"

"Kinda. She's mine to take care of until she's old enough to take care of me. Then I get a return on my investment."

Else's nose wrinkled. "I wouldn't have sex with anyone I didn't love."

"Oh, she loves me alright. I saved her from getting chewed on by her brother. He'd died of a fever. They were living in a car and she'd got herself trapped in there with him when he came back. She leapt into my arms and didn't let go until I set her down on the deck here."

"So this is a religious community?"

"Not all of us. I myself say the words and take the blessings and just do what I gotta to get by. The fishermen, they have their own thing going on. And the engineers, they're as far gone as the believers.

"Are their geeks on board this ship?"

"Not quite. The engineers live deep in the ship. They work on the engines and all the other crap that's rusting away down there. They're the ones who want to get this boat fired up and moving. But they can't because the Captain won't let them do that, and the Captain, well his word is law.

"How can I meet this Captain?"

"You meet him when you are chosen. Or when you die. The priest says he's gonna judge us all."

"There's electricity here. I saw a camera watching me. That has to be powered from somewhere."

Hob swept his hair back with a filthy hand. "Well damn, you are a smart one. There's batteries. Solar powered. The engineers rigged it up. They keep the bird crap off the panels and the Captain says how the juice gets used. The crew keeps an eye on us holders. Make sure we ain't doing anything other than fucking and feasting."

"And that's all you want from life?"

"Sure. I get fed and I get to fuck. What more could I ask for?"

"Freedom."

Else started back up the stairs to the deck. Hob followed her and leaned past when she struggled to open a door that led outside.

"Don't you wander off now," he said as Else stepped out into the dim light of evening. She followed a worn trail through the crusted guano along the deck. Birds circled and scolded overhead. She could see boats of all shapes and sizes floating out in the calm sea. Figures on them were cleaning nets, and the lights from the ship sparkled off the day's catch.

She walked until she reached the front of the boat. This deck was wider, and the birds flocked in greater numbers here. She watched as they dived and fought, snatching up scraps of fish guts. Men stood at long tables, slicing fish open and cleaning them. A flapping tarpaulin kept the birds off and the shrieking gulls seemed to have learned to wait for their share.

After a moment Else was noticed. A lean, tanned man with long hair and a beard crusted with salt and twisted into tight braids came towards her. He wiped his knife clean as he approached and sheathed it through the belt holding up his cutoff shorts.

"Hi," he said.

"Hi. I'm Else."

"Quint. What do you want?"

"I want my baby back. I want my baby and I want Lowanna too. She's not my baby, but I told Jirra I would take care of her. She doesn't have anyone but me."

"Babies go up to the crew. They don't come back," Quint said.

"Why? Why do you let them take the babies? Why don't you just fight them?"

Quint shrugged. "We have a good thing going on here. We have food, a safe place to live. We don't get bothered. We just get to live."

"You could live on land. You could live on the beach, or in the forest or in the mountains. I have seen all these places."

"The dead are there too. They would come and eat us. We wouldn't be safe," Quint said with a rueful smile, as if speaking to a child.

"You would be free. You could fight for survival. You could build something real."

"This is real. The sun, the sea, the fish. It's all real."

"What about children? What about the future of the human race?"

"The human race?" Quint looked around. "There is no human race anymore. The race is over and we lost. All that's left are the scraps. It's not even our world anymore. We had our chance and we blew it. We ruined everything. Here we have a chance to live out our last generation. Live and then return to the sea."

Else scowled. "I'm not ready to quit. I haven't lived long enough to lose interest."

"Look out there, you see that?" Quint pointed to the black-green polish burning under the setting sun. "Compared to the oceans we are nothing. We are a tiny mote in God's eye. The ocean has been here long before us and will be here long after. We are nothing by comparison. Our lives are meaningless on that scale."

"I have a son. He was born two, maybe three days ago. To him I am everything. He doesn't know any of your bullshit. He only knows that he is alone and that I am not there to take care of him. So you can take your philosophy of giving up and you can shove it." Else turned on her heel and started walking down the guano-encrusted deck. She couldn't stand still any longer. She couldn't wait for her baby to be eaten by the crew. She couldn't fail him like she failed his father.

Quint watched her go. That woman had a fire in her that he had not seen since his surfing days, and the way she walked the deck reminded him of someone he used to know. By the time Else had vanished among the stacked crates and piles of salvage scrap, he remembered who it was.

CHAPTER 6

The ship had several decks and their layout confused Else as she went up the metal stairs and around piles of wood and plastic junk. There were burn marks on the metal deck where people had lit fires. The walls were marked with scrawled murals of graffiti, their details long lost to the scouring of the salt water. When whatever they painted with had been used up, the artists started scratching messages in the spreading rust. Words of hope and lost meaning—*Don't believe the hype!* and *Happy Hour 7AM till Fuck nose when!*—were carved large into the corroded steel. The birds watched and scolded Else at every step. She kept an eye out for Hob or Eric, not wanting to be taken by surprise again. She worked her way upwards. The crew, the walking dead, the evols who ran this supposed sanctuary lived somewhere above. The doors she tried were locked or rusted shut. Peering in through salt-frosted windows showed only dusty rooms plundered long ago.

There was no sound other than the breeze and the cries of seabirds out here. Else moved faster, jogging up the stairwells that connected each deck, scattering birds in angry clouds as she burst out among them. Their noise morphed into the cries of children. She started yelling, "I'm here! I won't leave without you! I'm coming for you, baby!" The setting sun blinded her as she ran along the highest deck. The wide deck was open, up to a wall of steel that ran from one side of the ship to the other. Twenty feet up, the top of the wall turned to glass. Massive windows reflected the view in three directions. Above the glass, spires of old antennae reached up to the first of the stars that smeared the twilight sky.

Else found another set of stairs and started climbing again. The doors on the highest deck were locked too. Seabirds had nested in every available space and she stepped around their heaped-up donuts of shit and dry seaweed. Solar panels erected along the high points of the deck were dull in the spreading gloom, their photoelectric cells waiting for dawn to start converting sunlight into electricity again and feed it down into racks of batteries stored somewhere inside the ship. Another way the crew held sway over the captive population.

"You shouldn't be up here." Sarah's voice took Else by surprise. The girl moved like a ghost.

"And you should be?" she replied.

The blonde child narrowed her eyes. "I can go anywhere I want. No one can stop me." She cocked her chin and stared up defiantly.

"Show me how to get in there." Else pointed to the tower of steel and glass.

"That's the bridge. Only the crew goes there. That's where the Captain lives."

"Show me," Else repeated.

Sarah backed away a few steps and then bolted. Else gave chase. The smaller girl flew down the deck, leaping over bird's nests and darting past sealed doorways in a way that made Else feel like a lumbering cow.

Reaching the back of the ship, Else stopped; Sarah had disappeared. She crouched down and examined the crusted deck. Small bare footprints, blurred by speed. Sarah had run through, turned right, and headed across the deck. She wouldn't have time to reach the opposite rail. So where did she go?

Else walked forward slowly, looking up the high steel wall. No way the girl could have climbed that. The footprints led to a small hatch. Else squatted again and tugged at the steel doorway. It was locked from the inside. She could see a smaller handprint on it. Sarah had gone to ground. Rising to her feet, Else wondered what other openings might exist up here. She turned sharply at a zipping sound. A shadow dropped through the moonlight. Pressing back against the wall, Else prepared to fight.

Hanging in a harness at the end of a rope was a hairless woman painted black with grease from head to toe. She wore only a ragged pair of stained shorts and a pair of dark tinted goggles pushed up to her forehead. Brushes and screwdrivers jangled in the harness as she twisted at the end of the rope.

The girl regarded Else with a somber expression. "Who the fuck are you?"

"Else. Who the fuck are you?"

"Ratchet. They call me Rache. What are you doing up here?" Rache swung gently in her harness, her dark goggles giving her an alien expression, as if she had four eyes.

"I'm looking for a way inside. I need to get my son back. What are you doing up here?"

"Maintenance. Someone's gotta clean the panels. Salt and bird shit don't do much for them."

"You're an engineer?" Else asked and Rache's chest puffed with pride.

"Yeah."

"Why are you covered in that stuff?" Else asked. Rache's expression soured.

"It's grease. Grease comes from hard work. Hard work is what will save us. One day this ship will sail to a safe place."

"The man who believes in God told me that this ship is an ark," Else said.

"He's crazy. There is no God. There's only the engines. The engines are what we need to get us moving."

"Why don't you just start the engines and sail away?"

Rache glanced upwards, staring at the flaking paint and the rust patches on the white-painted steel. "The Captain is the only one who can set the ship free. We are ready. We keep the engines clean and maintained. All the ship's systems are ready to go. We just need the Captain to give the order." Rache sounded wistful and evangelic at the same time.

"You don't need to wait for the Captain. Why not just start the engines and take over the ship?"

Rache reached up and pushed the goggles higher on her forehead. Her eyes were green, the same brilliant jade of the sea. "Are you kidding me? If the crew heard you talking like that they'd tear you apart and throw you over the side."

"Why do you let them rule over you? Why do you let them take the newborns and give you nothing in return?"

"They give us a safe place. They give us hope," Rache countered.

"They imprison you. All of you. You don't need to stay here. You could take your boats and go anywhere you want. You could start a new life, raise children and rebuild society."

"I dunno anything about that. I ain't never had kids." Rache's eyes dipped to the deck. "Not for lack of trying, though."

"They would take your baby away from you. Just like they did mine," Else said. "But I'm going to get him back. I just need to find a way inside."

"You can only get in from down below. All the deck hatches are sealed. You'd need to go the way the engineers do. Up through the maintenance ducts."

"Show me." Else stepped forward and grabbed hold of the rope suspending Rache off the deck.

"I'll take you to the Foreman. But I ain't promising nothing."

Rache grabbed a loop in the rope and heaved herself up with one hand until the line to the harness went slack. She unclipped it, dropping barefooted onto the deck.

"This way," she said, slinging the harness over her shoulder.

They wound their way down to the lower decks, Else following the engineer as she opened a door and they descended deeper into the ship. This area was marked differently from the hold where Hob and his people lived. The walls here were covered with schematics and scientific formulae.

"The ones who remember teach those who haven't yet learned. Then when they die, the ones who learned become those who remember," Rache said.

"If you let the crew eat your children, there will soon be no one left to learn," Else replied. They carried on down the stairs until they passed the waterline and entered the deepest area of the ship.

It was dark down here, darker than the night sky, always so full of stars. On the nights when clouds covered the moon, even the clouds seemed to glow with silver light. This was nothing like that. For a moment Else felt like she was descending once again into the depths of Woomera. She was plunged back to the place under the desert where the geeks hid from the evols and worked their genetic magic to make better weapons and zombie-killing Tankbread. So safe and perfectly contained—until the lights went out. Then the true darkness was suffocating. A darkness as complete and thick as velvet curtains stinking of burnt flowers pressed against her face.

"You okay?" Rache said in the dark.

"Dark," Else managed.

"Well yeah, lights are limited."

"Can't...breathe."

A scratching sound came from somewhere below, a steady winding grind. A few seconds passed, with Else feeling a cloying panic pressing the air out of her lungs. Then a flare of sodium-yellow light cast long shadows up Rache's dark face and made her eyes shine.

"It's okay," she said calmly. "You're safe down here."

"Don't like being trapped in the dark," Else gasped.

Rache shrugged. "Follow me and the light will stay on."

Else pushed on down the stairs, following the moving circle of light. Rache stopped in front of a door, which she rapped on with the knuckles of one hand. Else felt her heart thudding; the close darkness terrified her.

Claustrophobia is an irrational fear, she reminded herself. *But it doesn't make it any less real*, she mentally retorted.

The steel door ahead rang with the sudden strike of metal. Else growled a warning that Rache ignored. The door cracked open and then swung inwards. A warm glow emerged from the other side. Rache immediately pushed on it and stepped through the gap. "Almost home," she said over her shoulder.

Else followed the light. Behind the door and to one side of the corridor stood a young man, painted in black oil against the shadows. The whites of his eyes vanished when he blinked, rendering him almost invisible. Else watched him warily and kept moving after Rache. The girl ahead ignored the doorman and he watched them go before pushing the door shut in their wake.

Rache walked with Else on her heels until they stepped onto a walkway that ran around a chamber as wide as the ship. Below them, pipes and domed machines were being crawled over by oil-stained figures as black as the shadows. The air hummed with the vibration of feet and the clang of tools striking metal.

"The engines are always ready," Rache said with pride in her voice.

"Then why don't you sail away?" Else asked again. Rache ignored her. A trio of blackened, tool-carrying mechanics came swaggering down the walkway. Like Rache, their heads were shaved and they did not smile as they approached the two women.

"Hey Giz, Prop, Bolt, this is Else." Rache crossed her arms, the goggles on her forehead glinting in the light.

The three nodded. "She's no black. What's she doin' down here?" Giz asked.

"She's from ashore. Came here looking for her sprat."

The three young men sneered. "Grabbit wants you on turbo stripping," Giz said. "The landy can turn around and go back to the hold. Ain't nothing for her here."

"She's walking with me, all the way to the Foreman," Rache said, drawing herself up to her full height.

"Well you'd both better walk your arse to the turbocharger," Giz said. The three boys pushed past.

"I can't stay here," Else said, looking for a way out.

"You can leave anytime you want. No skin off my knuckles." Rache headed off down the catwalk. Else hesitated for a moment and then hurried after her.

The engineers lived in conditions similar to those of Hob's people. Else saw no babies, just pregnant women with white eyes shining in their dark-stained faces and men with bodies sculpted into lean muscle from hard work. Two guards, armed with swords hammered from sheet metal, stood in front of a steel door.

"Got a landy. She needs to see the Foreman," Rache said.

One of the guards pulled a lever and stepped through the door. Else caught a smell of cooked fish and sweat before the door closed again. The remaining guard moved in front of them and stared. The three of them stood in silence, unmoving until the door opened again.

"Come," the first guard said. With Rache leading the way, Else ducked through the door into a room at the bottom of a set of metal stairs. Women lounged naked on ragged cushions and crumbling furniture. The guard climbed the stairs, Else and Rache following close behind. The room at the top contained more cushions and a bed of sorts, with more naked women. Else had only ever seen one fat person, the Greek near Woomera. The man on the bed looked like he had eaten the Greek and his pigs for lunch. The women massaged the sprawling folds of his abundant flesh. Else could smell the sour stink of his sweat and filth across the room.

"Foreman," Rache said and went down on one knee. Else just stared.

"Who is this lovely creature you have brought us, child?" The Foreman's voice was a breathless wheeze. His face seemed half-formed in a swollen ball of fat topped with thin black hair that hung over his shoulders in greasy strands.

"She's come from ashore," Rache said.

"Ashore..." The blob waved one of the girls stroking his arm away. "Come closer."

Else stepped up to the edge of the bed. The smell was overpowering, a nostril-clogging stench like rotting vegetation.

"What is your name, child?" the Foreman asked.

"Else. Someone on this ship took my son. I'm here to get him back."

The swollen head nodded. Else could see now, it was more than blubber that encased his body. The lower legs were amputated at the knee, and the Foreman's thighs had spread under the pressure of some growth that deformed them into obese bags of quivering skin.

"Your child must have been new; such salvage are given as tributes to the Captain and crew."

"Not my son," Else growled.

The Foreman's hand waved again. "Such is the way of things. You are young and we have plenty of men here. You can have another child."

One of the naked attendants leaned over with a plate of cooked fish, broken into natural slices. The Foreman took a pinch of the white meat in his fingers and stuffed it into his mouth.

Else cleared the edge of the bed in a single leap. She sent the girl with the plate flying back, fish splattering against the walls.

"You're not listening to me," she snarled, her fingers pressing deep into the soft, wet folds of the Foreman's fat neck. "I am here to get my son back. You can either help me, or I will burn you along with everyone else who stands in my way."

The Foreman's eyes bulged, crumbs of fish tumbling from his tongue and quivering lips.

"Stand back," he squeaked, and the guards closing in with weapons drawn hesitated.

"What you ask…It can't be done. We must render unto the Caesar what is Caesar's."

"And unto God what is God's. Yes I've read that book too." Else's fingers pressed deeper. There seemed to be no end to the soft rubber of his flesh.

"You must understand…" the Foreman started to choke. "We are powerless. We must…obey."

Else released her grip. "Why must you obey?"

"We wait for the day when we are called upon to bring the engines to life," Rache spoke up.

"You are waiting for a day that will never come. The evols are not interested in guiding you to a new paradise. They simply want to continue feeding off your young until you forget what it is to be human," Else said without looking around.

"No…that is not true," the Foreman said. "We have an important job to do. The Captain himself has given us the responsibility to be ready. We do his work."

"How did you lose your legs?" Else asked and slid off the bed, wiping her hands on the cloth.

"I…It was a long time ago. I don't remember," he said.

"You cannot question the Foreman in this way," one of the guards said.

"Why not? Did the Captain tell you that it was forbidden?" Else scowled at the guard. "Tell me, I want to know. What price did you pay for your place on this ship?"

The Foreman swallowed hard. His body quivered and he whined deep in his bulk. "I am the master of the engine room. I know the engines. I alone hold their secrets."

"You're using a combined gas and steam turbine installation, consisting of two General Electric LM2500 gas turbines and a steam turbine coupling. But you have no fuel. You've got people living in your gas tanks."

"You cannot know this!" the Foreman quivered and waved his hands in impotent rage.

"Someone has very carefully painted the propulsion system schematics on the walls. I see things and I remember them. I also read books. Face it, you are living a lie and leading these people to a long and miserable death at the hands of a few evols that you could easily conquer if you just rose up and said enough." Else stepped away from the bed and walked to the door, Rache and the guard moving out of her way.

"You're pathetic," she said to the Foreman. Else opened the door and went down the stairs, needing more than ever to feel fresh air on her face and be away from the stink of so many people living in confined space.

"Wait!" Rache called, flying down the stairs and pushing past the knot of curious engineers gathered to see the strange landy woman.

"Come with me." She pulled Else's arm, guiding her away from the watchful eyes of the black-stained workers. Else allowed herself to be led. They went to a room, closed off by a ragged cloth sheet. Inside the small space, piles of stained bedding and clothes were heaped and strewn about. Under the pile of bedcovers someone snored, farted, and mumbled their way back into deeper sleep.

Rache pulled a small metal box out from under a sagging shelf.

Opening it, she drew out a creased and finger-marked postcard. "I want to go here," she said.

Else took the card and stared at the photograph of a tropical island with the once proud ship in the background.

"You can't go there on this ship. It's dead. Dead as the crew, dead in the water."

"How can I get there?" Oily tears welled in Rache's eyes.

"Fight. Stand with me and escape the crew. Life on land isn't easy, but it's better than what you have."

"This is all we have. All I remember. Did you mean what you said to the Foreman? That the ship will never sail?"

"I'm no expert, but I've seen enough and read enough to know that this is not the way. There are other ships; you could find one and get it going and sail anywhere you wanted."

Rache blinked as the idea of having her own ship to sail rolled over in her mind.

"You said you could get me up to where the crew is," Else said.

The engineer nodded and wiped her nose on the back of her hand as she sniffed the tears back and put the postcard away. "Yeah, up through the ducts. It's an easier way to get up high. We stay out of the places the crew go, but we can do maintenance without bothering them."

"Show me," Else said firmly.

The young woman guided Else along the narrow catwalks that spanned the bowels of the ship. She could see at a glance how much had been stripped out already. Half the engines were scattered in rusting pieces. Entire sections were being slavishly toiled over, dismantled and rebuilt over and over again. *Give them hope and they will work themselves to death*, Else thought. The ladder to the maintenance shafts was guarded. Rache motioned Else to stay back while she went forward.

Rache approached the young male guard. She put her hands on

his oil-stained chest and spoke softly to him. They exchanged a few words that Else could not hear.

Else watched curiously. Her experiences in how people related to each other were mostly limited to books and the occasional encounter with a survivor group. She had seen crude seduction, rape, and prostitution of both sexes, but with limited direct exposure to other people, she found it difficult to read the guard's body language.

With Rache leading him, the man went willingly into a smaller sleeping area curtained off from the main chamber. Else waited for a few moments and then, unsure of what was happening, she approached the curtain and took a cautious look inside. She blinked twice, her eyes adjusting to the dim light. Rache was on her hands and knees, almost invisible with her blackened skin in low contrast to the gloom. The young guard knelt behind her, his hips thrusting against the young woman's buttocks. Else watched impassively; they mated the same way as most animals she had seen.

The man's back arched and he let out a guttural groan, shuddering against Rache. She waited until he had collapsed on the padding and rags before rolling over into a sitting position and wiping herself clean with a stray cloth.

"Sleep well," she said to the prostrate boy, who just waved weakly in reply. Rache crawled out of the sleeper alcove and pointed up the ladder. "We head up, through that hole and into the pipes."

Else nodded and clambered up the metal rungs after Rache, who climbed like a cat. The space at the top of the ladder got smaller and darker the closer Else climbed. She focused her attention on Rache's feet and pushed on into the tight confines of the pipe.

"I don't like the dark," Else whispered, her voice echoing in the narrow tunnel.

"It's not dark," Rache replied, pressing herself back against the curved wall of the pipe. "Look."

Else blinked. Above her, beyond the fading light of the engine room below, the walls glowed with patterns and signs. Luminescent paint, green, yellow, and blue, shone coldly in the gloom.

"The first engineers, they had the secret of painting in light. It shows up best in the dark. You can never be lost in the pipes if you know how to read the marks."

"Chemical luminescence…" Else whispered, intrigued by the vivid brightness and complexity of the art that spiraled up the pipe.

"Do they make words?" she asked as Rache resumed climbing.

"Not proper words, like in the manual, but they say where to go and where you will be if you come out a hatch."

The two women climbed in silence through intersections and along changing angles of dull, echoing metal. The pipe changed from heavy round steel to thinner square ducting. The ladder ended and now they crawled on their bellies.

"Keep quiet," Rache whispered over her shoulder. "We're getting close to the crew territory."

Else nodded. Her focus remained on breathing and keeping calm while the space shrank around her.

The duct vibrated under the impact of a crash somewhere ahead. Rache froze and Else wormed her way forward to try and see.

"What was that?" she whispered.

Rache's eyes flared wide in sudden fear. "Crew." The engineer wormed her way to the side of the duct, leaving a panic-inducing amount of space for Else to slither into position beside her. Light flared in pale lines through a grille just beyond Else's face. She peered down into a bare room with iron water and gas pipes running in tight clusters along the ceiling. A man hung from a chain looped over the pipes. The chain had been fastened around his wrists and he thrashed and growled with bestial fury.

"Evol," Else breathed. "Why have they chained him up?"

Rache couldn't see anything and was afraid to move with this strange monster so close to them. The only door to the room banged and then swung open. A man stepped inside, his uniform crisply pressed and well laundered. He looked normal until he turned his head, and then Else saw that most of the right side of his face lay open in a ragged wound, still seeping yellow fluid. Above the wound his eye sagged over a rim of scraped bone. A fringe of tendon and flesh ran along the line of his cheek. The hair and skin on the right side of his head had been burned away; even the ear had melted into a charred nub.

"How long has he been like this?" the scarred evol asked someone behind him.

"Two days," came the slurred reply.

"Feed him," the officer commanded and stepped aside. A crewmember, wearing the same dark clothes of the guard Else had killed, stepped into the room. He carried a squirming baby boy upside down by the ankle. The tiny figure, so new his skin was still smeared with white, waxy vernix, squalled and wriggled. Else felt her heart leap into her throat. *Baby!*

The crewmember lifted the tiny person up in front of the chained evol's face. The zombie immediately started sniffing and straining forward, his teeth snapping on the air.

The baby swung in the hand of the crewmember, who seemed to be enjoying the game of teasing his comrade. In a moment, the arc of the baby's swing came close enough that the lunging evol's clashing teeth caught on tender flesh and the newborn shrieked in agony. The zombie thrashed against his chains, shaking the baby and snarling until he tore a large, bloody chunk of meat from the tiny body.

Up in the duct, Else exploded into screams. Her fingers scrabbled at the grille, desperate to get out and punish the killers. Rache wrapped her arms and legs around the yelling woman. With one hand clapped over Else's mouth, she hung on until Else's rage had spent itself in wild thrashing and scraping of fingernails along the dull metal walls of the duct.

In the room below, the noise of their struggle was drowned out by the dying screams of the baby, the laughter of the crewmember, and the snarling of the evol who feasted on the stem cell–rich flesh of the newborn.

The transformation of the dead man came quickly as he absorbed the flowing blood and torn flesh of the child. The snarling reduced and his body shuddered; the grey color faded from his dead skin as it flushed with stolen life. The crewman unlocked the shackles and the evol dropped to his knees before slowly rising to a standing position.

"Are you ready to resume your duties?" the officer asked.

"Yes…sirggh…" the evol said slowly.

"Clean him up and have him report," the officer said and marched out of the room. The two remaining evols followed him out and the door closed with a dull boom.

Else, still struggling, bit down hard on Rache's hand. The girl squealed and let go.

"You crazy bitch!" she yelped, clutching her wounded hand.

"They killed him! They fucking killed him!" Else threw herself at the grille and this time managed to knock it out of its frame. Slithering out, she dropped into the room that stank of fresh blood and the arrested decay of evols. The only remains of the child were a few crushed bones and a smear of gore. Else could see nothing to indicate it was her baby, her son. She opened the door. The corridor was deserted. She sniffed the air, seeking her prey, but only smelled fresh blood. She turned left, heading in the same direction Rache had been leading her.

After Else had vanished around the corner, a small shape crept into the hallway. Moving silently, Sarah went to the open room where the evol had been restored. She stared at the splash of blood and pieces of mashed red meat on the floor. She darted into the room and crouched down, carefully scraping the mess into a battered tin can until it was full. Returning to the doorway, she peeped both ways before slipping out into the corridor and hurrying off the way she had come.

CHAPTER 7

Else went slowly up a stairwell, every sense alive to signs of the undead. Dust and salty grime crusted everything. Boot prints in the dirty carpets showed a lot of people had been walking around up here. She strained for any sound of babies crying. The fear that her son might have already been eaten nearly choked her every time she dared think it.

In Else's experience evols did not make noise. They did not breathe, engage in small talk, or move around unnecessarily. Like ambush predators they would stand, still and silent, waiting for something to get their attention, and then they would strike.

Growing rage soon threatened to overwhelm her caution as she tried every door handle and slammed doors on empty rooms. Marching down the silent corridor, wanting to shout and scream and demand the crew come out and face her.

Behind the door labeled as "Boardroom" she found a group of evols all wearing faded blue uniforms. They stood like abandoned dolls in the dark until the door opened, then a dozen heads turned in her direction.

"It is forbidden," said the nearest dead man. Else picked up a wooden chair and smashed it across his face.

This act of violence roused the others and they marched on her as a group. Backing up, Else held the splintered remains of the chair's leg like a stake. A woman raised her hands, reaching for Else. "Forbidden," she echoed. Else spun on the balls of her feet, slamming the ragged end of the chair leg into the woman's throat. Black blood splattered across the others, startling them into deep-throated growls of aggression and unease.

"Come on!" Else yelled, the noise of her voice unsettling the dead further. They attacked in one group, teeth and hands reaching for her, the thin veneer of civilization sloughing away like dead skin as they succumbed to the instinctive drive to kill and devour living meat.

The pieces of chair shattered against bones and jammed deep in dead chests. Else backed up, using the door to bottleneck her attackers. She lashed out with feet and fists, destroying knees, shattering noses, and smashing snarling heads against the metal doorframe. An evol stumbled through the door, feet tangling on the twisted corpses that littered the floor. Else grabbed the zombie's arm and twisted; the dead sinew cracked and the arm dislocated at the shoulder. Else kept twisting, a howl of hatred and rage fueling her strength. The arm ripped free from the glistening socket. Armed with this makeshift club, she laid into the remaining dead.

Soon only three remained and the doorway had clogged with the still writhing bodies of the broken evols. The survivors hung back, a primal survival instinct flaring somewhere in their rotting skulls.

Else wiped the gore and slime of carnage from her face and spat the foulness of them from her mouth.

"Tell your Captain," she panted. "Tell him. I am Else. I am going to kill you all. And him. Him I will kill last."

With a final glare she threw the gore-soaked arm down and walked off down the narrow corridor. Climbing another flight of stairs, she found the way forward blocked by a sealed door. Else pounded on it, determined to bring her enemy out to face her. No one came.

Frustrated, she ran up the next flight of stairs, the adrenaline of the fight fading fast, leaving her tense and shaking. Moving into a hallway that ran along the length of the ship, Else slowed her breathing as her nose picked up a range of strange smells. Feces and a sour acid stink filled the air.

The smell came from a dimly lit room where three crude cages had been constructed from pipes of steel and heavy plastic. The pens were small, with barely enough room for a single occupant. Else came closer, disturbed and curious at the same time. In front of each cage hung an empty metal tray and she could see that trapped inside each cell was a naked, adult woman.

"Why are you in here?" she asked. The nearest woman raised her head. Greasy, matted hair and eyes sunk deep into a face smeared with grime stared out through the bars. "Why are you in here? Are you being punished?" Else asked again.

"We..." the woman's voice croaked. She coughed, her gaunt shoulders heaving. "We feed the young," her voice rasped, and Else could smell the sweet acid of malnutrition on her breath.

"The babies the crew eat?" Else asked, pressing forward and rattling the enclosure.

"Not all of them...Some are kept alive, until they are needed. A week...maybe two..." Her breasts were swollen and dripping thin milk. It ran in rivulets down the corrugated surface of her ribs as the woman slumped in her pen. There was no room for her to sit or lie down. She could barely bend her knees and Else could see where the pressure of the bars had ulcerated her skin, leaving deep, foul-smelling wounds that oozed pus.

"Where are the babies?" Else demanded. She found the fastening bolt for the cage, the other two women stirring as she rattled the bolt open. The wet nurse in the cage fell forward as the cage swung open. Else caught her, gently lifting the woman and laying her down on the floor. Her body was wasting away; below the ankles her feet were an open sore, stained with smears of bodily waste. Her skin was breaking down with infection and malnutrition. At the points of her shoulder blades and elbows the skin had rubbed raw and wept blood and fluids. Writhing maggots dripped like melting wax from the fist-sized holes in the woman's skin.

"I will get you out of here. I will take you to the hold; they need to see what is happening here. They have medicine, they can help you." Else hurried to the other two cages while explaining what she intended. The women in the cages cringed away from her. One of them started shrieking as the cage door swung open, thrashing in the tiny space and smashing her skull against the bars. Droplets of fresh blood stained her naturally red hair and masked her face in a crimson sheen.

Else ignored her, leaving the door open as she moved to unbolt the final cage. The blonde-haired woman in this one was younger and fresher. Starvation and imprisonment hadn't yet taken her strength or sanity. She stepped out on her own, watching Else with wild eyes.

"Come with me," Else insisted. "I can take you to safety." The fresh-faced woman sank to the floor, her face blank with horror, hands crawling up her face to press against her ears, blocking out the screaming of the redhead.

"You have to get up." Else went and tugged on the blonde girl's wrists. She whimpered and pulled away. "You can't stay here, you'll die," Else said.

"We are already dead..." the woman on the floor moaned. "There is no safe place...not since they took over."

Else looked at the three women with disgust, not at their physical condition but at their weakness. "They only win if you stop fighting," she said.

The door opened and a woman with a dried-up bite that had torn a chunk from her scalp stood in the doorway, processing what she was seeing. Else didn't give her a chance to speak. Charging forward, she slammed the evol back against the wall. She followed up with a hand strike to the throat that tore the dead flesh away and exposed the yellowing ringbones of the trachea.

"Forbidden," the evol gurgled, her teeth snapping at Else's arm. She grabbed the zombie's head and twisted it off.

The women from the cages whimpered and moaned. The blonde girl screamed and scuttled back into her cage, pulling the door shut. The woman on the floor had gone quiet and still. When Else checked on her, she was dead.

Else sealed the room on her way out. The women in the cages should be safe when their dead roommate got up again. If the crew were keeping babies alive until they were needed, then her son might still have a chance.

The hours had blurred into one another, the sun a fiery disc rising over the horizon when Else climbed out on a high deck. The seabirds were rousing for the day in their nests, and the salt air seared Else's dry throat as she looked for a way up higher.

"You're in trouble," a singsong voice warned. Else scowled.

"Sarah?" she asked.

"I'm going to tell the Captain," Sarah's voice sang from a different direction. Else turned slowly, scanning the walls and hidden decks. Sarah climbed like a cat and knew every inch of the ship. She could be anywhere, watching and taunting Else.

"Tell him what exactly?"

Sarah's giggle echoed off the steel and set the birds muttering. "That you did stuff an' you went where you're not allowed."

"I'm looking for my baby. You know that." Else turned her head. Sarah was right there; she was sure of it. How did she get up so high?

Sarah's voice came from another place, this time behind Else. "The Captain's going to kill me. Kill me proper, so I come back smart. He'll do it cuz I'm going to tell. Then the first thing he'll give me to eat is your baby."

Else heard the faint sound of bare feet slapping on the deck and then the creak of a door swinging shut.

"Sarah! Wait!" Else yelled at the sky.

The engineers knew the way up to the highest points on the ship, where the crew waited with her baby. After sweeping her gaze across the high steel walls, Else turned and climbed down to the safer decks where the ship's passengers eked out their existence.

CHAPTER 8

Else made her way into the engine room, where the engineers toiled with the fantasy of seeing the ship sail once again. Rache was nowhere in sight when she entered the main chamber and tapped the nearest worker on the shoulder. "I'm looking for Rache," she told him.

"Haven't seen her." The oil-stained man folded his arms and glared down at Else.

"You don't belong here," the next woman she approached said before Else could ask where Rache might be.

"None of us belong here," Else replied. "If I can find Rache I can help you all escape."

"We belong here. You, you're just trouble." The engineers came onto the catwalk, sliding down poles and clambering up over the rails. In moments Else found her way blocked by a crowd of hostile faces.

"Rache!" she shouted over their heads.

"Go on, piss off!" someone shouted and the mob pushed forward. Else was shoved against the railing. Doubling over, she pressed back before they could force her over the side to plummet to the floor meters below. More engineers were gathering down there. Angry faces turned upwards; they raised their fists and shouted for Else to leave or die.

Rache appeared, pushing her way through the group on the

catwalk. She shoved men aside and glared at anyone who dared snarl in response. "You need to leave here now, Else," she warned.

"Please," Else said. "You know how to get up to the bridge. I need your help."

Rache hesitated, "I...I can't. You're on your own. I'm sorry."

"Rache!" Else shouted at the girl's back as she pulled back into the crowd that pressed in, seizing Else by the arms. Her feet lashed out, catching one man in the side of the head with enough force to send him spinning over the railing. Screams came from the crowd below.

"Kill the bitch!" a voice howled. Others took up the shout: "Kill! Kill! Kill!"

Else let out a scream of her own, a raw, primal howl of fury, and she tore free of the greasy hands that clung to her.

"Fuckers!" she screamed. "I'll fucking kill you if you get in my way!" Teeth bared she charged them, striking the first man low in the midsection, knocking him down and using his chest as a platform to leap for a pipe that ran overhead. A dozen pairs of hands reached up for Else as she climbed to the topside of the pipes. If she crouched down there was enough space here to scramble away from the crowd. Angry voices followed her and when the pipes abruptly angled upwards into the ceiling she took a chance and leapt across a yawning gap to catch hold of a hanging chain. Swinging back and forth she started to climb down, hand over hand. The crowd of engineers on the high catwalk parted and a heavyset man stepped into view. In his hands he carried a blackened metallic tube with a blue flame burning at the end. A hose ran to a pair of squat tanks on his back. His right hand pumped a lever vigorously as Else stared at the strange apparatus without comprehension.

"Kill her!" the crowd roared. Else paused in her climbing. The faces looking up at her from the floor far below had the same wild eyes and bared teeth of those on the catwalk. Climbing down would get her killed too.

With a dull cough and a high-pitched hiss, the short tube spewed fire and rolling black smoke. Else had time to yell "Fuck!" and let go of the chain before the inferno swallowed the spot she had hung from a second before.

The crowd below broke her fall. They were packed too tightly to give her space to land on the steel plate floor. She heard screams of pain and opened her eyes long enough to see through the tangled pile of limbs and stinking bodies. A wrench came arcing through a gap in the melee and her vision shattered into a thousand shards of dark unconsciousness.

—∞◆∞—

Else's eye cracked open, her sight blurred red from the crust of blood cementing her eyelids together. A yellow bulb burned in a wall bracket, giving everything a jaundiced look.

It took her a moment to realize that she was hanging from the ceiling by chains wrapped around her ankles, while her fingertips waved a foot off the ground. Everything tasted of blood. Her head pounded and a delicate examination with her hands found a healing gash on her forehead where the wrench had knocked her out. Blood from half a hundred bruises and cuts burned across her face and body. Milk pressed from her breasts and dripped in her eyes, blurring her vision further and stinging against the cuts on her face.

Everything hurt, which Else took as a good sign. It meant she wasn't paralyzed or dead. She experimented with lifting her head to follow her hands in the upwards traverse of her body. Her clothes were gone and her spine creaked as she curled up to touch her toes.

The chain securing her feet had been wrapped around a steel girder in the ceiling and looped around her ankles. Else bent further, shallow breaths hissing from between her clenched teeth as she craned upwards. Her straining fingers reached the edge of the chain, and then strength failed her and she fell back, gasping for breath and swinging upside down.

After a few long moments of recovery she tried again. This time she folded up at the waist with more force. The chain slapped against her fingertips and then she gripped the closest links. With her finger grip taking some of the strain, she pulled herself into an even tighter fold. More of the chain came under the grip of her hands and she bent her knees outwards, pulling her body up to lift the strain off the chain loops that held her feet. As the links went slack, Else wriggled her left foot and then her right until they slipped out of the loosened chain. Hanging by her hands, she dropped lightly to the floor and immediately collapsed, her feet completely numb from the lack of blood flow.

"Fuck," Else whimpered as her legs exploded with a painful burning, prickling sensation. Flexing her legs and ankles helped until normal circulation returned. Standing up with more care, she had to crouch again, the change in gravity's direction making a bathroom break her first priority.

The door had been locked from the outside. Else sat down in the lee of where it would open when someone came to check on her and leaned against the wall. Her head still ached and the healing wounds on her body itched and burned. With her knees drawn up, she lowered her head and went to sleep.

CHAPTER 9

The squeak of the door handle being twisted open roused Else into pitch darkness. With no natural light she had lost sense of time, though her throat was dry and her stomach rumbled, suggesting hours had passed. She pushed herself up; first she would fight her way out and then find some food.

Else pressed back against the wall as the door swung open, her fist ready to smash the new arrival's face. Rache raised a smoking oil lantern, gaping at the empty chains, and then turning in time to see Else advancing on her with bared teeth.

"Wait!" she yelped, hands raised in defense.

"Get me out of here," Else demanded.

"I will, but listen. It's not safe. There's been some kind of disease outbreak. The holders, they're getting sick, dying and coming back feral."

"The holders? The people living in the hold?" Else asked.

"Yeah. They're going crazy and attacking anyone they can find. It's getting really fucked up."

"Where's the Foreman?"

"Up in his office I guess. He's just telling us to lock up tight and wait for the crew to restore order."

Else's sudden smile was a death mask grimace in the dim light.

"Is that what you think is going to happen? The crew is going to restore order?"

Rache blinked, her face opening in complete shock, "But.. . they have to."

"They don't have to do anything. They will only try to stop an outbreak to protect the herd. They only need enough of you to keep breeding. That's the only reason they'll destroy the ferals."

"So what do we do?" Rache asked.

"What I've been saying all along. We fight. We destroy every last motherfucker. Then you will be free."

"Free? Like being able to set sail and go anywhere?"

"Sure, you can be the captain of your own boat if you want." Else peered out into the cathedral of the engine room. Engineers were huddled in small groups around drums that flickered with oil fires. Weapons of hammered steel with gleaming edges lay close at hand.

"Ohh..." Rache breathed. "Captain Rache..."

"Can you get your people to follow you? We need them to help save the holders, find any survivors and bring them back here. The fishermen too."

"We can't go out there, there are zombies," Rache said with genuine terror rising on her face.

"I'll need some clothes, and one of those blade weapons your people have."

Rache slipped out the door. "Wait here," she said and vanished into the gloom.

Else idly scratched at a scab on her chest; the rough edge of someone's boot had split the skin and cracked a rib. The bone felt restored, and the dried blood lifted from a pink line of healing scar tissue as she scratched. Her body tingled with the itch of healing and she rubbed her back against the edge of the door while waiting for Rache to return.

The girl came hurrying back with a bundle of cloth cradled

against her chest and a short-handled, scythe-like blade in her other hand.

Else took the clothes offered. "I have seen material like this before," she said. "The soldiers at Woomera wore the same color."

Rache held up a pair of boots. "I don't know if these will fit. I only had a moment to grab the first pair I saw in the stores."

The boots were too large, so Else tore strips of fabric from the trousers and wrapped her feet before sliding the boots on and lacing them tight. Taking the scythe, she tested the strength of the wire binding that held the blade to the handle.

"We are ever vigilant," Rache said, her eyes reflecting the chrome of the blade.

"Eternal vigilance is the price of freedom," Else replied, swinging the blade and getting a feel for the weight of it. "I read that in a book," she added.

"I don't know if they will follow us." Rache's eyes were wide and white against her blackened skin.

"You want to be a captain, you need to be able to lead." Else gave her a minute to think it through. Rache took a deep breath and left the room. Else rested the blade over her shoulder and followed the girl.

"Hey! Hey!" Rache yelled across the cavernous chamber. People turned and looked, some rising to their feet.

"Have they broken through?"

"Is it the dead?"

"They're here!"

Voices clamored from all directions. The clash of weapons being snatched up echoed off the walls. Rache walked out into the gathering crowd.

"We…We need to fight the dead," she said, her voice lost in the growing alarm of the swelling mob.

"Where are they?"

"Someone tell the Foreman!"

"Listen to me!" Rache yelled, her voice stronger this time. "We are engineers! This ship is our home! We will not hide like holders! Like children! We will protect our home! We will fight for what is ours!"

The engineers stopped hurrying about in circles looking for the enemy and started turning towards Rache. Listening to her voice calling them to stand together.

"Who are you to tell us what to do?"

"That's Rache, she's just a panel scrubber!" another voice jeered, and others laughed with him.

"Yes!" Rache shouted them down. "I'm a panel scrubber. I keep the shit off the solar panels so you can have water and light. I believe in the ship! I believe in the Foreman! I want to see her sail!"

The crowd shouted—"Yeah! Sail! Sail! Sail!"—drumming their weapon handles on the metal floor and against pipes in a rhythmic pounding that swelled across the engine chamber.

"We take the fight to them! We take this ship! Then we sail her!" Rache's face rose above the crowd as the nearest engineers lifted her on their shoulders. Fists punched the air and a deafening chorus of cheers rolled around the room.

Hands fell on the barred gates and doors, pulling levers and tearing away the barriers. The crowd surged forward, pouring out of the room and into the stairwells that led out into the ship. Rache waited until the last of them had left the room and Else stepped up beside her.

"You'll make a good captain," Else said and followed the line of warriors going to war.

"Where did the outbreak start? Do your people even know where they are going?" Else asked Rache as they followed the crowd.

"In the hold, some people got sick and then turned. They died hard and came back feral. You know how it spreads, right?"

Else nodded. She knew the Adam virus didn't spread; it was

already in everything. Lying dormant in the air, the soil, the water, and in every living person. When the body died, the virus activated, bringing the person back to kill and feed on living flesh.

"Where are the survivors? Do they have somewhere to go?" Else asked.

"Dunno," Rache replied. "We can start in the hold and see who is left."

Shouts from the engineers ahead told them the first of the new evols had been encountered. They heard the clash of steel on bone and flesh, the screams of the dying, and the snarls of the hungry dead driven into a fury by the presence of life.

The corridor clogged with squirming bodies. Else hefted her blade, the familiar rage building in her chest. The fine blonde hairs on her arms rose as adrenaline flooded her system. She charged into the fight, swinging the scythe up in a wide arc, point first into a dead woman's head, splitting her skull in a spray of brackish grey blood.

The freshly dead had more muscle, more reserves of nutrients for energy, and they moved quickly, driven by a desperate need to consume. The engineers fought hard, shrieking war cries giving voice to their fear as they smashed their enemy. The battle of the corridor eased as the dead fell. Else dragged a groaning engineer out of the fray, his arm contorted by the missing chunks of flesh ripped from him by evol teeth.

"No...no...no..." the wounded man moaned. Else ignored his protests and swung her blade, piercing his skull. His eyes dulled and with a shudder he went still.

"Which way is the hold?" Else asked as she hooked and dragged limp corpses from the pile blocking the corridor.

"Down there," Rache pointed to a darkened doorway. Snarls and growls echoed up from the gloom. The engineers milled around the descending stairwell, no one ready to be the first to go down into the darkness.

Else took the lead, heading down the stairs and into a narrow corridor that ran along the deck below. Three evols were feasting on a fresh corpse; the broken body of a teenage boy shook as they ripped and tore at his soft entrails.

"Hey, motherfuckers," Else called to get their attention. The trio's heads snapped up and they leapt forward snarling, hands outstretched.

The curved blade whistled through the air, striking the first evol through the back of the neck and jutting out through his throat. Else let go of the handle and kicked the second one in the chest, knocking him back on the floor.

The third evol, a woman, dodged Else's punch and grabbed her wrist in two hands. Bloodstained teeth bit down on her skin and Else twisted her arm out of the slick grip of the dead woman while punching her in the head with a flurry of short jabs.

The zombie started to convulse. Tasting Else's blood destroyed the virus controlling her brain in spectacular fashion.

"Weapon!" Else yelled over her shoulder. The woman lunged forward again, grappling Else and forcing her down onto the blood-slicked floor.

A blade clattered past and Else snatched it up. Swinging the handle around, she forced it under the woman's chin and pushed backwards. The evol howled, thick drool spilling down her chin. Else jerked the blade handle sideways and threw the woman against the wall. Rolling to her knees, she swung the blade down in a chopping motion and buried it in the dead woman's head.

The engineers came down the stairs and hacked the remaining evol to pieces. Else handed her weapon to Rache and went to the evol struggling to stand up with her scythe blade sticking through his neck. Grabbing the handle she twisted it, snapping his neck with an audible crack. The evol slumped and Else yanked the blade free.

"They will never hesitate. They will never stop. They will kill you if you don't destroy them." Else shook the gore from her blade and addressed the wide-eyed engineers. "You must be like them if you want to win. Destroy them without mercy. Smash the brain or cut the spinal cord. Do it however you can. But never hesitate, or they will make you one of them."

The handle of the scythe weapon creaked in her grip as Else stepped towards the engineers. "And if that happens, I will not hesitate to kill you myself."

"You're...you're bit..." Rache stared at Else's wounded arm with wide eyes.

"I'm different. They bite me, they die. They bite you, you die," Else said.

"What are you?" Rache asked.

"It's a long story," Else replied.

"Well...why don't you just go around letting them bite you and kill them all?"

"For one thing, it fucking hurts, and for another, there's not enough of me to destroy them all. It's more efficient to kill them."

The engineers regarded the woman with open-mouthed awe. Rache stamped her foot and punched the air in the sudden silence. "Yeah! We're taking the ship!"

The crowd shouted their approval and drummed on the floor with the hafts of their weapons.

Else stepped aside and let Rache lead the charge down the empty corridor. These were her people and the engineers needed to see Rache on the front line, leading them to some semblance of freedom.

The flood of people impacted the doors that led to the hold. A crush ensued as the doors were forced open and then they plunged onwards, down another stairwell and into the close and stinking confines of the holders' dormitory.

The place lay in ruins. Bedding and the few salvage items they claimed as their own were strewn everywhere. Blood had sprayed up the walls and pooled on the floor. Around the room, torn corpses, some writhing and struggling to move, made guttural moans and clawed at the air with blackened fingers.

"They're all dead!" Rache cried as her engineers set to and dispatched the evols that remained.

"Some of the holders might have survived," Else suggested as she casually lopped off a snarling boy's head.

"Where are they then?" Rache asked.

"The Hole," Else said. "They might have gone down to the fighting place they call the Hole."

"Do you know where it is?" Rache asked.

"Yes," Else replied. "I remember everything I've ever seen."

The engineers swept on, down corridors into the belly of the ship. The evols were ahead of them, crowding around a door and snarling at the scent of terrified flesh almost within reach.

"Kill them all!" Else shouted, her blade swinging and cutting deep into the neck of the nearest evol. Rache's people followed her into the fight, howling their own rage and smashing the risen dead into black-blooded piles of severed limbs and shattered skulls.

They fought their way into the room. Else could see the surviving holders; they had retreated into the fight ring, where they now fought a desperate battle against the ranks of risen dead who pressed in on all sides. Men and women leaned in, flesh tearing on the crude barbs woven into the tight wires, clawing at the living just out of reach. The holders fought back with scraps of salvage and anything they had been able to snatch up in their desperate flight down to the Hole.

The engineers fell on the dead from behind, cutting them down until the floor ran with slick blood and the greasy smears of crushed brain matter. When the holders realized they were being rescued, they counterattacked with renewed vigor. Else could see Hob, a metal pipe nearly as long as she was tall swinging in his hands like a club. He brought it down on an evol's shoulder, nearly tearing the dead man's arm off and driving the zombie to its knees.

The evols reacted slowly to the attack from a new front. They turned to face the engineers and were cut down. Heads flew from shoulders and squirming bodies were hacked up, the guts spilling out across the floor.

Finally, stillness descended. The walls dripped dark fluids and the sound of panting breaths echoed through the room.

Rache's engineers ended the lives of seven friends and loved ones who mostly sat slumped, grim faced and silent, clutching deep bite wounds on their arms, necks, and hands. The wounded engineers died without a sound. The survivors struck hard and moved on, keeping their grief to themselves.

Hob and five other holders crawled out of the ring, all looking haggard and wide eyed.

Else regarded the three men and three women they had found. "Are there others?" Rache asked.

"Yeah," Hob snorted and spat a wad of phlegm on the pile of dead. "Some of us came down here. Rest ran up topside, or fuck knows where."

"That means there will be more evols. Feral ones like these," Else said. "Where is Sarah?" Else asked, looking around the room.

Hob narrowed his eyes at the sound of his daughter's name. "Isn't she with you?"

Else scowled at him. Her instincts were to not trust any of the holders, Sarah especially. Not knowing where the girl was made her uneasy.

"Last time I saw her she was up on the high decks," Else said.

"Who's Sarah?" Rache asked.

"My daughter. She knows this ship better'n anyone. She'll be fine. I'd like to find her, though," Hob growled.

"What about the fishermen and the church man?" Else asked Rache. "They might need help too."

"You lot," Rache gestured at the engineers and surviving holders. "Head topside, secure the open decks. Check on the fishermen; find that god fella too and if he's not turned, bring them all back to the hold."

The holders and engineers moved off without a word. Else noted that not one of them had questioned Rache's seizing of the leadership.

Else waited while the group filed out of the room. She put a hand out and stopped Hob as he walked past.

"You and I, we need to talk about your kid," she said.

CHAPTER 10

The crowd in the Hole seethed with trapped tension. A lust for violence lay thick in the air. It showed in the flash of their eyes, the baring of their teeth, and their clenched fists that curled around crude weapons crafted from salvage.

Else held back until, at Rache's urging, the engineers lifted her above the crowd and carried her up to the barbed wire ring, where she could be seen and heard above them.

"My name is Else," she said. The mob swelled and heaved like a debris-strewn ocean. The murmuring voices fell silent and someone shouted from the back, "Speak up!"

"My name is Else!" She lifted her head and spoke to those against the far wall. "My name is Else, and I am Tankbread."

The crowd muttered in confusion. They had been out here, trapped in this sanctuary for so long they had never heard of the solution that ended the war that was nearly the extinction of them all.

"Tankbread," Else repeated. "Scientists made us from cloned cells. We are like people, but grown real fast. We were fed to the evols. In return they left the survivors of Sydney alone. Tankbread is what ended the war. They ate us, so they didn't eat you." She looked out over the sea of grim expressions. The engineers with black painted faces and the symbols of tools scratched in the dark grease painted on their skins. The holders with colored and chrome

104

markers tied in their hair and beards, and the fishermen with their salt-crusted dreadlocks and deep tans. But so few children. Less than ten here were younger than Sarah, a girl on the verge of becoming a woman. She represented a new generation of savage who knew nothing of the old world. These children would only ever know fighting, and fucking, and dying for a scrap of salvage and the promise of immortality through the rebirth of being chosen as crew. Else took a deep breath and spoke to them all.

"There's a world out there. A whole world. The land on the edge of the sea is wide and open. You can live in the sun. You can make your own salvage. You can stop fighting each other and start fighting the dead. Working together you can defend your homes and be strong. You can have babies and raise them. You can create a future."

The murmuring started within the ranks of the holders. Else ignored the priest, Jonah, as he pushed his way through the crowd. He climbed up next to her and banged his driftwood staff on the floor of the ring.

"Blasphemy!" he roared. "This woman is possessed! She seeks to destroy us all!" The believers among the holders echoed his anger. A scuffle erupted in the audience. Engineers shouted down the faithful and a brawl erupted as the fishermen started throwing punches at anyone who was not one of them.

Rache's shouts for order went unheeded as the crowd in the Hole erupted into a free-for-all, with blood being shed as angry snarls took the place of words.

Else kept silent. She had no patience for those who would not listen. Let them fight; she would tell her story to the survivors, or she would fight them, rescue her son and baby Lowanna, and then be on her way.

Hob slid under the wire of the fighting ring, Standing up, he nodded at Else and then turned to face the rioting crowd.

"Shut the fuck up!" he bellowed. His voice echoed off the

walls and ceiling, rattling the lights and drowning out the crowd's angry shouts.

The fighting crowd settled. Blood streamed from noses and split lips. A few loose teeth were spat on the floor and the last grumbling voices were shushed to silence.

"Y'll listen to her and y'll show some fuckin' respect!" Hob snarled. "Right," he nodded, "Y'were sayin'?"

"My name is Else," she started again. "You don't have to live like this. You can make your own place on land. No crew telling you how to live. No one taking your babies from you. You can live and build your own society."

"The dead are everywhere out there!" someone shouted from the crowd.

"Yes," Else nodded. "The dead are a threat. But you can fight them. You can build walls and fences. Teach your children to fight. Protect yourselves and live by your own laws."

"We belong here!" a woman yelled, and others shouted their agreement.

"You belong in a stinking hole? You belong in a floating prison where your lives are worth nothing? A place where your only purpose is to breed food for the dead?"

They started muttering again, "Whaddya gonna do about it?" a man in the front row demanded.

"I'm here for one reason. I have a son. He's only a few days old. The crew keeps the babies alive. They keep women in cages; these women feed the newborns until the crew eat them. I'm here to get my son back and Jirra's baby, Lowanna, too. If I have to destroy every evol on this ship to get them back, then that's what I'll do. But that's just me. You want to be asking yourselves, 'What am *I* going to do about it?'"

The muttering rose again. People turned and started telling their neighbors what they thought. The volume climbed and Hob scowled at them, waiting for the first fist to be clenched.

As Jonah opened his mouth to speak, Hob turned on him. "And not one more fuckin' word out of you cunt."

Jonah blinked and stared at Hob for a moment, before stepping back, his gaze dropping to the floor.

Rache slipped under the wire and stood in the ring. "I'm Rache, of the engineers. I dunno about you lot, you holders, fishermen, and other limp pricks, but us engineers, we're here to sail this ship. We've waited too long. Listened to too many empty words and promises. From the Foreman, from the Captain, and from all you other fuckers. If this ship ain't sailing, then we're leaving. We're taking our smarts, our tech, and our people. You know 'em, the ones who keep the lights on, keep the rust from eating the hull, and the ones who were gonna fire up the engines when the Captain gave the order!"

The engineers in the crowd cheered and pumped the air with their fists. Rache grinned. "We're going to be free! Free to sail our own ships and go anywhere we want!" The crowd erupted in a frenzy of excitement. Holders, fishermen, and engineers jumped and hooted.

Rache raised both fists in the air. "But first we're gonna have to fight! Destroy the crew! Take the ship for ourselves! Live free!"

Hob lifted Rache by the legs and sat her on his shoulder for a victory circuit around the ring. The roar of the crowd's bloodlust brought fresh memories to Else's mind. She climbed over the wire and pushed through the close crowd, the air in the room getting too thick to breathe.

Gasping for air, she stumbled out into the stairwell and headed upwards. The crowd responded to Rache's orders and surged out as well. A tide of humanity, foaming at the mouth with pure savagery, spilled out onto the open deck. Else got to the rail, leaned over, and threw up. Thin, acidic bile rained down on the choppy water below.

The sun had set and the lights running from the solar-powered batteries were already dim. The war party didn't seem bothered by the lack of light as they swarmed up the outer stairwells and started forcing the doors open on the upper decks.

Evols came at them from all sides, mostly the recently deceased, with crew behind them, giving orders and pushing the more frenzied ones in the right direction. Some of the crew had guns and they aimed carefully, shooting the rebellious ship dwellers in the chest or gut so they would have a better chance of rising again and joining the crew's side.

Else wiped her mouth and snatched up a dropped weapon. The fight still needed her, her son still needed her. She sidestepped a fisherman, locked in a life-or-death grapple with an evol, and swung her blade into the back of the zombie's head. The dead man howled and struggled to break free of the fisherman's grip. Else jerked the blade free and decapitated him.

"Use weapons," Else said in response to the fisherman's gasped gratitude. She pushed on into the fray, slashing the salvage blade left and right, cutting limbs from the dead. Blood, still turning black from the activated virus, sprayed from the stumps and made the footing treacherous. Else dropped to her knees, sliding in the wash of gore under the grasping hands of the evols bearing down on Rache's forces. Her blade flashed and evols tumbled, amputated legs twitching and standing on their own.

As the first wave of dead fell, Else spun to her feet, striking out at the crew that goaded their shock troops into battle. The barrel of a rifle blocked her first strike. The crewmember swung the butt of the weapon, aiming for her head. She ducked under it and hit him with an uppercut, snapping the evol's head back and cracking the neck with an audible pop.

Slashing with her blade, she cut through the exposed neck. Air bubbled through the black blood spilling out of the zombie's gashed throat. Else snatched up the rifle and tossed it to a waiting rebel. Rache ran up brandishing a gun of her own.

"We are winning!" she yelled. Else just nodded; there was nothing to celebrate yet.

CHAPTER 11

In the last hours of the day, under the light of a gibbous moon, Rache called a council of war.

The crew had fallen back, leaving their dead, both walking and dismembered, to fend for themselves. Rache scratched lines in a pool of blood on the deck, marking possible entry points into the upper decks and indicating areas where a counterattack could come.

Else made little comment. This was Rache's show now, and she needed to cement her control over the rebellion she had started. The men who huddled around the girl nodded and leaned on the hafts of their weapons. They had salvaged two guns, automatic rifles that had a full magazine of ammunition between them. Most of the rebels didn't know how to use a gun, but they picked it up quickly after Else's demonstration.

The council meeting broke up with Rache's people moving off to give orders and organize the rebels into squads positioned at the identified points where they expected the crew to appear again.

"We should press the attack," Else said. "I don't know how long they will keep my son and Lowanna alive."

Rache nodded, her face sorrowful. "The lights have gone out. We can't attack in the dark, they will wipe us out. I'm sorry, Else, but we will need to wait until dawn and try then."

Else stood up. "That is exactly what the crew will expect you to do. They will be ready. They will be waiting."

The curved blade of Rache's scythe whistled as she spun the weapon like a baton. "Ready or not, we will destroy them."

"Yes you will, but I can't wait that long." Else snatched the spinning handle from Rache's hand and swung it over her shoulder, sliding it into a holster on her back fashioned from scraps of cloth and blanket. She took a machete from the deck and holstered it too before walking away along the deck and vanishing into the darkness.

On the high deck the engineers were assaulting a sealed door. Their hand tools had only scraped the paint; now they were arguing among themselves on the best way to cut through the steel.

"I don't suppose you have an oxyacetylene torch?" Else asked. They shrugged, their blank faces reminding Else that these people were more savages than old-world, educated technicians.

"Wait here," she said, "I have an idea." Finding her way down to the fore section of the lower deck took awhile. Edgy rebels nearly attacked her twice, and the hastily erected barricades turned the stairways into a maze.

Arriving inside the ship, Else paused to listen. She heard the usual creak and groan of the decaying steel infrastructure, the dull boom of the rising waves beating against the hull, but no other sounds.

The door to Eric's sanctuary was locked. She tapped on it, whispering his name and telling him who was knocking. Her tension rose as the door remained closed. "Eric, open this fucking door right now," she growled in a low whisper.

With a muffled click the bolts started to slide back, and then Eric's eye glinted through the crack. "Fuck off," he whispered.

"We need you, Eric. The engineers, the fishermen, the holders. They're taking the ship. They're rising up against the crew. We need your help."

"Fuck. Off," Eric said firmly.

"I will not." Else felt her patience burning away like dry tinder touched by a flame of indignation.

Eric rolled his eyes and pushed the door shut. She jammed her foot in the way and shoved him backwards. Busting into the room Else looked around, a realization dawning on her face.

"You are leaving?" she said.

Eric swept his long hair back with one hand, "I…well you got me thinking, this place is fucked. So yeah, I'm leaving."

"Fine," Else snapped. "Could you give me your supply of explosives before you go?"

Eric hesitated. "That stuff is dangerous. You could get seriously hurt messing with it. Maybe even blow a hole in the hull."

"I'm counting on it," Else replied.

Eric was still shaking his head when he opened the pool supplies locker on the deck where he kept his chemistry set.

"This stuff is stable, until you upset it," he warned.

"How do I set it off?" Else asked.

"Well you can use a detonator, or a fuse." Eric warmed to his subject. "I've been experimenting with different caps. That's primer, or shit that blows up and sets off the bigger bang."

Eric lifted a plastic crate lined with salvaged seat cushions and stuffed with packages wrapped in oil-soaked paper.

"That's the big boom; each one of those is enough to blow a hole in anything." He ducked back into the locker and a moment later reemerged with a small glass jar of thin tubes that looked like home-rolled cigarettes and a roll of coarse, black cord.

"This is the dangerous shit," he said, holding up the jar as if it contained live scorpions. "Stick one of these into one of the packages, twist the end of the fuse cord on to the paper at the other end of the detonator. Run yourself a decent length of fuse, light it, and then…"

"And then?" Else prompted.

"Fuckin' pray," Eric said solemnly.

"I need your help," Else said. "You know how to work with this stuff; you can put the bombs where they will do the most damage."

"Nuh," Eric grunted. "I'm getting myself on a boat and buggerin' off. You go and have a nice war, though."

Else's blade flashed in the moonlight, the tip stopping a few millimeters from his throat. "Please," Else said.

"Well," Eric swallowed hard. "Seein' as you're askin' so nicely."

Else watched as Eric unpacked a second plastic crate of homemade high explosive. The first crate was transferred into two sacks that Eric pulled from the locker.

"I could sure use a smoke right now," Eric chuckled as he opened the jar and gently slipped the detonators out into his hand. "Don't get these buggers wet," he said, handing a cluster of the paper tubes to Else. "An' if you catch fire, get rid of this shit, all of it."

Else nodded, carefully sliding the caps into her shirt pocket and lifting one of the heavy sacks. Eric draped a coil of fuse around her neck. "Remember to make sure you're a helluva way back before you light the fuse."

"Got it." Else picked up a second bag of dynamite. "You know what to do?" she asked.

"Yeah, yeah," Eric grumbled, not meeting her eye.

"If you fuck this up or run out on me, I will find you and I will hurt you in ways you cannot imagine."

"Cross my heart," Eric said, his face going pale under his deep tan.

Else headed down the deck, back to Rache and her rebels. It was time to bring the whole thing to an end.

CHAPTER 12

A storm was rising in the predawn darkness when the engineers reported the last of the explosives were in place. They had been loud and angry in their opposition, until Else explained that there were other ships, enough for all to be their own master and sail their own destiny. "To do that, we have to destroy this place. Let go of the past and start fresh," she insisted. The engineers looked at Rache, who nodded her agreement. Else was pleased they were deferring to the girl; the last thing she wanted was to become the focus for their new hero worship.

"Tell them to blow the door," Rache said. Else headed up the stairs to where two engineers crouched in the lee of a steel wall. The wind was blowing hard now, spray and rain lashing her cheeks with salty tears.

"Light it!" Else shouted over the howl of the wind. The two engineers nodded. Huddling over the end of the cord, they uncovered the flickering oil lamp and touched its wavering flame to the fuse. For a moment nothing happened; then the fuse sparked and hissed, and a bright flare of white flame blossomed and raced up the line. Else hurried to follow it, to make sure it wasn't quenched by the rain or a break in the fuse. The nearest engineer grabbed her and dragged her back down the stairs, his face etched with fear and excitement.

Else counted to ten, then eleven, twelve, thir—

A dull *whumph* sound echoed over them, a cloud of smoke swelled and collapsed under the rain, the clang of steel striking steel, then silence.

"Cool," one of the engineers said. Else pulled away and ran up the stairs. The door that they said led into the highest decks lay open and twisted. The heavy steel frame had buckled, marked by black powder burns and the melted residue of Eric's homemade nitro explosives.

Else drew her short-handled scythe and ducked inside. The corridor was filling with the dead. The explosion had overwhelmed their unfiltered senses and left them stunned and disorientated.

In the close confines of the steel hallway, Else started the killing. The engineers cheered and filled the doorway at her back. One of them aimed a semiautomatic rifle and squeezed the trigger; the round spanged off the wall and hit an evol in the throat. Else ducked at the sound of the gunshot and sliced a zombie through the hips, bringing its head low enough to be cut off.

"Hold your fucking fire!" she yelled.

With the engineers hacking and stabbing, the corridor quickly cleared. Else moved on, a growing sense of urgency filling her. If she did not find her son soon he would die. She couldn't think beyond that. Her mind drew a blank.

The sudden sound of a baby crying snatched Else's attention. At the end of the corridor a metal door swung shut with a squeal, the baby noise rising behind it. Else started running, the grinning face of Sarah visible in the closing gap as she pushed the door shut. Else thudded against the metal a moment after the latch on the other side slammed home. Peering through the small glass porthole, she shouted, "Sarah!? Sarah, open the door!"

She heard a high-pitched giggle and through the dust- and

salt-encrusted porthole she could see the blurred shape of Sarah vanishing down a stairwell, a tiny bundled figure in her arms.

"Help me here!" Else yelled back down the corridor. The engineers, splashed with black gore, were finishing off the risen and responded to her shout.

"We need explosives. I need to get this door open."

"There's none left; they're all wired up," an engineer reported.

"Fuck!" Else screamed and beat on the steel door with her fists.

"Let's have a look." The engineers worked on opening the door while Else, unable to stand still, ran back up the corridor and started opening doors, looking for another way deeper into the ship.

In a decaying cleaner's closet, years of leaking chemicals had corroded the floor. A glint of light came up through the lace-thin metal, Else crouched down and started punching through the rust with the butt of her scythe handle.

Opening a way through to the deck below took a few moments and then she dropped down, feet first, through the narrow gap, tearing her clothes on the jagged edges as she squirmed through. The sense of vulnerability that came from having her legs dangling down into the corridor threatened to bring on unfettered panic. A snarling, like a dog discovering an intruder, echoed through the space under Else's feet. Instinctively she drew her knees up, the weakened metal resisting her attempt to wiggle her swollen bust through. The creaking of the metal clashed with the sound of claws scraping on the deck. Else couldn't see what was happening below her, but nothing sounded reassuring.

The snarling echoed around her feet again. Else waited for the sharp pain of clawed evol fingers tearing at her flesh. Pressing back against the edge of the hole, she widened the gap and dropped, landing in a crouch ready to kill whatever horde waited for her. The corridor was empty. She turned, scythe at the ready. Else reacted to the sudden scratching of claws on the steel floor and a snarl of something coming at her from the shadows by charging at the darkness, snarling herself.

A large dog, with a brindle pattern to its fur and a mouth full of gleaming teeth, leapt out at her. Else parried the attack, knocking the animal into the wall. She spun the blade around, sending the beaten steel whistling towards the dog's chest.

The first blow struck the wall, the dog twisting away and then charging in to slam Else to the floor, teeth snapping at her throat. Holding the handle of her blade in both hands, Else pressed back against the dog's chest. The animal wasn't starving; he'd been taken care of, probably trained to act as a guard for the crew. Else swung her legs up, wrapped them around the dog's body, and with a heave she rolled the animal on to his back, sitting astride him and pressing down with the blade handle. She pushed until the snarls became wheezing gasps and only stopped once she heard the crunch of the animal's throat being crushed under the pressure of her attack.

Gasping for breath, Else stumbled to her feet. The dog lay on the floor, convulsing with bulging eyes as it choked to death. With an overhand swing she slammed the blade into the top of its skull.

Jerking the weapon free, she started jogging down the hallway. If her sense of direction was right, this corridor should take her to the stairs. The door to the stairs on this level was open and it smelt strongly of the dog marking his territory.

Else crept down the stairs, drawing the machete and hefting it in her other hand. Somewhere below she could hear a door opening and closing, the thin cries of her son acting as a beacon. Above she could hear the pounding of the engineers working on opening the door. There was no time to wait for them—she had to keep going. Finishing this the way she started, alone.

Reaching the next level, Else lifted her blades and ducked down. The doors were wooden, with grime-encrusted panes of colored glass. Figures moved on the other side. Else tucked the machete under her arm and reached out and turned the handle. The door brushed over faded carpet; this part of the ship must have been where the passengers lived. She ducked back as two crew turned to look in her direction.

They moved silently on the carpeted floor. The first one, a woman with blonde braids that had coagulated into two thick, tentacle-like dreadlocks, opened the door.

"Hi," Else said, and swung the scythe down into the woman's shoulder. The zombie grunted, turning her head to stare at the curved sliver of steel impaled between her collarbone and shoulder. With a frown she tried to reach up and pull the blade out. Else jerked the weapon upwards; the wound welled black blood.

Else struck again, with the machete this time. The ceiling was too low to swing overhead at the woman's skull, so she swung upwards, like the pictures of golfers she had seen. The blade burst through the woman's jaw and punched out the top of her head. She collapsed, dragging the blade down. Else yanked it out, readying both weapons as she stepped through the door.

The second crewmember lunged at her. Else sidestepped and, with a truncated swing, buried the scythe in his back as he stumbled past. The evol collapsed; she pulled the blade out and split the zombie's skull with a final blow.

Signs on the walls indicated various attractions available to on-board guests. A murmuring rose as Else headed down the wide hallway. Double doors opened into the balcony restaurant that overlooked the grand ballroom. She walked out into the deserted room. Tables, draped in white cloth, waited for diners who would never come. A brass rail ran along the edge of the balcony and Else peered over into the scene of carnage below.

Blood lay in thick swipes along the ballroom floor, splatter patterns ran up the walls, and an audience of hungry dead moaned and clawed at the doors at the other end of the room.

Else leapt on the rail, caught in a moment of momentum, her arms flung wide, her head back, eyes closed. She dropped in a graceful dive that folded into a somersault before landing with a dull boom on the marble tiles of the dance floor. The seething crowd of dead, mindless and frenzied in their blood hunger, stopped clawing and hammering on the door opposite. In ones and twos they turned their limited senses towards a new sound—the sharp scrape of sharpened steel on ironwork.

Else crouched on one knee, twisting slowly, back and forth, the tips of her blades inscribing two gleaming crescent lines in the floor. The shriek of metal on stone took on a rhythmic pulse, like the dying heart of a metal giant beating its last.

Snarling, fresh blood and torn flesh spilling from their mouths and dripping from their hands, the evols advanced. The noise and the pulsing warmth of Else's body drove them into fury. As one they surged forward, bearing down on the crouched figure that, in the last moment before they reached her, spun to her feet. The blades in her hands flashed bright and cold as the killing began.

Else saw only teeth and dead flesh. She struck, slicing through bone and virus-laden muscle. Everything within her was focused on destroying the walking dead. Skulls shattered and severed limbs flew across the hold to bounce off the rusting walls. The freshly risen dead oozed blood that was still darkening to the black ichor of the waste-laden slime of the older zombie.

Else ignored the pain of the teeth that sank into her body. She cut, slashed, and cut again. Stabbing one evol through the eye, striking another and splitting his head down to the jaw. She almost lost her grip on the machete as the blood sprayed and made the handle slick.

Trampled corpses crawled towards her through the rain of blood. Broken bones jerked like marionettes desperate to join the feast of her warm flesh.

Those unlucky enough to draw blood from Else convulsed and spewed dark blood as they staggered. They writhed in a frenzied tarantella dance, the antiviral cells in her plasma tearing through their infected flesh.

Else fought on, killing them all. Killing them for the father of her baby; the man who gave his life that this nightmare might end. Killing to avenge Jirra. Killing for Bindi, for Lowanna, and for her own son. Killing for all the children yet to be born if humanity was to ever have a chance to survive. Else killed because it was all she had ever known, and she did it well.

The stinging wounds on her arms and body burned. Else pirouetted and decapitated a dead fisherman whose face was a screaming mask of blood and hate. With a snarl she raised her weapons to kill again, but there were no volunteers. The ballroom was awash with the spilt blood and severed body parts of a hundred dead. Blades ready, Else picked her way through the battlefield. A broken body bared its teeth and snapped at her ankle. She stabbed it through the ear and twisted, destroying enough of the brain to end the viral control.

The door at the end of the ballroom creaked open. Else stared into the gloom, ready for an attack. Instead a pale blonde girl stepped into view and surveyed the carnage.

"Sarah?" Else asked. "You're alive. Hob was so worried about you."

"You have ruined everything!" Sarah shrieked. She stamped her foot, splashing blood across the hem of her faded sundress.

"Where is my baby, Sarah? Where is my son?"

Sarah's mouth curled into a sneer. "He's on the butcher's block!"

Else took a deep breath to stop from screaming. "This isn't the way you should live, Sarah. The crew can't give you anything."

"The Captain said he would make me one of them. I could live forever! Up in the bridge! I would be safe and special and everyone would be afraid of me!" Sarah's face contorted in frustrated rage.

"The Captain is going to die," Else replied, her voice steady and commanding.

"No!" Sarah extended her right arm, a shard of glass glinting in her left fist. Else rushed forward as the girl slashed a deep wound along the white skin of her own forearm.

"Stop!" Else screamed.

Sarah plunged her bleeding arm into the shattered remains of the fallen dead at her feet.

Else grabbed the girl around the waist and pulled her back, almost throwing her against the wall.

"I did it," Sarah giggled. "I did it. I put the blood of the crew on everything so the holders would die and then kill you. Then the Captain would choose me. Just like he promised."

Else squeezed the girl's arm above the wound, muttering "no, no, no" as she watched the dark lines of virus-tainted blood surging through the girl's veins.

"I'm going to live forever now…Up on the bridge, where you can see the whole world and never want for nothing." Sarah's eyes started to lose the focus and shine of the living. She tilted her head back and laughed one last time. "The Captain says I can eat your shitty little baby too…"

"I wanted to save you!" Else screamed as Sarah slumped in her arms. She laid her down, not ready to strike the final blow until it was too late.

"Saraghhh…" a phlegmatic gurgle spoke from behind Else. She stood, turning slowly, the hot fury of battle now tempered by the death of the child.

"You must be the Captain," she said to the evol looking down on her from behind the balcony rail. He was in excellent condition for a dead man. His skin was firm and almost pink, the uniform he wore was well mended, and his beard was neatly trimmed. Even the buttons on his crisply pressed uniform shirt were polished to a high sheen.

"You argh the mainlander. The woman who has been causing so much distress to argh tight-knit community," he spoke well enough. A trace of thickness and a slight slur to this speech was the only sign that his heart did not beat naturally.

"I am Else. I was created to destroy your kind, and I was made well."

The Captain's lips twitched; it was less a smile than a grimace. "I'll kill you and your dreams tonight," he said.

Else stepped forward, her eyes fixed on the erect figure high above her. The ship shuddered and the sound of tearing metal echoed through the infrastructure. Else dropped into a crouch while the Captain steadied himself against the balcony rail, looking about in sudden confusion.

A second explosion followed and then they came in a rapid series, each shuddering blow making the metal moan, until something buried nearby detonated and the ballroom floor cracked. Spars of rusting steel burst up through the floor in a gout of black smoke and searing fire.

Else rolled aside, narrowly avoiding being impaled on a broken girder. The Captain backed away from the balcony edge and vanished from view. Else yelled at him over the metallic screams of the wounded ship. She holstered her weapons and ran up the broken girder, jumping over the rising flames. Leaping off the jagged tip, she flew through the air, her fingers brushing against a rotting wall hanging. Sliding down, she gripped the cloth, which disintegrated in a cloud of dust and mold.

Else snatched at a supporting cord; it held as the mass of rotting cloth crumpled onto the spreading fire on the floor and exploded into flames. Climbing up, she felt the threads parting under her slight weight. The rising fire below caught the rope and started climbing after her. A few brief seconds later, Else seized a grip on the edge of the balcony. The rope parted and dropped past her, the floating embers of the fire catching on other dry curtains and flaring up into a boiling wall of flame that quickly licked the ceiling. Pulling herself up, Else dropped onto the balcony. Another explosion rocked the ship. The world turned on its side as the room suddenly sagged. She grabbed the rail as the floor tilted.

With the fire spreading behind her, Else scrambled for a nearby table. The restaurant chairs tumbled past but the tables were bolted to the floor. Shielding her head, Else rode out the attack of the falling chairs. Gripping the carpet with her fingertips, she crawled towards the exit.

The steel of the ship's bones moaned as an explosion tore through its guts. The smoke was rising, clouding Else's view and tightening in a band around her chest.

She tumbled out of the restaurant, the spreading fire sucking the air from the corridor in a howling wind. Else lost count of the explosions. The destruction had spread beyond Eric's dynamite; some ancient reserves of oil fuel had been ruptured and were now burning deep beneath the deck.

The door the Captain had fled through hung open. Else jumped and grabbed the doorjamb, pulling herself up and onto a staircase that with the current degree of roll would have given M. C. Escher eyestrain. The ship moved again, rolling back on an even keel, the force of the motion slamming Else into the stairs.

Climbing to her feet and coughing against the rising smoke, she ran up the stairs. The Captain would tell her where her son could be found. She would burn him until he told her exactly where he was.

A sign warned that she was approaching an area restricted to authorized personnel only. Else yanked the door open and ran up the last flight of stairs to the bridge itself.

The Captain stood at the controls, staring out through the wide windows that overlooked the prow of the ship. The storm had arrived with the full fury of nature. The sky was lit up with the white-hot flash of lightning, and the wide windows ran opaque with rain. Five evol crew stood at their positions around the bridge, rifles held across their chests. They tilted with the pitch of the ship as it rocked in the stormy water and the sundering explosions in its belly.

Else drew her blades, ready to get started, when a sixth evol stepped into view from behind the Captain. A tiny naked figure hung by its ankles from the evol's hand, his face red with outrage and his howls stifled by the dead hand clamped over his mouth. "My baby," Else said.

"Yes," the Captain agreed. "Will you watch him die, or will he watch you die?"

Else just shook her head. Everything ached and her lungs burned from the smoke curling up through cracks and vents. "Your ship is going down, Captain. Are you ready to go with it?" Her voice came out as a croak. The Captain narrowed his eyes. "Enough," he spat. A drip of black spittle landed on his chin. He took a perfectly folded handkerchief from his pocket and scowled as he dabbed at it.

"Kill her," he ordered. The evols stepped forward, rifles rising to the ready.

Else readied her weapons. If it ended here, she would die fighting. She didn't care how many bullets they fired; she would cut them down. If her son was going to die, then his last moments would be in her arms.

A blaze erupted on the forward deck, the fire's light reflecting off Else's steel. Her head snapped to the wide glass windows that spanned the bridge. The evols charged forward, guns firing. Else threw herself to one side as the windows exploded inwards in a hail of gunfire. A man wrapped in smoldering black clothes swung into the bridge at the end of a braided rope. His long hair and beard singed and trailing smoke, he crashed into the control console and fell to the floor. Scrambling up, he yelled something, the words lost behind the thick covering of his gas mask.

"Eric?!" Else yelled.

"Geffuggow!" Eric shouted. He reloaded his automatic rifle while the evols stopped, confused and overwhelmed by his sudden entrance.

"No!" Else leapt up and shoulder charged Eric, knocking his weapon aside and sending a burst of bullets through the face of the closest evol. "My son!" she screamed.

Eric ripped his gas mask off. "What?"

Else ignored him and spun on the balls of her feet. Her machete sliced through an evol's skull, shearing the top of his head off and sending blackened brain matter splattering against the console.

The scythe followed, the tip burying itself in the head of another evol, punching through the ear canal. Else levered downwards, twisting the blade and coring the zombie's brain like a rotten apple, dragging the weapon from her grip.

The evol holding the baby lunged forward. Else dropped the machete from her left hand and scooped her son up, punching the evol in the face with her right fist.

The dead man snarled; the skin on his face split and dripped black blood. Else punched upwards, the heel of her hand crushing the dead man's nose and driving shards of bone up into the brain. The evol snorted, his eyes rolling up in his head. Else stepped back, cradling her wailing son against her chest as the zombie collapsed, quivering on the floor.

Eric's automatic rifle barked and another zombie's head vanished in a spray of dark gore. The last two evols started shooting. Else spun down behind a control console, clutching her son to her chest as bullets ricocheted around the bridge. Eric roared something unintelligible and emptied his magazine into the two dead men. The Captain was caught in the spray of bullets and went tumbling back into the smoke.

"We gotta go!" Eric yelled. "This whole place is coming apart!" The ship rocked with a fresh explosion, the temperature in the bridge rising as the air darkened with fumes.

Else leapt up and ran to Eric. "Has everyone got to the boats?"

"Yeah, that Rache girl gave the fishermen what-for. They're evacuating everyone right now!"

A hand appeared through the smoke behind her and slammed down on Else's shoulder, dropping her to the floor. "Take my baby!" she yelled at Eric, thrusting the tiny body up at him. Eric nodded and grabbed the child. "Get him to the boats!"

Else spun around, lashing out with a foot, only vaguely aware of Eric running out the door, her baby squalling as he was carried to safety. Her boot slammed the Captain in the chest. His composure had melted in the heat, a ragged flap of skin hung down from his right temple. The bone underneath glistened a dull grey.

He sank down and ripped Else's discarded scythe out of the crewman's head. The curved metal end hung steady an inch from her face. The Captain opened his mouth to speak; instead Else knocked the handle of the blade aside and flipped up onto her feet, snatching up the machete and swinging it at the Captain's head. He blocked and riposted, the steel blades clanging together as the combatants smashed into each other.

A wall of flame erupted in the doorway; the Captain flinched back. Else pressed the attack, her machete slamming into his shoulder. He grabbed the handle and pulled the blade free. Swinging the other weapon, he forced Else to duck. Disarmed, she backed away across the bridge, feeling the linoleum underfoot bubbling in the heat.

The Captain ran forward, the curved blade rising over his head like an axe. Else leaned back, inhaling with a sharp gasp as the sharpened steel sliced downwards, cutting through her shirt and drawing blood in a long line down her stomach.

Else stomped down on the scythe's wooden handle, shattering it and knocking the Captain off balance. Grabbing him by the throat, she jammed her mouth against his neck and bit hard.

The Captain howled. Jerking back tore a chunk of meat from his neck.

"It is forbidden!" he hissed. The air he drew in to speak whistled through the ragged hole in his throat.

Else wiped the back of a hand across her mouth, smearing the black blood of him onto her cheek. She spat his sour grey flesh from her mouth. "I'm your ending," she said, her eyes burning from the smoke. "My children will live on, but you will burn and your bones will rot. The human race will recover and rebuild. I will not rest until that comes to pass. We will purge your kind from the world."

The air outside the bridge swirled orange and black as a geyser of burning oil burst upwards through the foredeck.

"We are eternal…" the Captain croaked. The lethal elements in Else's cells were already devouring the parasitic particles that drove his dead flesh.

The floor creaked and the ancient linoleum began to smoke and curl upwards, charring in the heat from the inferno that had spread to the deck below. The Captain sank to his knees, his wide-eyed gaze reflecting the tendrils of flame curling up the walls as the air in the bridge became stifling.

"Not as long as I live," Else said. She lunged forward, snatching up the broken weapon, the blade swinging in an arc that would have taken the Captain's head off at the neck. Instead the floor gave way and they both plummeted into an upwelling cloud of fire.

PART II

PART II

CHAPTER 1

The survivors rowed for shore as the ship behind them shuddered with explosions. Silhouetted against the flaring light they could see the writhing forms of burning people, alive and dead, dropping over the railing into the storm-tossed swell.

Hob pulled on the oars. The small boat had no salvage that would help them on the unforgiving shore. The women and few children huddled together, moaning in terror every time the sky was lit up by another explosion. Hob kept rowing. Land had to be there somewhere; they had disembarked on the right side of the stricken ship.

When the roar of breakers was louder than the death rattle of the ship, Hob yelled at his passengers to hold fast. The small boat rose on a swell, surfing the crest of a breaking wave and powering forward, the oars sweeping through the air, nearly throwing Hob on his back at the sudden lack of resistance.

When the wave passed and the boat dropped, Hob heaved on the oars again. The boat bobbed and the next wave pushed it onto the dark sand of the storm-lashed beach.

"Get out!" Hob yelled, feeling the tug of the sea dragging the boat back out. He rowed hard, trying to keep the small craft straight on. If they turned, the first breaker to hit them would capsize the boat.

The passengers clambered over Hob, jumping into the surf and carrying howling children on their shoulders. Once the boat was empty, Hob shipped the oars and jumped into the freezing water. Wading ashore, he dragged the boat behind him. "Give me a fucking hand!" he yelled. Other survivors came and seized the boat. Working together they pulled it above the reach of the storm surge.

As the sun rose the wind fell. The people from the ship had spent a cold and miserable night huddled on the beach, terrified of every noise and crack of wind-snapped trees behind them.

Hob crawled out from under a sodden blanket, stood up, and stretched. The lack of movement underfoot made him dizzy. He took a few steps to regain his composure. Opening his pants he pissed on the sand, shivering in the morning chill and the sense of relief.

Small boats and chunks of wreckage were rising and falling on the surf. Other salvage had come ashore and already people were moving about, picking up anything useful and piling it above the high-tide mark.

Looking around, Hob swallowed the fear he felt at the line of trees. The dead ruled the land. His people only came ashore when they needed salvage. Being out here, exposed in the open, terrified him.

Most of the faces he could see were familiar. Holders, fishermen, engineers. They all had a look of shock etched deep into their faces. He guessed his expression was the same.

"Sarah," he said. Turning in a slow step he looked up and down the beach. "Sarah!" he yelled. Walking down the beach he grabbed the first salvager he found by the shoulders. "Where's Sarah?" he demanded. The woman shook her head and went back to gathering driftwood.

"Fuck!" Hob swore. Shielding his eyes against the sunlight now reflecting off the whispering surf, he peered out to sea. Only a dark smudge of smoke remained, rising above the horizon. "Sarah?" he asked. There were bodies floating out there; some still moved or clung to flotsam.

"Hey, man, you seen the crazy chick from the land? Else?" Hob turned and scowled at the dark-haired man who looked familiar.

"What? No, fuck off," Hob said automatically.

"I've got her kid," Eric said, gesturing with a flush of embarrassment to a small group of forlorn holders.

"Which one?" Hob asked.

"She has more than one? I've got the boy."

"How the hell did that happen?" Hob turned away from the wreckage-filled sea and started walking towards where Else's baby was being comforted and fed by one of the women who had recently sacrificed her own newborn.

Eric fell into step beside him. "Well, it's a long story. Ya see, she came to me and asked me to blow up the ship. So we did that, and she was fightin' with the crew and the Captain on the bridge. I came in through the window. She told me to take the boy and get to the boats..." Eric trailed off as Hob finished processing what he was saying and turned to glare at him. "You blew up the fuckin' ship?"

Eric swallowed hard. "It was an accident?" he suggested.

"Fuck me," Hob muttered. "That bitch turns up and the entire place goes fuckin' crazy. Where's that cunt thinks she's in charge?"

"Rache?" Eric offered.

"Yeah, her." Hob had a direction for his anger now. It would be good to work out his fears on Rache's whimpering flesh. He strode off along the sand, glaring at the knots of survivors as he passed.

"Else had a point," Eric said, hurrying after Hob. "We weren't doing so well. I mean, okay I was doing fine, but you lot. You holders and engineers, your situation was pretty much shit."

"We were fucking safe there!" Hob snarled.

"Yeah but there's more to life than being safe," Eric muttered, not willing to risk a physical confrontation with the enraged Hob.

"Rache!" Hob roared.

A figure stood up from a small campfire, handing a wrapped bundle to one of the women sitting cross-legged next to her. Rache's skin was still stained with oil, but much of it had washed away, leaving her with a grey pallor, much like the dead.

"Whaddya you want, Hob?" Rache asked, her body language set to fight.

"Where's that fuckin' bitch and where's my daughter?"

Rache hesitated. "You mean Sarah?"

"Yes, I fuckin' mean Sarah and that crazy bitch that got us in this fuckin' mess."

Rache looked up and down the shoreline. Bodies rose and fell on the long regular breath of the ocean. She yearned to be out there, riding that swell and fall. Sailing over the horizon until there were no more horizons. "I haven't seen them," she said finally.

"Is that her kid?" Hob said, stabbing a finger in the direction of the campfire.

"Yeah, and Lowanna, the abo girl Else had with her," Rache replied. Hob made to push past her, but Rache stepped up in his face. "You go near that baby girl or Else's boy and I fuckin' swear, Hob, I will feed you to the first dead fucker I can find."

Hob's knuckles cracked as he clenched his fists. Rache's eyes never wavered from his. After a moment he snarled something and turned away.

"Fuckin' asshole," Eric muttered when Hob had stalked out of earshot.

"Rache," Cassie, a survivor from the campfire, said as she approached. "What are we gonna do for food?"

"We'll just…" Rache looked from the sea to the tree line. "Get everyone together. Gather the salvage. We'll make some weapons and then we'll go find some food. All of us. Together."

First Cassie and then Eric walked away, stopping at each group of huddled people to pass on her instructions, to share the hope that Rache had given them.

CHAPTER 2

The sand melted into glass under the intense heat. It glowed from banana yellow through to cherry red. A cycling, vibrant palette of colors that made the swirling plasma seem almost alive. Then the water washed over the burning sand and it screamed.

Else sat up, her eyes flaring wide and then snapping shut as the full glare of the morning sun hit her face. Her body was a crawling mass of burnt skin that hung in peeling strips. As a fresh wave beached itself, the water washed over her wounds with a searing agony that birthed a new shriek of pain.

Moaning, she climbed to her feet and backed away from the hissing surf. The beach was littered with washed-up wreckage. In the distance the remains of a small fire smoldered on the sand.

Else focused on that; walking in that direction gave her something to do. She had lost her son and Lowanna. Tears welled and stung on her raw cheeks. Through her blurred vision she saw the footprints and marks where salvage had been dragged up and piled above the high-water line. She wiped her face, hissing at the sting. Someone had been here, different feet. Else walked on down the beach, following the meandering trail of footprints. The trail widened as more people came together, joining the ragged procession. Else saw where they stopped, milled, and stood watching as some altercation took place in the sand. Then they moved off again; this time the footprints headed towards the tree line. Else knew the river lay beyond the narrow forest of mangroves. Whatever the survivors had in mind, they were heading towards an area overrun with feral dead and even more dangerous, feral crocodiles.

Else stopped and listened. Birds, the breeze in the trees, but no sound of screaming yet. She focused on putting one foot in front of the other, climbing the gentle slope of the dunes, through the hard spines of grass and on into the wet mud of the mangroves.

The tracks ended here. The tidal mudflats oozed and filled any holes made in seconds. On the roots of the mangrove trees that looked like many-fingered hands plunging into the rich earth, she could see the fresh splatter of mud splashed up by people passing by.

The group had spread out, picking their way through the treacherous ground. She plunged in, the cold compress of salty mud both soothing and agonizing against her legs. Wading through the sucking mud, Else sank up to her knees with each step. She held on to the mangrove roots and pulled herself along, eyes alert for any sign of crocs or evols.

She found the first body caught in the tangled roots of an old mangrove tree. Only an arm remained, the rounded nob of bone at the elbow gleaming white and pure in the morning sun. The water around it was still; either the croc had swum off, or the dead had moved on. Else slid down into the water until only her eyes and nose were above the surface. Moving slowly, she felt for changes in the currents, or surges of pressure.

A croc, close to six feet long, surfaced silently ahead of her. It looked like a floating log; just its eyes and a few knobbly points of her long muzzle were visible. Else moved carefully; without weapons she would be entirely defenseless against an attack. The croc dropped beneath the surface with a slight *bloop* sound. Else followed, her eyes wide open against the brown water.

The croc came at her like a great bolt fired from a bow. Else twisted her body as the beast snapped its open jaws at her exposed flesh. In the fraction of a second that the croc slammed her mouth shut, Else grabbed it by the jaw and held the mouth closed. The croc exploded in a thrashing frenzy; Else wrapped her legs around the armored body and hung on. The raw burns covering her skin made her pain a living thing that hurt so much she almost passed out. Every time her head broke the surface Else took a gulp of air and tried not to scream in agony.

The crocodile could stay under for at least five minutes, even while fighting, so drowning it wasn't an option. Else didn't think anyone had ever successfully ridden a crocodile like a horse, so the next thing to do was dismount safely.

Dropping her legs, she pushed her feet into the thick mud under the water. Getting some kind of stable footing, she wrenched the croc towards a mangrove tree. Moving and setting her feet again, she heaved a second time. The croc slammed into the wide trunk of the mangrove tree, thrashing and hissing as she battered Else with her tail. Else slammed the croc's head against the trunk hard enough to dent the tree. Stunned, the croc went still. Else dropped the animal in the water and pushed away, swimming through the submerged roots until she found dry land. The croc didn't follow.

The small island in the tidal zone had a mat of fallen leaves and signs of crocodile nesting sites from past breeding seasons. Else scooped up a branch; it seemed firm enough and would do in a pinch. The only sign of recent life on the island were the scuffed leaves and hurried footmarks of the group from the beach.

Else followed the trail, losing it among the trees but finding other marks of their passage: a torn snag of fabric, mud smeared fresh on a mangrove trunk. There were still no sounds, and that worried Else more than screaming would.

She started to run, taking long strides that carried her across the deep mud on stepping-stones of high mangrove roots. Else reached the edge of the trees and the long and gently sloping riverbank that lay beyond. The mud here was wiped slick and smooth by the bellies of crocodiles. They warmed in the sun on the bank and then slid into the water to hunt prey.

Looking upstream Else saw the survivors some distance away, still on her side of the river. They were a huddled knot of women and children, surrounded by a ragged line of defenders. Assaulting them on all sides were a dozen feral undead in various stages of dismemberment and crocodile-induced damage.

The drying mud caking Else's skin was a soothing balm to her burnt flesh. She only had the stick, but she ran anyway, charging at the evols and swinging hard. The stick smashed to splinters against the first dead-head in range.

The evol grunted and tried to reorientate herself to the new attack. Else stabbed her in the eye with the jagged tip of the wood and shoved it in hard enough to pierce the brain. The zombie dropped into the mud. The defenders cheered as they fought back, cutting the remaining dead down with renewed strength.

When the last of them were dispatched, Else ran her eyes over the group. One woman held a baby, and the mewling cry of the tiny form hit Else like a hammer blow in the chest. Ignoring the people trying to thank her and pat her on the back, she shoved through the crowd, pushing people out of her way until she stood in front of the cowering woman.

Sinking down to her knees, Else pulled back the edge of the faded blanket that wrapped the baby. The face was still new and soft, like a young butterfly whose wings had not yet fully expanded and dried.

"Baby..." Else whispered.

The woman nodded and lifted the tiny bundle up. "The girl too," the woman said. "She's safe an' all."

Else nodded, sinking to her knees on the wet ground, fresh tears burning on her cheeks as she cradled the tiny boy against her breast.

CHAPTER 3

"We are going to die out here," Cassie whined for the third time. Else resisted the urge to slap the woman across the face. The sun was still high overhead, beating down on the walkers. The pain of the deep burns had faded from Else's skin. Her hair was completely gone, giving her a strange, alien appearance. The healing flesh itched maddeningly, which did little to improve her mood.

Rache came jogging up the line of straggling people. Engineers and men with blades crafted from salvage walked on the outside of the line.

"Much further?" Rache asked cheerfully.

"Yes," Else said and moved her son to the other hip. The deep drawing sensation that seemed to come from deep inside and flowed down her swollen breasts and out through her nipples when he suckled buzzed like a completed circuit in her mind. A sense of rightness had settled over Else during the day's march and she didn't appreciate the interruption.

The baby slept now, eyes screwed shut against the bright light, his tiny limbs quivering against her body.

"I'm not even sure where we are going," Rache said and gave a slight giggle. Her eyes darted over the landscape, the size of it leaving her with a sense of vertigo. "I can't believe we made it to onland."

"You'll see stranger things than dirt and trees," Else replied.

The first herd of kangaroos they saw sent the survivors into an uproar of excited chatter. Those old enough to remember grinned and shouted as they watched them run, while those who had never seen such creatures before stared with open mouths.

Rache organized the fishermen to do what they did best as night fell. Fires were set along the bank and they reeled in enough catch to feed everyone to satisfaction. There was only one casualty, an older fisherman, who hobbled into the river to unsnag a line from a floating log. The crocodile took him before he knew it was there. A splash, a truncated scream, and then nothing but ripples carried away on the light current.

They fished from shore after that.

Else tended her baby, sitting by the fire with a mother called Sheila who gave advice on the practical care of babies. Sheila, who said she had born seven children since the Great Panic, only to have all of them taken away by the crew, nursed Lowanna and wept silent tears when Else told her that the baby girl would need a mother who could take care of her until she was fully grown.

Only one mob of evols came upon them in the night; a disfigured and desert-scarred group that numbered less than six. They were attracted to the firelight, and the sentries cut them down without injury or fuss.

After dawn, when the survivors had breakfasted on leftover fish, Else started walking again. Heading upriver, following the bank and retracing her steps to where Jirra's people had their camp. She carried her baby in the sling and two of the short-handled scythes across her back.

Rache, Sheila, Hob, and the others fell into step behind her. Else ignored them. The sooner she could get back to her house in the bush, the sooner she could get back to rebuilding her life and raising her child.

Rache asked questions constantly, and Else found that each

answer she gave prompted more questions. She told the engineer about the cities she had seen, the abandoned boats and vehicles, the once shining towers of glass now dulled by a decade of dust and decay. All things that Rache was barely old enough to remember from the time before.

"How did you find Lowanna?" Else asked.

"Eric, he found her when he was putting his bombs everywhere. He killed a couple of crew and took her. Reckoned it was her, cuz she was the only Abo baby there."

"He left the others?"

"Didn't have much choice. Only having two arms and needing to run and fight and god knows what."

"He saved me too," Else admitted.

"You wouldn't think it to look at him, but for a crazy guy, he's got steel."

"He knows things, useful things. And he's a leader, like you," Else said.

Rache blushed a little under the grime on her cheeks. "Nah, he's too old for me."

"You want to have smart kids, you find a smart man to have them with," Else said.

Jirra's people kept a simple camp, a few shelters made from foraged wood, bound and thatched with the paper bark stripped from gum trees. Else gestured for the ragged convoy to halt. Standing at the edge of the camp, she frowned at the cold remains of cooking fires and the silence broken only by the buzzing of flies.

"What is this place?" Rache asked.

"This is where Lowanna was born, her people live here." Else went down on one knee, her gaze intent on the deserted campsite.

"Where is everyone?" Rache whispered.

Else didn't respond. The baby grizzled against her and she hefted him gently. Hob came striding up the line, muttering and cursing the heat, the flies, and the delays.

"What the fuck is going on?" he demanded.

"I'm looking to see if it is safe for us to go in there," Else said.

"Fuckin' place is deserted. Why wouldn't it be safe?" Hob wiped the sweat from his dusty face and scowled with a look of thunder. "We stand around in this fuckin' heat we're gonna fuckin' die."

"If you're hot, go for a swim," Rache said sweetly.

Hob glanced at the slow-moving river, muddy grey and filled with unseen dangers. "Go fuck yourself."

Else stood up. Sliding a sheathed blade from where it hung on Rache's hip, she walked out into the camp.

"Billy? Sally? Anyone here?" Else walked around the camp. The drying fish were gone, stripped from the wooden racks. The shelters were empty and the group following her picked over the few scraps left behind.

"You were expecting someone to be here?" Hob asked.

"There were people here. They would have helped you," Else said.

"They would have helped us? You mean you won't?" Hob stopped stirring the dust with his foot and turned on Else.

"I can't help you. I'm lucky to keep myself alive. I have to take care of my son."

"You dragged us all off the ship! Because of you we're stranded here in the middle of onland! You have no fuckin' choice. You have to help us!"

Else opened her mouth to respond, then thought better of it. The other survivors gathered around, eyes wide with fear, yet a shadow of hope lurking in their expressions. They were desperate now. On the ship they had been protected, at least in a way. Now they had nothing except themselves and the constant threat of death by evol, crocodile, or in the weeks ahead, a slow death by starvation.

"Okay. Okay…" Else raised her voice to be heard by everyone.

"I thought there would be people here. People who could give you food, shelter, and support. I don't know where they have gone. I don't think they are dead. They've just moved on for some reason."

"Can we find them?" Rache asked.

"We can try," Else replied.

"So what are we standing around here for then?" Hob turned to address the group. "Pick yourselves up, you useless fuckers. If you want to live, then stand up and walk." Hob strode amongst them, kicking those who moved too slowly for his liking.

The holders started moving without complaint; they seemed used to the abuse from people like Hob. The fishermen scowled but didn't say anything. The engineers looked to Rache, who nodded, before they stood up and started walking.

Else walked on. Her skin itched, and the regular feeding demands made by her son left her feeling weak and drained. It wasn't just the survivors who needed food. Her genetically engineered cells burned a lot of energy to fuel her rapid healing. She put aside her physical concerns, focusing on the steady striding rhythm of one foot following the other. They were beyond the saltwater mudflats now, the risk of crocodile attack lessened by the fresh water flowing in the nearby river. Within an hour of walking along the riverbank, following the dried remains of bare footprints, they found where the Aboriginal camp had crossed the water. A collection of carefully stored canoes and dinghies could be seen on the other side of the river, drawn up and lashed to trees to keep them in place during any further floods. Else summoned Rache, Hob, and Quint the fisherman. Eric lurked in the background, trying not to be noticed while listening in on the conversation.

"We need some people to swim across the river, get the boats, and bring them back," Else said.

Rache and Hob looked at her as if she had gone mad. Quint nodded, "Yeah, I'll send some of the guys over."

"What about crocodiles?" Rache asked.

Else looked her in the eye. "You don't get the dangerous ones this far from the sea."

Hob opened his mouth and closed it again. Quint called three of the fishermen forward and ordered them to swim across the wide river and collect the boats. They didn't seem convinced that they would be safe from crocodile attack, but they obeyed his orders. With a minimum of splashing they struck out for the far bank. Else watched with an almost detached curiosity while the other survivors lined up along the bank and gave whispered encouragement. The swimmers arrived on the other side without incident. They climbed out of the water, turning to wave to the people on the opposite shore.

The evols came out of the trees, looming up behind the fishermen in a ragged line of a dozen walking dead. The three of them reacted to the shouts of warning from the other survivors.

"Fuckin' stupid idea," Hob said, spitting into the mud.

"They might make it," Else suggested, her gaze fixed on the desperate battle taking place beyond the river.

The fishermen slashed out with the salvage-forged blades they carried. Dead flesh parted and the mud soaked up the dark blood. One of the fishermen slipped in the mud; a dead woman bore him down, snapping her teeth at his throat as he screamed and struggled.

"We have to help!" Rache cried. Else slipped the blanket sling from around her shoulders. Turning to Cassie, she let her take the squirming bundle that was Else's son.

Else ran into the water. She swam hard, vanishing underwater and reappearing less than a minute later with a splash on the opposite bank. Her steel blades flashed; the dead fisherman hadn't resurrected yet, so Else decapitated the woman that was tearing strips of skin away from his bones. One of the other fishermen had climbed a tree and two evols were scrabbling at the bark, peeling away the dry sheets and reaching up to pull him down. The third fisherman had vanished, running into the trees in panic.

Else sidestepped a swinging clawed hand and, countering with her blade, she cut the reaching limb off at the elbow. A follow-up blow split the zombie's skull. For each one that fell, two others came shuffling forward to feed on her.

The woman flicked the brains and matted hair from her blades. Crossing her arms, she took a deep breath and waited until the remaining zombies were close enough. She unfolded like a bird of prey. Instead of talons or wings, her arms ended in sharpened steel. This was her dance, the only one she had ever known. No matter where she went, the dead would be there. Killing them would be all she could ever do. There was no pleasure in it, no delight, just a grim satisfaction. For Else, their destruction was a need as basic as breathing.

She turned, scanning the ground and the trees. The dead lay in butchered chunks at her feet. The bush whispered and she caught her breath. After examining the woven bark that lashed the boats to the trees, Else sliced through it and tied the other boats to the first one. With a single oar as a paddle she floated the convoy across the river. In less than an hour everyone was across the water. The fisherman up the tree came down to the good-natured laughter and teasing of his friends. The man who ran into the bush did not return when they called his name.

"We need to keep moving," Else warned. The baby had nursed and now slept again, a warm and comforting shape against her chest.

No one argued. The stink of the dead lay like a fog over everything under the afternoon sun. They walked on, passing into the thin forest and starting at every sudden flap of a bird or bolt of a creature foraging in the dry scrub.

Else pushed ahead, leaving Rache to shepherd the survivors. Armed with her blades, Else moved quietly through the trees. A short time later she killed the first feral pig she came across with a well-aimed knife throw. The pig proved too heavy to lift or drag, so Else went back and directed the survivors to where they would make camp.

Once the pork was barbequing on spits over three open fires, the rumbling of empty bellies became almost audible.

Else slapped hands away like they were petulant children. "If you eat pig before it is well cooked, you can get sick," she warned again.

They ate after sunset, gorging on the juicy meat until they lay down, clutching their swollen stomachs and groaning. Else waited until the survivors were asleep, then she left the camp. Slipping past the sentries, who were engaged in some kind of belching contest, she orientated herself to the stars and moon. She felt certain that her house was within walking distance, but just how far that was she couldn't be sure. The baby grizzled, moving against her. Else absently lifted him out of the carry-sling and let his bowels and bladder empty without breaking her stride. The bush looked as familiar as every other stretch of salt-brush and gum.

Else kept walking, a ground-eating stride that was almost a jogging pace. She slowed as her son lost his grip on her breast. Walking, she cradled him in her arms, one eye on her surroundings and the rest of her attention caught by the way his tiny limbs moved and his jaw worked to suckle. He had the same hair color as his father. The long lashes that fanned over the baby's cheek came from him too. Else felt a deep sense of contentment spreading through her. A warmth that pulsed from the baby, through her breast, and into her body. She marveled at how perfect he was, while being so completely vulnerable and dependent on her for survival.

Not like the survivors, she reminded herself. They were on their own. She had brought them to the shore, to this mysterious place they called "onland." Now they would have to find their own food, make their own shelter, and live or die like everyone else.

The image of tiny Lowanna came unbidden to her mind. She

was also newborn and entirely helpless. Cassie would look after her. Cassie was nothing but a holder, a breeding machine trapped in the rusting hulk of a ship for over a decade.

The idea of Hob leering at Lowanna as she grew up, counting the days until she was old enough in his mind to take to his bed, flashed through Else's mind. If not Hob, then some other man. Would Lowanna ever have the chance to fall in love and trust the person she lay with? Else told herself there was nothing she could do about that. Her survival and the survival of her son were all that mattered. Lowanna would be dead if Else hadn't saved her. If Rache and Eric and holders like Cassie hadn't saved her too. So, a voice in Else's head said, if you let them all die, then all that struggle was for nothing? What did you save the holders and the engineers and the fishermen for?

Else stopped suddenly and shook the thought from her mind. Not my problem, she told herself. The baby settled again, his stomach full. She started running, cradling the baby so he wasn't bounced. She ran, feeling the energy of her last meal flowing into her muscles and bones. Running fast enough to leave the unfamiliar feeling of guilt behind among the dark trees of the Queensland rainforest.

The familiar pool that she swam and bathed in shone like broken glass in the moonlight. No crocs lurked in this water; it came from a deep mineral spring, clear and cool even in the height of the dry season. The wallabies, kangaroos, and feral livestock all came there to drink. Mona Lisa had been a young heifer when Else found her at the water's edge. She kept that cow; the ones before her had been roped and led home before being butchered to make enough dried meat and leather to last months. Mona Lisa was more of a pet than a supply of provisions.

Else stopped, sinking into a crouch and letting her breathing slow after her long run. The shore of the pool looked clear; no evols had wandered into the crystal green water. She skirted around the water, hearing the snarling and yipping of wild dogs. They travelled in packs, attacking wild sheep and breeding. The remains of the cow, would have been a feast for them.

Else counted eight of them, snarling and squabbling over the few scraps and bones that remained. The evol corpses remained untouched; no animals would ever eat zombie flesh. Else wondered why the carcass of a cow killed by the undead would be palatable to dogs.

She picked up a rock and threw it, sending a black and white dog yelping. More stones flew; the cunning dogs snatched up bones and soon the whole pack had run off barking and yelping into the darkness.

Their noise woke the baby. Else soothed him and carefully explored her home. The inside of her small house remained much as she had left it. Evols had crashed about inside, knocking her supplies onto the floor. Ants had been feasting on the fruit and vegetables she had stored. The meat locker was still intact, and the salt-cured meat hanging in it was okay.

Else lay the baby on the floor. Stripping the bed, she dropped the bloodstained sheets outside. She would burn them in the morning. The mattress was stained too, but she could scavenge for a new one some other time. With fresh sheets on the bed and the door barricaded shut, Else lay down on the bed, her son cuddled against her chest, and for the first time in a week she slept.

The baby woke in the night, and Else washed him clean, fed him, and cradled him until he settled again. His face was a constant source of wonder to her, and she fell asleep again smiling at the way his tiny nostrils flared with each inhalation.

Else lit her woodstove for breakfast and fed the baby. Wrapping him lightly in a sheet, she left him in the bed while she fetched a bucket of fresh water and filled the old oil drum she used for heating water. The fire underneath it devoured the filthy sheets, and Else used some of her precious supply of scavenged soap to wash the salt and mud from her hair and skin. Dressing in clean clothes felt luxurious after the long days in the same rags.

After checking on the baby and satisfying herself that he was fine, she went into her library. It was the third room of the house that Else built. Shelves and racks of books filled every available space. She would have put them on the floor but a fear of flooding and insects had kept her building more shelves. There was barely room to squeeze inside. She selected a chemical engineering textbook and walked out into the sunlight, scanning the index until she found the reference to explosives. She sat on a sawn-up tree trunk next to the laundry tub, reading until she heard her son crying. Putting the book down, she went and checked on him. He was warm, the air in the small house heated up with the morning sun and his hair now matted against his head. She took him outside, washing him with warm water and a soft cloth. She lay him on a blanket, his naked limbs kicking in the shade. With the baby taken care of, Else used sticks to lift the bedding out of the boiling water and draped it over the drying line.

The baby let out a gurgle. Else turned, a grin breaking across her face, telling him it was okay, momma was right here. The words died on her lips—a large, golden-colored dog with floppy ears was sniffing at the baby. The animal was bone thin, his fur matted with mud and burrs. He looked old and probably couldn't hunt as well as the others anymore, and out here that was a death sentence.

Time stopped for Else. She started moving slowly, soft words spilling from her lips in a breathless tumble. "Good dog, nice dog. Please don't hurt my baby. Please just walk away. Good dog..." The dog glanced at her, his lips curling back in a snarl.

"There's no rabies in Australia. You're just hungry," she told the dog. "I can give you food, give you meat. Just please don't hurt my baby…"

The dog's muzzle dropped back to the baby, who flailed his arms and legs. Else nearly screamed; instead she sank into a crouch, her eyes never leaving the dog. Her hand curled around the stick she used for stirring the laundry boiler. It wasn't much of a weapon, but if she threw it, maybe she could drive the animal off.

In the few moments it took her to reach for the stick and start to rise again, the dog made up his mind. His mouth closed around the baby's tiny body and then he bolted. Else screamed, throwing the stick, sending it whirring end over end. It bounced off a tree and the dog, with the baby in his jaws, careened off into the undergrowth.

Else sprinted after them, a howling cry tearing from her throat. Branches lashed at her face. She sidestepped around trees and dug her toes into the leaf mulch, her leg muscles bunching and exploding with each running step. The dog was a splash of tawny yellow in the dusty green and brown of the forest. Else ducked her head under a branch and ran harder. She would never leave her baby alone. Never again. Never for an instant would she take her eyes off him. Not for as long as he lived. *Please let it be longer than today, please.*

Ahead of her she heard a sudden yelping. The cry of a dog in great pain. Else ran harder—if the dog had stumbled into a mob of evols, then her baby was in even great danger. She sprinted, arms pumping as she ran.

Bursting out of the trees, Else skidded to a halt. A man stood in the grass less than a hundred feet away. Wearing nothing but a leather thong around his waist with a flap that covered his groin, his hair and skin had the dark coloring of an Aborigine. He pulled his spear out of something lying in the grass. Else could smell the fresh blood. With a snarl she charged, knocking the startled hunter flat on his back, the baby howling as he landed in the grass.

"Stay the fuck away from him!" Else screamed.

"He's okay. He's okay," the hunter wheezed and then started chuckling. "Jesus! I think you scared ten years outta me, lady!"

Else ignored him and picked up her boy. To her sobbing relief there were no puncture wounds in his skin.

"He didn't hurt him," Else said through the tears flooding down her face.

"Nah, missus, that dog, he's got enough of the retriever breed in him to carry prey in his soft mouth. Safe as in his momma's arms."

Sinking to her knees Else cuddled her howling boy, comforting him into silence. The hunter set to and skinned the dog, gutting it with quick and efficient knife work before butchering the body and wrapping the little meat that was there in banana leaves.

"You out here on your own?" he asked, sliding wrapped cuts of dog meat into a sack containing similar packages. He had been hunting dog before Else's arrival and carried an ample supply.

"Are you from Jirra's tribe?" Else asked, not willing to admit she had no backup to a stranger.

"I know a few Jirras. My name is Joel." The hunter extended a bloodstained hand, which Else ignored.

"Billy and Sally, Jirra's woman was Bindi. She died. They had a baby girl called Lowanna."

Joel nodded. "You're the crazy white girl, lost her baby in the flood last week?"

"I got him back," Else said with an almost growl in her voice.

"Is Jirra with you?"

"He died. Lowanna is okay. I left her with some people."

Joel lifted the sack onto his shoulder and gathered his spears in his other hand. "Sorry to hear about Jirra, he was a decent bloke. I heard he went with you because you were going to take care of his girl."

"I did," Else insisted. "I kept her safe, until the people on the ship took her away from me."

"Boat people, aye?" Joel scratched his right knee with the toes of his left foot, leaning on his spears as he stood on one leg.

"I got Lowanna back, and my baby. I got everyone off the ship! The crew were evols, and they were eating babies to stay smart!"

Joel nodded. Little of what Else said made sense to him, but it was important to be polite. "So where is Lowanna now?"

"With Cassie, and the other survivors. Cassie can take care of her, feed her and protect her from Hob."

"The girl is Murrai tribe. Jirra and her grandparents, they would want her to be with her people."

"I tried to find them," Else said. "The camp was empty. It's not my fault!"

"We gone on walkabout," Joel said. "Maybe you take me to the people who got Lowanna. Then I take them back to Billy and Sally. See if you people wanna go walkabout with us."

Else nodded. Everything was going to be fine once she had her son back. She would take care of him the way she had taken care of herself for the last nine months. Now she felt a rising panic and sense of helplessness. Maybe she wasn't good enough to take care of him on her own? With other people around, there would always be someone to hold and protect him. He would never be alone while she went hunting or scavenging for supplies.

"I'll show you where they were," Else said and together they walked off into the trees.

Else led Joel to the survivor's camp via her house. She gathered a few items of her own. A bow and hunting arrows, a pack load of clothes, her boots, some food, knives, an axe, and a soft clip-on carrier for cradling the baby against her chest as she walked.

She kept an eye on Joel while she packed. He crouched in the dirt and wiggled his fingers, chuckling at the tiny baby who gurgled and kicked on the folded blanket Else had laid down for him.

When they left her house, Joel took the lead, finding Else's trail from the night before in a few moments and loping along the forest floor with a mile-cutting stride that Else worked to keep up with.

Joel followed Else's trail without pause. She had to call a halt after a couple of hours to tend to the baby. Joel stood, one foot resting against his other knee, and sipped water from a bag while she tended to her son. After a drink of water for herself, they set off again.

They heard the survivor camp before they saw it. Angry voices, male and female, loud enough to draw every evol within a mile to investigate the fuss. Else hesitated—rushing in with the baby strapped to her chest would put him in danger. Instead she shed her pack and bow, moving forward with an axe in one hand and the straight-bladed sword in the other.

Hob had been pushed to his knees, his arms raised over his head and lashed to a thick branch that ran across his shoulders, effectively shackling him to the wood. His head was bowed and blood hung in long scarlet drips from his nose.

"Rache!" Else stepped out of the trees and shouted above the angry voices. Joel followed her, standing beside her and regarding the noisy strangers with open curiosity.

The arguing died out and Rache nodded at Else, the blade of her salvage weapon resting over her shoulder.

"What's going on here? Why is Hob tied up?" Else asked.

The tumult of voices flared again. Else raised her hands, motioning them to silence. "Rache, tell me. Everyone else, just shut up."

"Hob attacked Anna. So now we're gonna kill him," Rache announced. The holders started shouting and Rache turned on them, yelling her own anger in their faces.

"Shut up!" Else yelled. "Who is Anna?"

"I'll show you." Rache pushed through the crowd. Else followed, the people parting to allow her passage. Under a rough shelter a woman knelt, skin stained dark with the oil of the engineers, her head bowed.

"Anna?" Else asked, crouching down. The woman looked up, her eyes wet with tears. She shook her head and pulled a blanket back, showing a girl, her naked body bruised and battered. Else had read of young women being described as ripe fruit. Anna wasn't ripe. She had a lot of growing to do before she would be more than a girl whose body was changing with the onset of puberty.

"Is she dead?" Else asked.

The woman shook her head. "She's just gone away," the woman whispered. Her voice cracked as she reached out and stroked a strand of red hair away from the girl's unblinking eyes.

"He raped her," Rache said softly. "He said…He said she'd had her first bleed so she was ready to breed. We were out looking for food and heard the screaming. By the time we got back, he'd done this to her."

Else stood up. The eyes of everyone were on her and she didn't know what they wanted. "What do you want me to do?" she asked the grim faces.

They all spoke at once, their anger and hate raining down like physical blows on Else. She wrapped her arms protectively around the soft cloth carrier that held her baby. He started to grizzle and she slipped the straps off. Sitting cross-legged, she wiped him clean and then fed him.

After a few minutes the people quieted down. Else ignored them until there was silence.

"Don't all speak at once. One person speaks. Then someone else speaks. The rest of us, we listen," she said. "Sit down, all of you." They did, slowly at first; then they all made a space on the ground and sat down.

"You," Else nodded at a man in the group, an engineer by the painted nature of his skin. "What do you want to say?"

The man stood up immediately. "Kill him!" he shouted, and others echoed the sentiment.

"One person speaks!" Else shouted and the crowd subsided.

"You," Else indicated another man.

He stood up and looked about. With a shrug he said, "Kill him. We can't stay here and we can't lock him up anywhere. What other punishment is enough?"

Instead of exploding into an angry uproar the group simply murmured a mix of assent and disagreement. Else moved the baby to her other breast; he didn't seem hungry anymore and just moved against her. "Who's next?" she asked. Two men stood up and one sank back down again, poised to rise when the opportunity presented itself.

"He's gotta die. You let this sort of shit happen and what next? What about when he kills someone? Feed him to the crew I say!"

The man nodded, agreeing with himself. Sitting down again the next fellow sprang up. "She's just a kid! You gotta make an example of him and maybe that means killing him. Let's face it, if we send him away, he'll just come back and kill us. If you don't want to kill him, punish him so that he knows what he did was wrong. Make him do hard labor or something."

Another man shouted without standing up. "He's got to be killed, make an example out if him. Do it so the next bastard knows what he's in for!"

A woman stood up. She waited until the voices around her had died down. "Don't we need him?" she asked. "He kept us together on the ship. Stopped everything falling apart. He hurt that girl and it breaks my heart. But I think we need him."

A younger woman who sat with the fishermen stood up and put her hand on the holder woman's shoulder. "He's hurt Anna and none of us will ever trust him again. I don't want him to die, but he's gotta pay for hurting her. What does her mother want?"

The engineers muttering grew in volume. "I say we brand him and then exile him!" one of them shouted.

"Kill him!" another voice demanded.

"What does the girl want? What does her mother want?" Voices around the group picked up on the idea and quickly drowned out those calling for execution.

"Bugger of a situation you're in," Joel said, crouching down next to Else.

"I don't know what to do," she admitted quietly.

"Maybe you're gonna need him, for a while at least. Maybe them fellas sayin' he's gotta be killed are right. Or maybe them that says he should be turned out on his own, they're right too."

The discussion continued; suggestions and arguments were made for a range of punishments. Hob remained silent through it all. The woman who had been tending Anna was brought forward. She shivered and stared at the ground and would pronounce no judgment, only saying, "He hurt my girl. He hurt her so bad."

The voices calling for Hob's execution continued. When Joel unpacked the fresh dog meat and started grilling it over the fire, it was agreed to take a break from the discussion to eat.

Else took Joel's water bag and knelt down in front of Hob. "You haven't said anything," she said.

Hob lifted his head. One eye had swollen shut; the dried blood and marks on his face gave him an evol-like appearance.

"Your problem is you think this fuckin' world is still safe. Y'think that old laws, old ideals and principles apply.

We're livin' in the new dark ages. Ain't nothin' gonna make a damn bit of difference now. Not in your lifetime and sure as fuck not in mine."

"What would you do, if they asked you to pass judgment?"

Else asked, tipping water into Hob's mouth. He drank greedily and panted a bit before replying.

"I'd fuckin' congratulate me on seein' the bigger fuckin' picture. You think that being nice and talkin' about shit is gonna save the human fuckin' race?" Hob stretched his neck against the branch that pressed down on his shoulders.

"I'll fuckin' tell ya what. If you don't get every fuckin' one of these cunts bred, we're fuckin' extinct."

"She's just a child. It wasn't about breeding a woman. It was about you forcing yourself on her."

"Forcin' myself?" Hob chuckled and spat blood on the dirt. "Ya shoulda seen the way she's been lookin' at me. Hot little cunt like that, she wanted it. Sayin' I attacked her is just engineers talkin' shit." Hob shuffled forward on his knees and whispered, "She fuckin' loved it."

Else set the water bag down, Hob's sudden erection pressing against her thigh. She lifted her gaze, staring him in the eyes, smiling gently. She slid her hand around his pulsing shaft, moving her grip down until she cupped his swollen testicles and Hob grunted and pushed forward against her wrist.

"I read a book once, it said that scars are what remind us that our past is real," Else murmured, her hand working Hob up and down.

"Yeah…" Hob said with a satisfied grin. "Thas' right. We all got scars. So she'll be a bit more careful next time. She'll get over it."

"There are those who say that you are an asset, so you can't be lost. There's those who say that you are dangerous and should be killed. Trust is going to be important in a group like this and what happens if your kind of thinking gets passed on through the genes. I know an expert on selective breeding and I'm sure she would agree." Else spoke softly, her voice as much of an arousing caress as the steady motion of her hand.

Hob's eyes fluttered closed as his mouth opened in a deep groan.

Whatever visions of sexual conquest he was seeing behind his eyelids were riding the sensation of Else's smooth stroking driving him towards a climax.

She watched his face, felt the convulsion of his orgasm and felt the hot splash of his fluids on her arm. In that moment where he was completely lost in the fire of his masculinity, she swept a knife up behind his ball sack and with firm pressure and an upward slicing motion she severed everything. Hot blood sprayed, painting her shirt and face. Else raised her hand, showing Hob his wilting manhood, now lying across her palm. The shock drained the blood from his face and his next breath was already a scream.

CHAPTER 4

"Carrying him will slow us down," Joel warned. Else shrugged. Hob's screams had only stilled when he fainted from shock and blood loss. The engineers and holders had moved quickly, responding to Else's command to put pressure dressings on the wound. She needed him to live and recover, to be a walking example of the law of the group. If he didn't die of an infection, then he might well serve a purpose.

They sat together under the trees, the rest of the group sleeping or sitting close together engaged in murmured conversations.

Else waved a fly away from her baby's face as he slept in the space made by her crossed legs. "I have medicine and books at my house. We can keep him alive."

"You got a powerful hate for this fella, aye?" Joel asked.

"Hate? No. I just compromised."

Joel nodded before saying what was on his mind. "If you want to keep him alive, maybe you shouldn't have cut his cock off?"

"He'll live," Else said. "I'm going to make sure of it."

Rache approached, a grease-splattered banana leaf with thick slices of dog meat steaming on it. "I thought you might be hungry," she said, offering the leaf plate to Else.

Else thanked her and ate quickly, the copper taste of fresh blood mixing with the strong game taste of the cooked meat.

"If you lead this lot back past your place, I'll go and find some stuff that might help him live long enough to get you what you want."

"I don't want anything from him," Else said, licking her fingers.

"Yeah, you want him to suffer," Joel replied and stood up. "I'll look for youse along the track to the house. If I'm not back by the time you get there, wait."

"Thanks," Else said. Joel nodded and vanished into the trees.

Rache came back and sat down carefully, as if waiting for Else to lash out with a knife at any moment. "Everyone's wondering who that guy was," she said.

"His name is Joel, he's with Lowanna's family, they've gone on walkabout. So he can take us to them."

"What are we going to do then?" Rache looked nervous as she asked the question.

"I don't know," Else sighed. "You're the leader, you tell me."

"I'm not the leader. You made everyone think about Hob and what he had done. You...cut him."

"I never asked to be the leader. I just want to go home and look after my baby."

"On the ship, when there was a baby that the crew didn't take, everyone helped. You can't look after a baby on your own."

The fresh memory of the dog sniffing her baby flashed in Else's mind. She shivered and stared down at the tiny form wrapped in a blanket, sleeping against her legs.

"As long as they know I'm not in charge. I don't want to tell people what to do."

"If I ask, would you tell me? Help me be like you, so I can lead them and they will follow?" Rache shot a glance at Else, who nodded.

"Sure, I'll be your advisor, but you can wear the crown." Else scooped up the baby and cradled him against her chest. "We should get moving, while there is still daylight."

Rache stood up. Moving amongst the group she touched

shoulders as she passed, quietly encouraging them to stand up and get ready to move. Else watched as the holders, the engineers, and the fishermen responded. Rache would be a good leader. She just needed to be more confident about it.

Else stood up, falling into step at the back of the group. Rache glanced back regularly and Else indicated the direction with a casual gesture. Hob lay on a rough stretcher of lashed branches. Four people carried him, and he slipped in and out of consciousness as they made their way through the trees.

The people shied away from Else, giving her a personal space that she enjoyed. Even Cassie, who normally wanted to chat incessantly about baby things, ducked her gaze and stayed well away.

The journey to Else's house in the forest took them until after dark. Else emptied her food supplies and they ate tinned fruit, vegetables, and dried meat stew, and the older ones spoke of long lost things like bread and peanut butter.

Joel came sauntering out of the darkness and crouched by the fire. Warming his hands in the glow he accepted a bowl of stew and, between bites, confirmed that Billy and Sally's people had made camp and would wait for Else's group to catch up.

"Good day's walk for this lot, I reckon," he replied when asked how far it would be.

Joel prepared a poultice of honey and leaf paste, which was applied hot to Hob's wound. He bit through the stick jammed between his teeth as a gag against the pain. Else also administered a handful of pills from her scavenged stock, some crumbling from age, but they seemed to ease his suffering and Hob drifted into sleep.

Rache, Eric, Joel, and Else talked together as the camp settled down for the night. "Where are Billy and Sally going on this walk of theirs?" Else asked.

"Wherever. They hunt, move around, see new stuff and check in on sacred places," Joel shrugged.

"I want to take them with us, all of us, and go to Mildura," Else announced.

"Mildura?" Joel scratched his beard. "That's a way down the road, aye?"

"We can find horses, or maybe some vehicles, fuel, that sort of thing. I once drove a steam train from Port Germein to Pimba."

"Steam train?" Joel's eyes crinkled over his grin. "I reckon you must've too."

Else smiled at the memory. "I was much younger then."

"My people are used to walking. We see more that way and usually get where we want to go," Joel said.

"My people have been living on a ship for the last ten years. They aren't used to walking long distances," Rache said.

"Lot of horse riding happen on that ship?" Joel asked. Rache flushed, "Of course not, but if we can find vehicles, we can make them go."

"You piss petrol then?" Joel asked.

Eric gave a cough. "I can brew something that should work for fuel. If I can find the right ingredients."

Else spoke up. "There's vehicles everywhere, plenty of farms around here with trucks and cars. Lots of garages and sheds. Keeps them protected from the elements."

Joel didn't look convinced, but Rache and Eric nodded their approval.

"What's in Mildura?" Rache asked.

"Friends," Else said. "A doctor. Technically she's a geneticist. She has this plan to rebuild the human race by selective breeding."

"What?" Eric asked.

"The important thing is that she is building a community. A safe place, where people can come together and work together. Grow food and live in peace."

"What about the dead?" Rache asked.

"Peace is a state of mind. We can work for it if we want it badly enough," Else replied.

"The dead will always be a problem. They don't decay, they don't change. They just want to kill and feed," Eric said.

"Which means we just learn to live with them," Rache declared and stretched until her shoulders popped.

"If you mean we learn to destroy every last one of them, then I agree," Else said.

"Goes without sayin'," Eric piped up.

"I always dreamed that there would be a place, somewhere in onland, that would be safe. Where the crew could never reach us," Rache said.

"One day," Else said. "One day we can make a place like that. We have to do a lot of fighting and a lot of killing to make it. Lot of people are going to die. Lot of people are going to lose everything."

Rache reached out and took Else's hand in both of hers. "Tell me it will be worth it," she pled.

"If you want a peaceful future badly enough, you'll do anything to make it happen," Else replied.

"I want it," Rache confirmed.

"We can start tomorrow." Else stood up, lifting her son and carrying him inside. Lying down on the bed, she fell asleep with his baby noises cooing against her neck.

CHAPTER 5

The rain came again before dawn, waking Else instantly and the baby a few moments later as the clouds opened and the water thundered down on the shingle roof.

Else dressed: jeans, boots, two layers of shirts, and an old oilskin coat with the hood pulled up over her head. The survivors had scrambled up when the rain started falling. They hunched miserably under the trees, nothing to protect them from the rain except a few scraps of cloth.

Joel stood in the rain, face turned up, mouth open, occasionally gulping like a dark-skinned fish. With the baby protected and her knapsack packed, Else sheathed her weapons and pulled the door shut on her house again. There might be no coming back to this place. She would miss her home, this place that had sheltered her during the long months alone while the baby grew inside her.

"Let's go," Else said and Rache jumped to rouse the others.

"Come on you lot, you'll get just as wet sitting here as you will walking. There's places to go and we can find shelter somewhere down the road."

The group stumbled to their feet, grumbling about stiff muscles and hunger. Hob had survived the night. "He's healing, going to be awhile though," Joel said as he redressed Hob's wound.

They fell into line, gathering their few children and supplies

166

while two volunteers dragged Hob's travois through the mud. A sodden troop followed Joel, Else, and Rache down the trail through the trees.

The rain drummed down on the ground and trees, making conversation difficult. They marched in silence.

One of the fishermen started it, a low rhythmic chanting, a work song with words of the net and the sea. A song of pulling together and getting the work done. The other fishermen joined in, and the holders soon picked up the words. They sang softly, afraid of attracting the dead with too much noise as the song murmured among the group. To Else, it seemed to bring them together, to give them a common purpose they had lacked on the ship.

"Sometimes I wonder if the rain will ever stop," Else said to Joel as they walked.

"Rain is what gives the earth life. Rain is life. If it ever stops, it won't matter what them dead fellas do. Everything will die."

"Sometimes I think that would be better," Else said. "If everything was wiped clean and the earth could start fresh."

"Back to the Dreamtime," Joel said, nodding.

"I'd like that," Else sighed. The baby stirred in his dry cocoon under her raincoat.

Joel waved them to a halt later in the day, then ducked down and crept forward. Else hesitated, wanting to stay close to him but not wanting to put her son in danger. She crouched leaning against a dripping tree trunk and scanned the trees ahead. Joel reappeared a few moments later. His way of silently moving unnerved Else, and she reminded herself to learn all she could from him.

"Road ahead, old highway," Joel reported as he sank into a crouch next to her.

"Any dead?" Else asked.

"No, it's all clear. We need to cross it, get into the bush on the other side. Keep moving that way," Joel indicated a direction that Else tagged as five degrees west of southwest.

"You wait here," Joel continued, "I'll go get the others."

Else nodded and Joel vanished into the trees. She went back to watching the forest ahead. After a minute she rose to her feet and crept forward. Even here, in the cover of the dense bush, she felt exposed. Too many directions for death to come from. A low bank of exposed clay and sandy soil that squished underfoot in the rain marked the edge of the highway.

Else looked both ways. The broad expanse of old asphalt disappeared into the mist in both directions, a black river dotted with tufts of green grass pushing up through the ever-widening cracks.

The shifting rain made shadows, and it wasn't until one of them moved against the rain that Else noticed the figure coming from the south. He was alone and moving with purpose. A wide-brimmed stockman's hat kept his face in shadow. Else slid a blade from the scabbard on her back, noting that if the man approaching was an evol, he had been eating well. There was no shuffle in his step, no confusion of dulled senses in his manner.

If he was a survivor, he might have friends and that could be just as dangerous. Else stayed hidden, watching the man as he came closer and then passed by. She wiped the water from her eyes and studied his face before pushing through the brush and stepping out on the road behind him.

"You—" Else said and hesitated. The figure had gone. Joel emerged from the roadside scrub.

"You okay?" he called softly. Else shivered. She dreamed of the Courier, but seeing a vision of him walking in the mist was an eerie sensation.

"Yes," she nodded. "We should keep moving."

The survivors emerged from the bush, gathering behind Joel and peering out into the open ground.

"We go that way," Joel pointed southwest again. Else nodded and waited while the group crossed the road.

"Does it always rain in onland?" Rache asked.

"No, this part of the country had a dry season and a wet season. This is the wet season."

"No shit?" Rache said with a wry smile.

"The rest of the year it doesn't rain at all."

"When it rained on the ship, we would just stay inside. Rain was a good thing; it refreshed the water tanks and washed the decks clean."

"It's a good thing in onland too. It makes things grow," Else said testily, still feeling unnerved by the apparition.

"The only green things we saw on ship was seaweed. Seaweed and fish. Salvage fruit and coconuts when we could find them."

"We'll take the road," Else said. "It goes south and we can travel faster."

Rache nodded and made the announcement to the survivors. They murmured their agreement, and the travois dragged over the rain-swept asphalt.

It was after dark when they came to the farmhouse. Set back from the road behind a stand of gum trees, the gates were locked but a truck had smashed through the fence, turning on its side and plowing up the ground. The truck was empty and rusting in the mud. Else walked with Rache at the head of the group, watching their surroundings carefully for any sign of movement.

"Who lives here?" Rache asked.

"No one now," Else replied. "Once, people owned this land and farmed it."

Rache looked intrigued. "Maybe they had cows, or sheep?" she asked.

"Papayas," Else said.

"Huh?" Rache frowned.

"This was a papaya plantation." Else nodded towards a sign, half eaten by mud, the paint faded to a ghostly shade.

"Can you eat papaya?" Rache asked.

"Yes," Else said.

They reconnoitered the house, finding nothing alive or dead. The paint had peeled, revealing boards that had weathered to the grey of dead bones.

"It's…creepy," Rache said.

"Bring everyone inside. It will be dry and we can make a fire."

The house fascinated the survivors. Some of them remembered living in places like this, and one woman sank into the dust-covered remains of a couch, weeping uncontrollably.

Else checked the house one more time. There were no human remains inside. Rache and Eric followed her into the kitchen.

"Don't!" Else barked as Rache went to open a large, white chest freezer.

"Never open those," Else insisted. "You'll regret it if you do."

"Freezer," Eric said. "Jeez, can you imagine what kind of shit would be growin' in there after this long?"

"Dead things," Else said.

Else wiped a kitchen window until she could see out. Joel strolled past outside. She watched as he crouched on the veranda and lit a fire in an old pot. Else opened the back door. "Joel, you should come inside, it's warm in here."

"Na thanks," he said.

"If you need anything, just ask, okay?"

Joel waved and went back to feeding sticks into his pot fire.

Eric got a fire started in the living room fireplace, and the survivors stripped down and dried their clothes. Years of living in close confines left them with no sense of modesty.

"Where's Hob?" Rache demanded.

"Couldn't get him in through the door," one of the stretcher-bearers said with a shrug.

"Well pick him up and carry him in. You leave him outside, he'll get sick and die."

Two men shuffled out and a minute later came in, Hob slung between them, shivering violently.

"Fuckin' cunt," he muttered. "Fuckin' cunts, all o' yer."

"Lay him down," Rache ordered, "on that soft thing." The men lay Hob out on the couch.

Rache peeled the dressing from Hob's wound. He hissed and dug his fingers into the couch cushions. "Ya fuckin' bitch," he snarled through clenched teeth.

The wound had crusted and fluid exuding from the gash had soaked into the dressing. Rache sniffed it; the smell of honey and salt seemed a good sign that the wound wasn't infected.

"You lie still, let that get some air."

"I'll give you some fuckin' air," Hob growled. "Stab ya in the fuckin' throat."

Rache crouched down and put her mouth near Hob's ear. "Listen to me, you fuckin' prick. She could have killed you. Half of them here wanted you dead. She could have let you bleed out, but instead she had you fixed up and kept alive. So quit your fuckin' bitchin' and give some goddamn thanks."

Hob subsided into muttering and Rache walked off to the kitchen to ask Else and Joel about how to make a fresh dressing for his wound.

Hob lay on the couch, his gaze sliding across the ceiling and away from the searing throb of his groin. He turned his head and his eyes fell on the girl. What was her fuckin' name? Anna? She sat near the fire, a steaming blanket wrapped tightly around her, safe in her mother's arms. The fuck did she have to look so fuckin' miserable about?

Anna twisted in her mother's lap, her pale blue eyes meeting his through the tangled fringe of her long red hair. Hob blinked in surprise. The hate he saw in her stare chilled him to the core.

"Crazy bitch," he muttered, turning his face back up to the ceiling. The emotion in the girl's stare echoed with him, though, even when he closed his eyes and tried to sleep.

CHAPTER 6

They slept the night in the house, eating the last of the meat that Joel hunted and the last of the cans from Else's scavenged stores. No one was keen to move at dawn. Else vanished out the back of the house, Joel strolling along beside her. They returned some time later, carrying bulging sacks.

"Papayas," Else declared and started handing out the bright yellow fruit to the confused survivors.

Eric let out a whoop and taking a blade he slashed one in half and sucked the juice that dripped from its core. The others quickly caught on, hacking the fruit into fist-sized chunks and stuffing themselves.

Rache grinned with her mouth full, the sweet juice dripping down her chin, leaving sticky trails on her skin.

Else cut papaya chunks into a bowl and went to where Hob lay, glaring at everyone.

"You should eat," she said.

"Fuck off," Hob snarled.

Else shrugged and set the bowl on his chest. "Don't wait for too long, we're moving out soon."

"Did you find vehicles?" Eric asked, and then let loose a thunderous belch that made the babies cry and the children giggle.

"No, just a tractor and it's rusted up," Else said.

After breakfast the group packed everything up. Their wardrobes were expanded with clothes salvaged from sealed plastic bags found upstairs, and everyone carried at least three fresh papaya.

Joel moved the empty bowl off Hob's chest and felt his skin. "No fever, mate. That's a good sign, aye?"

Hob grunted, inhaling sharply as Joel inspected his wound. "How you pissing?" Joel asked.

"How the fuck do you think?" Hob snarled.

"It coming out okay?"

"It burns like fuckin' fire. Then it fuckin' burns until the next time I gotta fuckin' piss. Then it fuckin' burns again. Stupid fuckin' thing to fuckin' ask."

"I found this," Else said, peering over Joel's shoulder. "It's an antiseptic spray, iodine."

Joel gave a noncommittal grunt. "Honey's good for preventing infection."

"Try this stuff too," Else suggested. Joel took the can and popped the lid off. Giving it a shake, he pressed down on the aerosol button. Hob's back arched off the couch. *"Oh you fuckin' cuuuuuunt!"* he screamed.

"If it burns, it's doing its job," Else said.

She left Joel to dress the whimpering Hob's wound. A weaker man would have died of shock and blood loss. Hob's anger would keep him alive.

They walked on down the road in better spirits. The children laughed and chased each other through the rapidly diminishing puddles. The adults had lost some of the haunted look that dominated their eyes.

Around midday, by Else's estimation of the position of the sun that had returned without mercy earlier in the morning, the Hob's stretcher came apart. A crowd gathered around him and concluded that the travois was beyond repair.

"Can you walk?" Else asked.

"Can fuckin' walk you into the ground, bitch," Hob snarled and with some help, he made it upright. He swayed slightly, the little color he had draining from his face.

"I'm going that way," Else jerked a thumb over her shoulder and turned on her heel.

The group gave Hob some room. He gritted his teeth and took a cautious step, then another. Anna stood behind him under her mother's arm and watched him hobble down the road.

No one cheered. The stretcher-bearers took on other loads, and the group moved on down the broken road.

They saw the first evol later that day, a lone male, tangled in a broken wire fence. The wire had cut deep, slicing the flesh from his arms and legs down to the bone. The group slowed to a halt, staring at this strange sight from a safe distance. The fear they had of the dead was changing to curiosity now that they were not under their authority.

"Should we kill it?" Rache asked.

"We always kill the dead. It doesn't matter who they were or where they are; we destroy every one we come across," Else replied.

Rache stepped forward under a chorus of advice and cries of caution from the group. She slid a blade from her back and with a nod at the audience she decapitated the snarling man.

Else turned and started walking while Rache brandished her weapon and grinned at the exultant praise of her people. With her back to the fence, Rache didn't see the second evol rise up out of the grass. This one was a young girl, bound to this spot by some lingering sense of security with the man who may have been her father.

Else heard the screams and ran back to the group. Rache was on her back, wrestling with the dead girl on top of her, the evol's shrill screams drowning out the cries of horror from the startled survivors. In three running strides Else arrived, her blade swinging down, hacking the girl's head off and dragging her body away. Rache rolled to her feet, teeth bared and eyes wide. "Fuckin' bitch," she spat and stepped forward, kicking her booted foot into the corpse. The toe of her boot punctured the necrotic skin and filled the air with rotten stink.

Else shoved Rache back hard enough to send her sprawling on her butt. "You think this is a game?" Else demanded, standing over Rache. "There is no room for complacency. This is about survival. For you, for them, for all of us."

Rache rolled to her feet, still amped on adrenaline and ready to fight. She subsided when she saw the look in Else's eyes; something in the deep blue of those irises terrified her.

"All of you, keep moving," Else ordered. The group picked up and marched on. Hob was already a quarter mile ahead, walking with a grim determination and a singular focus on the horizon.

Else marched after him, Joel falling into step beside her and scanning the trees on each side. "We're pretty exposed out here. Them dead fellas, they follow the roads."

"We move faster on the road," Else replied.

"Just don't camp here, aye?"

"There's farms all round an abandoned town, I remember from when I came up this way. Innisfail, it's a big town; shouldn't be too much further." Else glanced back; the survivors were hurrying along. Small children had been scooped up and rode on the shoulders of adults.

"Dunno how long they can keep up this pace," Joel warned.

"Well they'd better get used to it. The strong survive out here, the rest will die."

"Y'know my people, we've been here for maybe sixty thousand years. They don't come much tougher and I'm sayin' you should slow down."

The baby started crying at that point, ending the conversation and slowing Else's pace to a steady walk.

With a cloth from her bag, dampened in a puddle, Else cleaned the baby and then fed him while she walked. The survivors kept their distance, huddled together and watching her warily.

After an hour's walking in the sun, the steam rising from the ground made the air thick with humidity.

"We need to get some more water," Rache reported. "The fruit's all been eaten and the kids are hungry."

Else looked over her shoulder at the dusty, weary people. Why were they her responsibility? She should have stayed in her house with her baby and let them survive on their own. Except for the dogs. If not the dogs, then the crocodiles, or the evols, or a snake. So many ways to die out here in the bush. Safety came with community and with community came responsibility, no matter how much it rankled.

"Tell them we keep going until we find a house, then we can stay there for the night. It will be shelter from the rain, and the farms around here have lots of food growing."

"I should hunt," Joel said.

"How will you find us again?" Else asked.

Joel chuckled and shook his head. "You leave a trail like a herd of water buffalo. I'll find youse."

Else watched him lope off into the trees. Joel had a point. His people had survived for untold generations on this land. Hunting and moving around, never making the kinds of technological breakthroughs that other people did, but living in harmony with the environment.

"Where's he going?" Rache asked, jogging up to take position next to Else.

"Hunting," Else replied.

"I thought we were looking for his people," Rache said.

"Yeah, I guess they don't follow the roads."

"Is he coming back?"

"He will find—" Else stopped as in the distance Hob staggered and then collapsed on the road.

"Shit," she muttered. Hurrying forward, the two women reached him first. The rest of the survivors came running to see if he was alive.

"He's still breathing," Else reported. Blood and fluid stained the rough blanket skirt that Hob wore. They lifted the fabric away and saw the dressing underneath was soaked with blood.

"Let him die," one of the survivors muttered.

"He deserves it," a woman said.

The others muttered their own opinions. Else scanned the group until she saw Anna.

"What do you want us to do?"

The girl recoiled, pressing against her mother's side. "It's okay, love," her mother said.

"There was a wise man, named Voltaire, who once said that punishment should serve a purpose. A dead criminal is useless," Else said to the girl. "If Hob dies, then his punishment serves no purpose. It would be as if I had killed him immediately."

"I hate him," the girl whispered.

Else nodded. "You have reason to. Letting him die won't quench that. Let his punishment serve a purpose, not just his pain, but his scar for years to come."

Anna frowned, thinking hard about what Else was saying. "He will hurt me again," she whispered.

"No, he's harmless now. If he strikes anyone, I'll cut off his hand. If he threatens anyone, I'll cut out his tongue."

The girl nodded. "I'll watch him, always," she said.

"Okay," Else said. She unpacked medical supplies from her bag and dressed Hob's wound again. Using a sewing kit and thread she made some rough stitches in his flesh, closing the seeping wounds and finishing with a liberal spray of iodine over the area.

"Do we carry him again?" one of the men asked.

"Sit, rest, we will see how he is when he wakes up," Else replied.

The group sat down in the road. Some moved to the shade, with others facing the trees to watch for the dead.

Else dozed in the warm afternoon. Flies buzzed and crawled over Hob's stained cloth. Anna came forward, still wrapped in her blanket from head to toe. With a leaf-laden branch she waved the insects away. She then sat, watching Hob, out of reach but vigilant, until he stirred and asked for water.

"There isn't any left," Anna said. "You need to get up and walk until we find some." She poked Hob with the leafy branch for emphasis.

"Geddafuckout," he muttered.

"Else said if you hit anyone, she will cut off your hands, if you threaten anyone, she will cut out your tongue."

Hob's eyes narrowed. He regarded Anna, who sat on the road with her knees drawn up and her slight form draped in a blanket shield.

"Who the fuck put her in charge?" he asked.

Anna shrugged. "She's the strongest. So if you try anything, she will hurt you so bad."

"Gemme some fuckin' water," Hob said.

"You want water, you stand up and walk. You can stop when you find water." Anna flinched when Hob rolled on to his side. She rose to her feet, the blanket clutched tightly around her, only her face, feet, and the leafy stick showing.

"Get up, you shit," she said.

"I'm fuckin' getting' up. Why don't you give me a fuckin' hand?"

Anna didn't move. Hob made it to his knees, his mouth open and panting in the afternoon heat. He licked his cracked lips. The girl stood firm, her stick like a sword across her body.

"You have to learn to do things on your own. You have to learn to live with what you did," she said.

"Fuckin' smart cunt," Hob muttered, struggling to his feet.

"You speak like that to me again, and Else will cut your tongue out and make you eat it," Anna warned. "Now start walkin'." She lashed at Hob with the leafy branch. He raised his hands to protect his face and stumbled off down the road.

"You okay?" Else asked Anna, who stood trembling under her blanket in the middle of the road.

"He-he's ju-just a piece of fuckin' shit," she said. Tears welled in her eyes and carved pale tracks in the grime on her cheeks. "Just a dirty piece of fuckin' shit!" This time she screamed at Hob, who flinched but didn't stop walking.

Else hugged the girl, her body wracked with sobs until her mother came hurrying over and Else released Anna into her arms.

"Make sure they are okay to keep moving," Else told Rache before moving on to take up a point position ahead of the main group. With Hob in the lead and Else between him and the survivors, they trudged on until they reached the ruins of Innisfail well after dark.

CHAPTER 7

Else thought Innisfail must once have been a beautiful town. From what she had found on her way north months earlier, it had been a thriving town, supported by agriculture and a busy airport that flew tourists into the Queensland wilderness on their way to Cairns to the north.

On the maps Cairns was a big place, and Else hadn't been keen on going there. Her need to find a safe place to get ready for her baby pushed her onwards, into the rainforest, and it was there she found the abandoned hut that became her home.

Some tragedy had befallen Innisfail in the dark days following the end of the world. During the Panic it seemed that refugees had flooded into the city and they brought death and terror with them. Else had seen the scorched but strangely empty burial pits and the brick walls of buildings patterned with bullet holes and smears of blood where firing squads had gunned down people by the hundreds. Abandoned vehicles and luggage moldered in vast heaps at the highway entrance and on the airport grounds.

Painted graffiti declared that Innisfail was now the capital of a the new Australian republic and hand-printed pictures, now faded in the sun and rain, showed a smiling man who was the first and last president of the new Australia.

Else had found no survivors, only bodies among the many

burnt-out ruins of the buildings. Dogs roamed the streets in large packs; she heard them hunting at night, snarling and fighting over every scrap. She understood why Joel and his people avoided the roads and towns of the old world. In the cities survivors and the dead kept the animals in check; out here, their numbers grew and in the case of the rats, they had become a plague.

She spent one night in Innisfail, watching from a dirt-covered window on the second floor of a building as a pack of dogs brought a wild cow down and tore into her with their fangs. The rats had come before the dogs were finished with their meal. At first she heard the sound of dry leaves rustling over the ground in a light breeze; then it swelled to the chattering of rushing creek water sweeping gravel until, in the moonlight, Else saw a dark carpet pour out of the rubble of the burnt buildings. Rats, millions of them, their numbers bolstered by the ready supply of food in the town's grain stores and the rich fields of the outlying farmland. They had no natural predators, not once they reached these kinds of numbers. The dog pack bolted, scattering into the night, leaving the fresh kill to be swarmed over and within an hour the entire carcass was gone. Not even the hooves and bones were left.

She wondered if that was why the town had been burned and abandoned. The rats would have been unstoppable, burrowing into the mass graves and gorging themselves on the plentiful meat just under the surface.

Else had been pleased to leave Innisfail behind and continue north. Now as her group approached, she went to Rache to tell her they needed to steer clear of the place.

"We need to find food, water, and shelter," Rache said, peering out into the darkness and trying to make out the details of the town.

"We will, just not here. There are farms all around this place. Lots of them have supplies, vehicles even, more than we could ever use."

"Maybe the rats are all dead?" Eric suggested. "It's been what, six months since you were here last?"

"I don't know if they are dead, but I don't want to go in there and get eaten."

"Joel hasn't come back," Rache said. "We don't know what happened to him. He might have just buggered off and left us."

Else shook her head, "Joel wouldn't do that. It's...just not his way."

"Know him well do ya?" Eric frowned. "If I was him, I woulda dropped us like a cardboard box full of live snakes."

"Why don't we send Hob in?" Rache suggested. "If the rats eat him, we know it's not safe."

"We're not sending anyone in," Else said.

"Could be some good stuff in there, hidden supplies of chemicals and stuff. Big farming community, I could make some great explosives using fertilizer." Eric almost rubbed his hands together in glee.

"We go to the farms first," Else said and started walking. Hob pushed himself off the tree he had been leaning against and hobbled after her. Anna stood up and trailed after him.

Rache and Eric roused the remaining survivors. "Not far now," she said. "We'll find a warm place with plenty of food and water. We can stay there for a while and rest up."

"This'll be the last walking you need to do," Eric said, "We'll get some vehicles going and ride in style, aye?"

The idea of riding to their destination encouraged the survivors to keep walking. It started to rain and in the pitch darkness they almost missed the first farmhouse. Hob had recovered some strength after turning his face up to the sky and gulping great mouthfuls of fresh water, while Else focused on listening for evols stumbling around in the pouring rain.

After the group had passed through, Else and Eric dragged the gates shut. It wouldn't keep much out, but it would give evols something to slide past and continue on their way.

This house was larger than the previous farm they had explored. A long veranda ran along the front of the building that sagged with the slow decay of abandoned wood.

They followed the same procedure as before. Else and Rache went in first, checking the living room and commercial-sized kitchen for zombies.

"Clear," Else announced.

"Clear," Rache echoed from the kitchen.

"Check the rest of the ground floor," Else commanded, her eyes adjusting to the darkness. They moved together, opening doors and stepping away. The ground floor was deserted.

"You smell that?" Else asked. Rache nodded. A musty smell had permeated the house, like something long dead and mummified in the dry heat of so many seasons.

The women went up the stairs and into the hallway at the top. Else nodded to the left. Rache went first, opening doors into what were once children's rooms. Other than the dust that covered everything, the rooms could have been abandoned a few minutes ago.

Rache swallowed hard. "I remember a room like this," she said. "When I was a little girl."

Else said nothing, having no such memories and being less than a year old. She watched while Rache moved through the little girl's room, gathering up dolls and wiping the dust from their perpetually smiling faces.

"We should keep moving, the others are waiting," Else said.

Rache nodded and tucked one of the dolls into her shirt before following Else up the hallway.

The smell came from a home office. Papers were strewn over the floor, weighted down by empty liquor bottles. A desiccated corpse was slumped in a chair, a revolver on the floor next to his chair. Else poked at the skull. A black beetle scuttled out of the round hole in the side of the dead man's head, antenna waving until it overbalanced and dropped onto the rags that covered his shoulders.

"He killed himself," Else said, picking up the gun and checking the cylinder. Five rounds remained. Rache nodded, seeing nothing in the room to hold her attention. They continued on through the house, finding an empty bathroom, the tub half-filled with green-slimed water. The rest of the house was empty.

The survivors crowded into the living room. Eric set a fire in the grate and they stripped their wet clothes off and dried out in the heat.

"Any food?" Hob asked.

"Not yet," Else said. She lit a lantern with a stick from the fire and went to explore the kitchen. The pantry was full, jars of preserves and rows of tinned food waiting for the home cook to feed an army judging by the size of the cans.

Catering-sized pots and pans were arranged on shelves. Else took one of the largest pots and went back to the living room.

"We have food," she announced.

"And a pot to piss in," Eric said cheerfully.

Else slept badly that night. The baby fussed and seemed to have trouble breathing. Else held her palm to his tiny forehead; he seemed warm, and his cheeks were flushed.

Cassie crossed the crowded room and sank down next to Else, Lowanna feeding thirstily at her breast.

"He has a cold," she announced, looking over at the grizzling baby.

"He's burning with a fever," Else said, rocking her son gently.

"Best you can do is keep him indoors for a few days, keep him warm. Feed him when he will eat and it should pass."

"And if it doesn't?" Else asked, shooting Cassie a stricken look.

The other woman shrugged, "Then he will die."

Else stayed awake with the baby all night, listening to his breathing as it became a rasping wheeze. He slept in short bursts, until violent sneezes shook his body and he woke up crying.

The engineers, holders, and fishermen weren't bothered by the noise of crying babies. For them it was a good noise, a sound of hope and a child who had not been claimed by the crew.

At dawn, Rache organized a team to make breakfast. They built a fire outside and cooked up cans of beans and spaghetti between the heavy rain showers. After everyone had eaten she consulted with Eric, who was keen on exploring the outbuildings. Else had taken the baby upstairs, which left Rache in charge.

She led Eric and four of the men out into the farmyard and across an overgrown yard. Three sheds stood gleaming in the sunlight.

"We'll start there, aye?" Eric said. Rache nodded, watching the long grass carefully after her experience of the day before.

Eric went first, sweeping the grass with a stick. The others followed, climbing over a fence and into a weed-strewn driveway of packed gravel.

"Lock's on this shed," Eric reported. "I hope that means no one's been in it before us."

The men, two engineers and two fishermen, nodded and grinned. They were all armed with the scythe like stick-blades; Rache wouldn't let anyone go outside without a weapon.

Eric used his blade to lever the locking plate out of the door, the screws sliding out of the wooden frame with a shriek.

Rache looked around; no wandering dead were in sight. It seemed that the farm might be clear of evols.

The shed door rattled open, the noise echoing through the empty space behind it. "Ohh yeah," Eric breathed. The men and Rache peered inside. Farm and workshop tools hung on every wall. In the center of the shed a large, flatbed truck had been parked.

"Place like this should have fuel stores on site." Eric rubbed his hands together. "Fuckin' fantastic," he added.

They left the first shed and jimmied the lock off the next door. Inside they found more farm machinery, spare parts, equipment, and sacks of seed pockmarked with gnawed holes and reeking with the musty smell of rodents.

Rache flicked an empty sack away with the tip of her blade. The floor underneath the hessian fabric erupted in a boiling well of tiny brown shapes. Rache shrieked and started stamping up and down as mice poured out of the sacks and stampeded out the door in a furry tidal wave.

"Fuck! Fuck! Fuck!" Rache squealed and scrambled up onto a workbench. More mice ran over her boots to make their escape.

The men jumped out of the way, kicking aimlessly at the surge of tiny bodies.

"You okay?" Lug, one of the engineers, said, his face a mask of confusion.

"They touched me!" Rache sobbed.

"Did they bite you?" Eric asked.

"No!" Rache shouted back.

"Well, they're gone now," Lug said.

"Fuck!" Rache yelled one more time.

Eric moved on to the last of the locked doors. "You might wanna stand back, missy, there could be mice in this one too."

Rache glowered at him, embarrassment replacing her fear of the tiny things. "Mention the mice to anyone and I'll fucking kill you," she said.

The men grinned but nodded. Eric wrenched the lock plate off the door; the padlock clattered to the ground.

"What's that smell?" Rache said as the door started to slide open.

Eric peered inside. "Jesus, it stinks in he—"

A body lunged at him from the darkness. Small in stature, a boy of no more than ten years old, his dead skin as yellow and dry as old parchment. Latching on to Eric's arm, the boy growled deep in his throat like a rabid dog.

"Geddafuckoffame!" Eric screamed and jerked backwards, losing his footing and falling over.

The boy's blackened teeth bit hard into the sleeve of the leather jacket that Eric wore. Eric bellowed and started punching the kid in the side of the head. Rache stepped forward and swung her blade. It caught the boy in the ribs, lifting him off the ground and leaving him attached to Eric's sleeve by his teeth.

"You're not fuckin' helping!" Eric yelled.

The other four men started swinging their blades, hacking long, oozing gashes in the boy's emaciated frame. One of the wild blows bit into the boy's neck, cracking the spine as the blade cut through the vertebrae. The kid shuddered and collapsed.

Eric threw the body aside and sat up. "Fuck, there's more of them," he shouted while scrambling backwards, climbing to his feet and snatching up his dropped blade.

Two more young evols came shuffling out of the dark shed, one, a girl in filth-encrusted pink pajamas, the other an even younger boy, chewing on the ear of a stuffed rabbit, its once yellow fur now stained black with zombie drool.

"Kids…" Lug said, hesitating with his blade ready to strike.

Rache stepped around him and swung her blade. The girl's head rolled and the boy kept industriously sucking on the ear of the toy rabbit.

"Not kids," Rache said, swinging overhand and burying the curved point of her blade into the young boy's skull. "Walking dead. We destroy them. We destroy them all. Just like Else said."

Twisting the handle of her blade, she cracked the boy's skull wide open and jerked the metal free. "Never hesitate, never forget: they are not human anymore."

The third shed was empty except for the torn scraps of a woman's body, long rotted away to shards of bone and withered flesh.

"Don't you ever wonder what their story was, who they were before they died?" Key, one of the fishermen, asked while staring at the gnawed remains.

"Maybe the kids get bit, mother tries to take care of them. Father locks them all in the shed. Hears her screams as they turn and kill her. Blows his own head off," Eric said.

"It must have been hell," Key said.

"Where the fuck do you think we're standing?" Eric scoffed.

"Hey Eric, there's another room back here." Rache pulled horse tack and ropes off the wall and unbolted a door.

"Careful," Lug warned. They moved into ready positions and then nodded at Rache. She opened the door wide and stepped back, her own blade ready to strike.

The room beyond had a concrete floor and sheet metal walls. It was large enough to hold a five-hundred-liter tank, and the smell of oil permeated the air.

"Oh you little fuckin' beauty..." Eric whispered. He ducked down and peered under the tank, satisfying himself that the room was clear before stepping forward and tapping on the metal side. A dull booming sound changed in pitch about halfway down.

"Diesel fuel," he said with a wide grin. "Let's get you tinkers working on the truck. If you can get the engine in a fit state to run, we can drive as far as you fuckin' want."

———◦◦◦❈◦◦◦———

Else stood in the office upstairs, looking out the window towards the road, willing Joel to come loping out of the drifting rain. In her arms the baby shuddered and struggled to breathe. Else bent her head, closed her mouth around his tiny nose, and sucked sharply, drawing thick mucus out of his airways. She turned her head and spat on the floor. The baby shared half her genes; he shouldn't get sick. He should be strong like her.

"You are strong," she whispered to his fever-warm skin. "You will come through this and be okay."

She tried to feed him again, but the congestion in his nose and chest meant he couldn't breathe and eat at the same time. Instead she walked up and down the carpeted hallway, listening to the rain and speaking softly to her son of the things she would teach him when as he grew up.

─────⦿─────

In the shed, every engineer now crowded around the truck. They had rolled the chassis out into the rain, the tires flat after years of sitting. With the front of the vehicle under shelter, they managed to tilt the cab forward and expose the engine. They had scrubbed the green corrosion from the battery terminals and carefully topped the cells up with fresh rainwater. Another team had drained the fuel tanks and using a hand pump had filled a jerry can with diesel, pouring it carefully into the tank.

Now a heated discussion had broken out with different points of view on how to proceed. Rache slapped at a dozen hands that reached in to tug or point at the cables, aluminum, and other parts of the engine.

"Battery," one of the engineers declared. "It's a diesel engine; we need electricity to heat the glow plug so the fuel will ignite."

"We should strip it down, check everything," Lug insisted. "It's what the Foreman would have us do."

"The Foreman ain't here!" Rache snapped. "I'm foreman on this job and I say keep your fuckin' hands out of it."

"How do we make 'trickery without solar panels?" asked a blonde woman engineer.

Rache opened her mouth to answer but realized she didn't know what to say.

"With this," Eric announced. The engineers rose from their huddle and turned to look at him. He stood next to a squat, square machine on a frame with two wheels.

"Ladies and gentlemen, say hello to my little friend," Eric beamed and patted the machine.

"What is it?" Rache asked.

"This is a Milton model MD806, diesel-fueled, three-phase, two-kilowatt generator. It turns diesel into electricity."

The engineers climbed down from the truck and pored over this new discovery.

"How does it work?" Lug asked.

Eric shrugged. "Well it's a practical application of the Faraday principle of electromagnetism…" Eric trailed off and regarded their blank faces. "Magic, who cares? You put the fuel in and it makes electricity."

"We should still strip down the truck engine and make sure every part is ready to function," Lug insisted, and others nodded their agreement.

"Did you ever think that the Foreman had you stripping things down and rebuilding them constantly because that was the only way he could keep you doing what he wanted?" Eric asked. "Seriously, that ship was going nowhere. It was all about keeping control of the population while he sat up there in his office, stuffed his face, and got his dick sucked."

Under Eric's guidance they cleaned the generator, checking the fuel filter and cleaning corrosion off the terminals. They watched with intense curiosity as Eric filled the tank with fuel. He flicked a switch and waited.

"It's not working," Rache said.

"Give it a minute," Eric replied. After ten seconds he pressed a button on the control panel. The generator clicked but the engine did not fire.

"I told you, we should strip it down and put it back together to make it work," Lug said.

The other engineers spoke their agreement this time. Eric scowled at them.

"Touch this fuckin' thing and I'll gut you. Rache, don't let them touch it, I'll be right back."

Eric vanished into the back shelves of the shed, returning a moment later with a bent steel rod.

"What—" Rache asked but Eric waved her to silence.

Inserting one end of the rod into the machine Eric twisted it rapidly, the angled shape of the rod allowing it to spin easily in his hands.

"Okay," he panted after ten seconds of frantic turning, "push the green button." Rache jabbed the button and the generator coughed, shuddered, and then fired. A cloud of black smoke bubbled from the exhaust, filling the shed with a choking fog. Eric straightened up and made some adjustments, the generator's clatter smoothing out into a steady chugging.

"How long does it take to make electricity?" Rache shouted over the noise.

Eric grinned, and lifting two large alligator clips on the end of rubber-clad cables, he touched them together. A white spark crackled across the bare metal. "Step aside," he said.

He attached the clips to the battery in the truck. Climbing up into the tilted cab, he frowned at the empty ignition, then looked up and pulled the sun visor down. A set of keys dropped into his lap.

While the engineers watched with absorbed fascination Eric slid the key into the slot and turned it. The truck engine turned over, a long whining ignition cycle. The engineers exhaled with an almost religious awe.

Eric grunted, pumped the accelerator pedal, and turned the key again. The truck engine fired, the roar of it drowning out the shouts and cheers of the engineers. Eric climbed down and lowered the cab on its hydraulic struts.

"Can we drive it with those wheels?" Rache asked.

"There's a compressor, it'll pump them right up." The engineers jockeyed for position and gave each other advice as they rolled the compressor over to the truck and inflated the tires. To Eric's relief they all inflated and held pressure.

"Alright, turn it off or we'll have every dead prick in a hundred miles coming to have a look."

The engineers were jubilant. For many of them this was the first time in their lives they had made something mechanical actually work. The holders and fishermen had clustered in the backyard, watching with interest over the fence.

CHAPTER 8

It would take years for the cities to crumble, for the dry center of Australia to send enough dust and sand to erode the glass and stone. Burying everything under nature's relentless onslaught. In a thousand years, or a million, there would be nothing but a few preserved ruins, clues to the past and strange hieroglyphics that would speak of a civilization that once considered itself great and immortal.

Joel hadn't returned by mid-afternoon, when the flatbed truck and a four-wheel-drive SUV recovered from a garage next to the house rolled out onto the decaying roadway. Else sat in the passenger seat of the SUV while Eric drove. The engineers had spent the morning planning a roster system for who got to drive the truck. The first two were old enough to have driven before, and in true engineer fashion, they trained the others on the job.

Else insisted on leaving a note for Joel, telling him they were heading for the settlement on the north side of the lake called Gol Gol, north of Mildura.

The baby's fever broke during the morning and he had slipped into an exhausted sleep. Rache and Cassie sat in the back of the SUV; the cargo space behind them was loaded with food supplies, fuel tanks, tools, and weapons salvaged from the house and outbuildings.

"There's gotta be hundreds of places like this around here," Eric said. "We can get everything we need."

"Can you get us a safe place to live?" Cassie asked from the backseat.

"Yeah," Eric nodded, "I reckon we can do that."

The rest of the group, packed on the deck and in the cab of the truck, were in high spirits too. Most of them had never ridden in anything other than a boat powered by a sail and oars. They cheered and sang as the truck rolled out, following the SUV.

Eric kept them moving at under thirty miles an hour to start with. The road was littered with abandoned vehicles, and the occasional evol stumbled out of the debris to stand confused as they drove past.

"We should stop and kill them," Rache said as an evol bounced off the bull bars on the SUV.

"Keep driving," Else said. She felt the leaden weight of exhaustion pulling her down into sleep, the comforting weight of the baby sleeping against her skin under a blanket cover.

Else woke up after dark, the baby grizzling and squirming.

"Where are we?" she asked as she moved him into a feeding position.

"Somewhere south. There's a river up ahead. Not sure on the bridge, though."

"Let me see the map." Else took it and looked out the window into the darkness. At least the rain had stopped. "Did you see any signs?"

"Yeah, it's the Black River," Eric replied.

"Rache, take a couple of your people and walk the bridge. We need to know if it is clear and safe." Else remembered a bridge she crossed a lifetime ago and the shocking lesson in swimming that came from it.

Rache slid out of the cab, gesturing for engineer backup she walked out into the beam of the SUV headlights. Two men jogged past the pickup and into the light. Rache directed them to each side of the bridge and the trio started walking, weapons in hand.

"Townsville's down the road a bit," Eric said, staring into the darkness beyond the headlights.

"I never went there," Else replied.

"It was my hometown," Eric said.

"I'm sorry," Else said, it being what she understood was the right thing to say when someone spoke with such sadness.

"My wife took the kids to Sydney. We had a girl and a boy. It was right before everything turned to shit. She managed to get through on the phone a couple of weeks later, said she was going to try and get to Moore Park, some kind of evacuation center had been set up there. They were airlifting people out, she said. I never heard from or saw her or the kids again."

Else frowned. "Moore Park was never evacuated. People stayed there, they fought to survive. They fought hard and did it too. Right up till last year, when the treaty with the evols broke down; then they were overrun."

"Jesus…" Eric muttered. "My wife's name was Katie. Did you ever meet a woman named Katie at Moore Park? She was something, you would have liked her if you met her. She was the sweetest, most kindest person I ever knew." Eric's voice cracked a little; he kept staring out into the darkness.

Else lifted her head and looked at him with a steady gaze. "I know the name. I heard a story about a woman called Katie with children, a girl and a boy. She was one of the lucky ones that did get evacuated. People said she was very nice and kind."

Eric's head lowered to the steering wheel. A sob crawled up from somewhere deep down inside and hacked out of him like infected phlegm.

"I'm sorry," Else whispered. Her attention flicked to the head-light beams. A shadow passed in front of them, then another. It wasn't Rache or the engineers. Evols had come, drawn like moths to the light and the warmth. Else shuddered with relief, grateful that since the destruction of Adam she didn't feel them anymore. That she didn't hear their voices and their cravings deep in her mind.

"Evols," she said. "Cassie, take baby." Else lifted the well-wrapped infant from his covering blanket and passed him into the backseat. Cassie made space for him next to Lowanna, who barely twitched in her sleep.

"Stay in the car," Else said, sliding out and closing the door behind her.

The cold air and the standing up brought on an intense need to pee. Else suppressed the sensation and lifted the two blades she carried. Rache and her engineers were taking too long. They couldn't stand here all night; the people on the back of the truck were exposed.

Flexing her arms, Else moved onto the concrete bridge. Cars had crashed into each other, some of the wrecks still containing trapped bodies. They moaned and snapped their dead teeth at Else as she squeezed past. She stopped, went back, and smashed their skulls in with the point of her blade before continuing on. The river ran high, swollen with the rain falling in the higher plateaus, roaring under her feet and eroding the concrete until one day this bridge would collapse and be gone.

Climbing onto the back of an abandoned truck, Else stared out into the night. A ragged line of evols were caught by the barricade of crashed vehicles, almost halfway across the bridge. Else counted a dozen of them shuffling in aimless circles, and more, trapped in their steel coffins, adding their moans to the necrotic chorus.

Else jumped onto the roof of a sedan, and then with long easy running strides she ran over the rusting hulks, slashing at the dead who reached for her. Her blades found their targets; skulls split and bled black fluid. Heads rolled like balls across the wet concrete and she nimbly sprang onto the truck that had jackknifed across both lanes. The bridge beyond was clear of vehicles; only skeletonized corpses remained.

"Rache!" Else yelled, her voice rolling out over the swollen river and echoing off the sky.

"Else!" Rache's desperate shout came from somewhere out in the dark.

Else dropped to the road and started running. There was no time to go back and get help; getting every armed holder, engineer, and fisherman past the dead would take too long. Whatever trouble Rache and her men had run into could kill them if she didn't hurry.

Laughter and men's voices came to Else out of the darkness. Her feet were almost silent on the concrete, the rushing torrent under her feet covering any noise her boots made. A fence had been set up across the bridge. Else slowed to a halt—she had seen this kind of thing before. People died at places like this.

She could hear Rache now, fighting and swearing, no sound from her engineers. Maybe they were already dead, or maybe they were the ones laughing?

Else went to the edge of the bridge and sheathed her blades. Slipping over the rail, she lowered herself down to a narrow ledge, her hands gripping the concrete curb as her feet slid along the concrete lip.

Once she had passed the wall blocking the bridge, Else climbed the concrete buttress in a chin-up movement that let her peer over the edge and see what she was up against.

A fire burning in an oil drum illuminated a scene that Else had seen too often before. Four men armed with a variety of homemade bladed weapons, rifles, and shotguns stood around the fire watching as Rache struggled against two others who fought to hold her down and pull her clothes off.

The heads of her two engineers were mounted on spikes on the wall. Their bodies had been tossed into the river.

Else pulled herself up and dropped onto the bridge behind the spectators. She had studied a book that explained how to whistle in a dozen different ways, but every time Else tried it she couldn't make a sound. She settled for walking up behind the two nearest men and cutting their throats. Their companions were still laughing when they turned to see what was happening. Else stepped over the bodies and buried a blade in the third man's neck. With a jerk on the handle she pulled him between her and the fourth man as he fired a shotgun blast into his dying friend's back.

The third man screamed, his blood spraying over Else's face. The two men struggling with Rache scrambled to their feet, one of them pausing long enough to kick her in the face when she tried to stand up.

Else charged the shotgun man. The gurgling man with the blade in his throat stumbled and fell. Else left the blade behind and threw the second one. It spun, handle over curved blade, and hit the shooter in the face.

"Fuck!" he yelled, the shotgun drooping as he clutched his broken nose.

Else snatched the blade off the ground and with an uppercut swing she slammed the point up through the man's chin hard enough to burst it out the top of his skull. She scooped up the shotgun as it fell, turned on the balls of her feet, and fired from the hip. The blast sprayed shot over both the men bearing down on her, sending them spinning away screaming and bleeding from ragged wounds.

"You fuckers!" Rache screamed and kicked the nearest groaning casualty. "What the fuck is wrong with you people! We weren't a threat! We weren't trying to steal anything from you! But you fucking killed my friends! You fucking assholes!"

Else finished them off while Rache vented her fear and fury on the bodies. "Rache, we need to go. We have to find another way to cross the river."

Rache stood shivering, her arms locked around herself while Else found a way to open the gate in the wall. They returned to the others in silence, Else guiding Rache over the vehicles and getting her settled in the backseat of the SUV.

"We heard shooting," Eric said. "What the hell happened?"

"Rache ran into some locals. They killed the engineers, and frightened her."

"Shit," Eric muttered. "You okay?" he asked, turning in his seat to look at Rache.

The girl nodded. "We killed them, we killed all of them," she said in a flat voice.

"We can't cross here. There will be more like them in town." Else said. Lifting her son, she cuddled him as he cried. "We need to go back. The map says there is a road that goes west. We take that; it curves around and we can cross further upstream."

"Yeah, we'll head up Black River Road. As long as they haven't blocked that bridge as well," Eric said. "We can take the ring road and get back on the highway south of the city."

Else walked back to the truck. The survivors were huddled together and looking around fearfully. "We need to back up. There is a side road that will take us to an alternative bridge."

The engineer behind the wheel started the truck and got it rolling backwards. Making a ponderous turn, they pulled over to let the SUV pass them and then pulled out to follow.

The convoy did not stop again. The SUV burst through a wooden fence that had been constructed on the river road bridge. They saw no guards and speeding up they drove down the clear roads, skirting Townsville, which looked to be under siege from the dead. "There's a bloody good reason to stay away from populated areas," Eric said.

"They're populated now alright, with fuckin' man-eating walking corpses."

By sunrise they were south of Townsville, out in the wilderness and running low on fuel. The convoy pulled into a farmhouse yard.

"Stop!" Else yelled. The twitch of a curtain in an upstairs window caught her attention.

Eric skidded the SUV to a halt. Behind them the truck hissed and wheezed, its air brakes locking up on the gravel driveway.

"Back up!" Else ordered. The SUV reversed to a parallel position next to the truck.

"Back up!" Eric yelled through the open window.

"What's the problem?" Lug said from the passenger's side of the truck.

"There are people in that house. We don't want to stop here," Else said and Eric repeated the instructions to the truck.

"We're low on fuel. We need to stop somewhere and top up the tank. The folks on the back could use a break too," Lug reported.

"Fine," Else said, scanning the house for further signs of movement. "Just get back on the road, now!"

A shout came from the truck bed. Else twisted in her seat, then climbed up to kneel on it as she wound the window down and looked out towards the road. A metal gate had swung shut. Two teenage boys stood on the other side, rifles aimed at the truck and SUV.

"Get out of the truck!" one boy yelled.

"We can take them," Rache said from the back seat.

"No," Else said. "They haven't attacked us. We don't kill them unless they do."

"Yeah?" Eric did not look convinced. "Who's volunteering to die so we can get the green light?"

"No one dies," Else said and opened the SUV door. She slid out onto the driveway. Laying her son on the cushion of the car seat, she wrapped him up tight in a blanket and kissed his warm head.

"We didn't know this was your place," Else called out to the boys, her hands open and at shoulder height. "We were just looking for a place to stay the night. We can move on. We don't want anything from you." Else walked forward, her hands open, a calm expression on her face.

"Everybody get out!" the boy yelled again. His companion jerked his rifle from the SUV to the truck and back again. Else could see how wound up they were. They looked like they might start shooting at the slightest provocation.

"Everyone, move slowly and climb down. Leave any weapons where they are," Else called over her shoulder.

They moved slowly on legs made stiff from long hours sitting on the cramped truck bed. People climbed down and stood in a loose group at the rear of the vehicle.

Eric, Rache, and Cassie emerged from the SUV. "Hey guys," Eric said. "Sorry we rolled on up your driveway. We didn't know there was anyone living here."

"Keep your hands up!" the older boy yelled as Else let her hands lower. She hesitated but did not raise her hands again.

"You need to keep calm," Eric said. "We're not your enemy. If you would just open the gate, we'll be on our way."

The older boy said something to the younger, then leaned his rifle against the fence and climbed over the gate. Reaching back through the rails, he dragged his rifle through and resumed covering the travelers.

While the two boys were occupied, Else lowered her hands even more. The revolver she had taken from the farm lay tucked into the back of her jeans. She stood there, still smiling, and curled her hand around the gun butt.

"What would you like us to do?" Eric asked.

"I want you to start—" he began. Else's arm flew up, the gun level in her outstretched hand. She fired once, the heavy boom of the revolver echoing around the yard.

The older boy ducked, screaming for the other boy to get down. Everyone else hit the ground, mothers covering children with their own bodies. The younger boy screamed, an evol slumping over him, the oozing bullet hole in its forehead marking where Else's bullet had found a home.

Else lowered the gun. "You should bring your brother inside the gate, where it is safe."

"Michael!" the older boy scrambled to the gate latch. Yanking it open, he kicked the limp corpse off the younger boy and dragged him up.

The younger boy sobbed in terror, his face the color of milk. He clung to the older boy, crying into his embrace.

Else walked over to them. "I'm sorry I frightened you," she said. "There was no time to shout a warning; I saw her about to grab him."

"How did you know he is my brother?" the older boy asked.

"You smell the same," Else said.

Michael sniffled and lifted his head. "You're weird," he said.

Else grinned, "Yes, yes I suppose so."

Michael and his brother, Sam, had lived in relative safety with their parents during the Great Panic. They told their story to the survivors who settled in their house, sharing their food and the warmth of the fire.

"We did okay," Sam told them. "Dad kept us safe. We had everything, we grew all the food we could want. Dad taught us to shoot, and the fences kept the bad people away."

"Where are your parents now?" Else asked.

"Mum…" Sam started, then swallowed hard. "Mum died, she was having a baby. Dad had to lay them both to rest."

Michael crossed himself and Sam continued. "Dad cut his hand on some wire. He got real sick, and he died."

"When was that?" Eric asked.

"Dunno, I lost count of the days after that. Before the rains started, though."

"Did you take care of him? After he died?" Else asked.

"Yes…" Sam whispered.

"You're a brave lad," Eric said. "You're doing the right thing. Staying here, looking after your brother."

"There were others," Michael piped up. "The Alsops and the Delrays. They'd come and help us with harvest and we would go and help them. When Dad was here."

"They still on their farms?" Else asked.

"No," Michael said. "We haven't seen them in a while. I took Chopper, that's my horse, and went over to tell Mr. Delray that Dad had died. The bad men had come and made the Delrays like them."

"Did you lay them to rest too?" Else asked.

"No, ma'am. I rode out of there and came home. We've stayed on the place ever since."

Else asked more questions: Was there anyone else living here? Did they know of any settlements? Michael and Sam shook their heads to all the questions. Finally Else asked, "Who was at the window?"

"That was me," Michael admitted. "When we saw you coming, we thought you might be the bad men. So we sneaked out and came around by the gate."

"Do you want to stay here?" Rache asked.

"We don't have anywhere else to go," Sam replied.

"You could come with us," Rache said. "We're going to a safe place. There will be other kids your age and you would be welcome there."

"This is our farm now," Michael declared. "We have to stay and work the land."

"What happens if one of you gets a cut hand from some wire? Do you know what tetanus is?" Else asked. The boys shook their heads.

"It's probably what killed your father. He had bad spasms? His jaw locked up and he had a high fever?"

Michael nodded, reliving the horror of the terrible days when his father was dying.

"We can take you somewhere you can be safe. There's a doctor there who can treat diseases and infections."

"Sleep on it," Rache said. "We'll stay here with you tonight, and tomorrow we will be on our way. If you want to come with us, you can."

Michael and Sam didn't look convinced.

The survivors settled down to sleep and the two boys retreated to their rooms upstairs. Else followed them, the baby cradled in her arms.

"Michael, Sam," she said, catching up with them at the top of the stairs. "You are two of the bravest boys I have ever met. Your father and your mother would be so proud of you. They would also want to know that you are safe."

"We talk to them, up in heaven," Sam said.

"So if they are looking down on you, the best you can do is listen when God brings help."

"God sent you?" Sam's eyes went wide.

"Sure," Else said. "He works in mysterious ways, right?"

"We'll see," Michael said and took Sam by the arm. "Go and wash up for bed, Sam."

Else left them to it. She didn't believe in any kind of god, but faith seemed to have helped these boys through a living hell. She wasn't about to throw stones at the glass house of their belief system.

In the morning Michael announced they would come with Else's people. They took Else, Rache, and Eric on a tour of the farm, showing them the vehicles, still in excellent running order.

"I ride the quad bike," Sam said.

"Mostly we use a horse, or just walk. The engine noise tells the bad men where we are," Michael said.

"Would it be okay if we took the farm truck?" Else asked.

"Sure, I guess," Michael nodded.

The truck was smaller than the three-ton flat deck they already had, and the farm's diesel tank was almost empty. Eric and Rache agreed to load it up with supplies.

Michael and Sam had a locked cabinet filled with well-maintained guns and plenty of ammunition.

Their food supplies were mostly fresh fruit, vegetables, and eggs. Else and Michael went and opened the field gates so the remaining livestock could get out and take their chances.

With most of the supplies loaded on the second truck, the boys crammed into the back of the SUV. They looked close to tears as they drove away from the only home they had ever known, but Else kept them focused with stories of the wonders that would await them at Mildura.

There was still no sign of Joel and Lowanna's people. Else feared that driving had taken them beyond their reach. Expecting them to make their way to Mildura overland might be too much.

The highway rolled out in a black strip that was steadily disappearing under the relentless action of windblown dust, water, and weeds that took root in the unrepaired cracks.

Eric chewed his lip every time they topped up the fuel tanks. With three thirsty engines gulping down their supplies, he spent his evenings chewing on a pencil and scribbling calculations on a map.

"How far?" Else asked during one of their nightly council meetings around the campfire.

"Not far enough."

"How far?" Else repeated.

"Unless we find more fuel, we'd be two…maybe three hundred klicks short."

"Is that far?" Rache asked, frowning at the map.

"Far enough," Eric said.

Rache frowned at him. "And what does that mean?"

"It means we need to find more fuel or we are going to run out of food, water, and people by the time we get to Mildura."

"So we go somewhere else, somewhere closer," Rache said, her practical mind identifying the obvious solution.

"We go to Mildura," Else said. There was no room for compromise in her tone.

"Well, we'd better keep searching for diesel fuel."

"Where?" Rache asked, throwing her hands up in frustration. "Every tank we find is empty."

"I can make explosives, I don't know shit about making diesel."

"We need a refinery," Else said.

"Sure, there are refineries. But who is left to run them? What about shifting the oil to the refinery? What about drilling for oil and maintaining the equipment and machines?" Eric ticked items off on his fingers. "There's no fuckin' way we can continue to live in the old world. The oil barons of the future are going to be the guys with horse studs."

Else stood up, her body tense and quivering in the darkness.

"Evols," she said. It had been three days since they saw any new zombies. Each abandoned town they drove through gathered more of them. The slow-moving feral dead would turn in the direction of the engines and start following. Most of them got lost, or distracted by some other stimulus. A sizeable group continued to follow.

"Arm yourselves," Else said, marching out into the camp. The survivors scrambled up, snatching up guns, blades, and anything else they had scavenged.

"Get up, Hob," Else said, kicking him as she strode past.

"Fuck off," he muttered but climbed to his feet.

The walkers came out of the darkness, a ragged mix of men, women, and children. The children were the most disturbing. To the survivors, children were precious things. To see them decaying and monstrous brought suffering home.

Else commanded her people to use only blades and clubs, as the noise of firearms would attract more dead. They came in waves, slow moving, determined, and almost unstoppable waves.

Rache gave orders and the survivors spread out. Engineers stood with fishermen and holders, their weapons at the ready. They struck the first line of zombies down, and the next wave washed over them—dead flesh as dry and brittle as parchment, the tears and open wounds of a thousand blundered injuries, ropes of intestines dragged in the dirt.

Else waved her hand and the line of armed survivors plunged into battle. They hacked off limbs, crushed skulls, and kicked gnashing jaws hard enough to shatter blackened teeth.

Rache yelled a wordless battle cry. It was taken up by the others, a rhythmic howling that drowned out the hissing and moaning of the advancing dead.

Else hung back, watching and protecting the babies who cried from the safety of the SUV. The evols pressed harder against the defensive line. The noise and the smell of fear pushed them into a feeding frenzy. Zombies snarled and swiped at the living meat just in front of them. One of the holders swung her blade; the wooden handle snapped when it struck against the peeling skull of a dead man. She tried to step back, slipped in the gore underfoot, and three evols fell on her. Else tensed and yelled a warning to the others, but her shout went unheard in the heat of battle.

More evols tumbled across the defensive line. They slithered over the squirming mass of feeding dead before climbing to their feet and staggering towards the firelight. Else leapt the campfire, her twin blades reflecting the yellow flames. She crashed down on the first of the evols, her weapons slicing deep into the chests of two zombies. Yanking the blades free, she ducked a swinging arm and spun in a circle, the momentum of her blades cutting through the spine of another evol.

She killed in silence. There were no words or battle cries that could truly express her hatred for the dead. The fury she felt could only be eased by seeing them topple, brains destroyed, free to rot at last.

When the battle ended, Else spat the taste of black blood from her mouth. The woman who fell in front of her had been devoured; her remains now twitched as the Adam virus tried to articulate her ruined limbs. Else stomped her booted foot into the woman's forehead, crushing her skull.

When the fighting finished, over a hundred evols lay crushed and broken on the ground. Five of the 27 survivors were also dead, three of them having been executed to save them from the effects of zombie bites. Cassie, Eric, Rache, Hob, Anna, Michael, and Sam, all stood looking stunned and shaken by the ferocity of the fight.

"Load up the vehicles," Else said. "We keep moving." She walked back to the SUV, Eric hurrying after her.

"We've got maybe two hundred miles of fuel left. What happens after that?"

"We find more fuel, or we start walking." Else opened the door and lifted the crying baby out of the front seat. Cuddling him against her chest, she stroked his back and stared at Eric.

"And if we don't find more fuel? I'll tell you what happens," Eric continued. "We all die."

"I won't die. My son won't die."

"That's all you fucking care about, isn't it? You and the fuckin' kid."

Else's gun came up with the hammer sliding into a cocked position as the muzzle pressed against Eric's forehead.

"What else do I have?" she asked.

Eric swallowed hard. "You got all of us. You love the kid, sure I get that. But you brought the rest of us off the ship with you. We're your responsibility now."

"I didn't ask you to come with me," Else said.

"You made me blow up the fuckin' ship," Eric reminded her.

"Doesn't mean I have to protect you all."

"You're damn right it does. Each one of those people, they are looking to you to get us somewhere safe."

"Tell them to look at Rache. She's the one who wants to lead."

"She is leadin', but she's doin' it with one eye on you to make sure she's doing it right."

Else held his gaze for a several long breaths and then the gun angled upwards, the hammer clicking to a safe position. "Get everyone on board." She climbed into the front seat of the SUV and fed her son.

The convoy drove south on the Lynd Highway in silence, Eric scowling into the growing light of dawn. Else studied the countryside. The thicker bush of the north was thinning now to dry scrubland. The offspring of surviving stock could be seen moving in flocks and herds, always away from the road and the noise of the vehicles. They had to stop once when a mob of kangaroos exploded out of the bush and thundered across the road in front of them. Rifle shots rang out from the larger truck, and two of the animals skidded across the road, twitched, and lay still.

Else remained in the SUV while Michael and Sam supervised the butchering of the 'roos. The boys were skilled with knives, another lesson learned on the farm from their father. The skins and the meat were loaded onto the truck and in less than an hour the convoy was rolling again. Soon they drove through the ruins of another small town where dogs ran barking after the vehicles, but they saw no sign of the living or the dead in the roadside properties.

More abandoned towns flashed past, some with barricades and warning shots, one of which shattered the windscreen on the smaller truck and killed a young woman of the fishermen called Sal. They kept driving, Else refusing to let anyone stop and engage in a gun-fight with an enemy of unknown strength.

They stopped at each roadside petrol station and checked the storage tanks for diesel fuel. They all came up dry.

After a week on the road, the heavy truck sputtered to a halt. The other two vehicles pulled over and they measured out the remaining fuel in all three.

"How far?" Rache asked.

"We've come, eighteen hundred kilometers, nearly eleven hundred miles." Else said, poring over the paper map. "Eric, how much fuel do we have left?"

"Maybe two hundred miles."

"Not close enough," Else said. "It's more like three fifty, three sixty to get to our destination."

"Well let's not fuck about then." Eric leaned out the window. "Mount up, we've got miles to go!" he yelled to the other two vehicles.

The survivors stretching their legs scrambled back up onto the open decks of the two trucks. They rolled on, moving so much slower than Else would have liked, but the highways were breaking down and in places the road had been washed out.

"What state are we in?" Rache asked, peering over from the backseat at the map in Else's lap.

"New South Wales," Else replied.

"Where's Mildura?"

"Here," Else's finger stroked a point on the map.

"It's so close." Rache sounded disappointed. "We should be able to see it from here.

"Heads up," Eric said.

Else folded the map, looking out through the dusty windscreen. In the distance a lone figure stood on the edge of the road next to a bus laying on its side, a faded white cloth waving over his head.

The SUV stopped, the trucks parking angled left and right behind the four-wheel drive. Armed survivors jumped down from the trucks and scattered to the edge of the road. They had picked up the tactics quickly and with minimal training.

The man walked towards them, hands raised high, the white cloth stretched between them, fluttering in the light breeze. As he came closer they could see his gaunt frame and long hair. His clothes were faded by the elements and he wore a long coat.

Rache slipped out of the SUV and called out, "Are you alone?"

"What?" the man called back.

"Are. You. Alone?!"

"Yes!" the man yelled back, his eyes flicking to the wrecked bus on the side of the road.

Else narrowed her eyes. "He's lying," she said to Rache through the open window.

"Uh-huh," Rache replied. "Walk forward, and keep your hands up!" she shouted. The man started walking towards the SUV.

"Thank you for stopping," he called as he got closer. "I haven't seen any live people for weeks."

"Where were you headed?" Rache asked.

"Melbourne. I heard there's a sanctuary there. A Japanese supply ship came in. They have medical supplies and a cure for the dead."

A murmur ran through the group. Hope, as always, was open to suggestions.

"Bullshit," Else said.

"How do you know this is true?" Rache asked.

The man lowered his hands as he turned to look southward, his face wracked with confusion. "I...I was told, by a woman who said she had been told by someone who had seen the ship."

"When was that?" Else asked Rache.

"When was that?" Rache called across the distance between them and the man.

"I...I dunno. A month? Three months ago?"

"Tell the people behind the bus to come out," Else said.

"The people behind the bus have to come out," Rache called.

The man hesitated. "There's no one—"

"They come out or you die!" Rache shouted.

"They're just kids," the man said.

Else opened the door of the SUV. Her baby lay asleep in the back, between Cassie and Lowanna. Standing behind the door, Else drew her revolver.

"Everyone, out in the open now!" she aimed her pistol at the gaunt man.

"Okay! Okay! Jesus, chill the fuck out..." The man turned back to the bus and whistled. They came in ones and twos, filthy, wide eyed, and dressed in scavenged clothes with little understanding of size or fashion. Seven children, and none of them could have been more than ten years old.

"Where did they come from?" Else called.

"There was a settlement, over on the coast. They were in danger of being overrun. They asked me to take the kids and head to Melbourne."

"What happened to the bus?" Rache called.

"I fell asleep at the wheel and crashed." The gaunt man looked embarrassed at the admission.

"Are you messing with these kids?" Rache demanded.

"What? No! Jesus, I'm just trying to help."

"We cut the cock and balls off the last guy who messed with a young girl," Rache warned.

"Good for you," he replied.

"What is your name?" Else asked.

"Godfrey, Alan Godfrey," the gaunt man replied.

"I'm Else, this is Rache, the others can introduce themselves. Bring whatever supplies you have and find those kids some space on the trucks."

"Thanks!" Alan herded the children towards the trucks. Rache and two survivors went and pillaged the bus, returning with food, water, and a bag filled with paper.

"Do you know what this is?" Rache asked Else.

"I think it's money," Else said.

"Yeah, that's cash. Old world money. I wonder why they were carrying it?" Eric said.

"Maybe they thought it was still worth something," Else said.

"Maybe." Eric started the SUV and the convoy continued south.

The last of the fuel ran out on the edge of a town that by Else's calculations was around 200 kilometers from their goal. At 120 miles, Mildura was a lot closer than they had expected.

"So now what? We load everyone up with what they can carry and start walking?" Eric didn't look convinced. The sun was setting through a thin veil of cloud, giving the dry grassland all around them a sepia tone.

"We leave most of them here," Else replied. "We take a few people and explore that town ahead."

Turning from Eric, Else shouted out the window, "Rache, we need no more than five people. They should be armed and sensible."

While Rache gathered her patrol, Else fed and then washed the baby with a damp cloth. "Cassie, can you look after him while I am gone?"

Cassie nodded. Lowanna was grizzling and kicking on the backseat. She took the baby boy and laid him down next to the girl.

"You want me to come with?" Eric asked, unclipping his seat belt.

"No, you stay here. Keep an eye on things while we are gone," Else said.

"Sure. You know what to look out for, right?"

Else nodded and slid out of the SUV. The air was dry; the clouds to the west held no promise of rain.

Rache caught up with her on the road, five men with rifles, shotguns, and blades on her heels.

"We're going to look for fuel, right?" one of the men asked.

"We're looking for all kinds of things," Else replied.

At the first town they came to, the outlying houses were ransacked. The ones that were boarded up had been torn open, gutted like a carcass and the scraps left to rot in the sun.

Deeper in town they moved more carefully. While there were no signs of life, evols drifted among the abandoned cars and looted shops.

The group spread out. Moving in pairs they opened shops and houses, searching the interiors for tinned food, medicine, and Eric's shopping list of household chemicals and fertilizers.

As Else walked down the center of the main street, the evols slowly turned and focused on her. Moving closer they roused themselves, attracted by the beating of her heart and the whisper of her breathing. Else drew her blades, flexing her arms and waiting for the dead to come within range. Then in an explosion of movement, she cut them down, the sharpened steel of the scythe blades severing grey limbs and destroying necrotic brains.

More came shuffling onwards, slashing at her, the rags of their clothing hanging like their dried strips of torn skin. Else ran a man through with one blade, spilling his guts and tripping him as he walked. With the second blade she took his head, a wide swing shearing through his neck.

She killed them with a dancer's grace, spinning and turning to an unheard symphony. The hands reaching for her had no sense of rhythm. She danced with the dead anyway, taking the lead and ending the existence of five in quick succession.

When the mob had been cut down, Else walked into a store. The place had once sold clothes, and what rats and moths hadn't devoured lay under a thick cover of dust. Plastic wrapping cracked with age as Else sorted through the different items. The photographs of babies on the packets, some close to her son's age, fascinated her. Unpacking one of the packets she examined baby clothes, tiny outfits for a newborn. Gathering a selection, she carried them across to where racks of women's clothing hung. Else felt the texture of the dresses. She liked dresses; they were cooler in hot weather, and the swish of the fabric was nice against her skin. She could run and fight in a dress too. After making her selection from the brightly colored clothes that weren't filled with moth holes, Else went to look behind the counter for something to carry it all in.

A dead woman on her hands and knees looked up at Else as she came around the counter. Blood dripped from the woman's mouth; the severed head of a rat rolled in her mouth as she chewed on it.

Else dropped the clothes on the bench and with a smooth motion she pulled her pistol and fired once into the woman's forehead. She had once been a larger figure, dressed in the kinds of loose dresses that Else liked. Now she was just a swollen sack, leaking rotting meat.

Else found woven bags under the counter. She stuffed the clothes in them and stepped out into the dark street.

Rache came jogging towards her. "What the fuck happened?"

"Evol," Else replied. "It's okay. I took care of it."

"What did you find?" Rache regarded the bulging bags with interest.

"Clothes, for baby."

"When are you gonna give that kid a name?" Rache teased.

Else shrugged. "Names are important. I need to give him the right one."

"Lot of babies on the ship, they never got names," Rache said.

"Everyone will have a name now," Else said.

They continued their sweep of the town, the other salvagers joining them, all laden with a variety of salvage looted from shops and houses. Else went through their loads, tossing things aside. "CDs? Coins? Keys? Find any food? Fuel?"

The salvagers shook their heads. "Everything's been swept clean."

"There's a sign up there, that's one of those fuel places." Rache pointed down the road. "Let's check it out."

Else nodded. The moon was bright enough to see on the street, but the darkness of the shop fronts and houses made her uneasy. They walked down the centerline of the main street. Somewhere in the darkness a dog howled. It was answered by others.

"Dogs," Rache said with a shudder.

"If you come across a dog, attack," Else replied. "Charge at them, make noise, show your teeth. Be a bigger predator than they are."

"What if we come across a pack?" an engineer wearing a CD as a necklace asked.

"Shoot the biggest one and run like hell."

They arrived at the gas station, fanning out and checking through the windows for trapped evols. Else waited till everyone reported back that it was clear.

Opening the door Else slipped inside, her eyes wide in the dim light. She inhaled through her nose, sorting through the myriad scents and confirming there were no dead here.

She found what Eric had shown her on previous searches of gas stations, a metal rod under the counter and an articulated stick with marks on it. Taking the two items outside, she used the rod to open the metal disc that covered the diesel fuel storage tank, then she unfolded the marker stick and lowered it into the tank. It came up wet to the hundred-liter mark.

"There's fuel in this tank!" Else called across the forecourt.

The others came running. "Where is the pump?" Rache asked. The salvagers looked blank. "Go on, find it," she ordered. They trotted off, returning a few minutes later with a hand-cranked pump. A long pipe hung from the base of the cylindrical pumping unit. The output pipe was a heavy plastic tube.

"You," Rache pointed at one of the salvagers. "Run back to the trucks, get everyone to bring fuel tanks." The man sprang into action, vanishing into the darkness as if a swarm of rats were on his heels.

"We should keep exploring," Else said. "There could be other useful stuff around here."

Leaving the pump they walked on to the far edge of the town.

"Listen," Else said, raising a hand to stop the procession. They strained in the dark, ears tuned to the slightest change in the background noise.

"What is that?" Rache asked, her eyes wide at the strange sound.

"A piano. And people singing to the music," Else said.

"It's beautiful," Rache sighed.

"It's coming from that way," Else said, turning from the main street and walking deeper into the town.

They tracked the music to a small wooden church. A fence had been built outside; six-foot-high posts and layers of chicken wire were topped by rolls of barbed wire and surrounded with sandbags. Heavy orange road barriers were arranged at angles, putting the church inside a diamond shape, the purpose of the configuration lost on Else.

She froze and gestured the people behind her to move into cover as evols came wandering into view around the perimeter fence. They were attracted by the noise from inside the building and as they shuffled along, the smooth plastic lines of the barriers gently turned them away from the fence.

Else watched, fascinated at the way the evols were being guided. They didn't bunch up against the fence; instead they were being channeled, funneled into a corridor of barricades until they reached the end of the barriers, somewhere out there in the darkness.

"There's got to be a way in," Rache whispered in Else's ear.

"A gate, between those two bigger posts," Else replied, her eyes fixed on the evols moving away down the barrier. "Okay, let's go." Else led them over the plastic barriers and into the evol run. Then, after clambering over the other side, they approached the gate. It was securely latched but not padlocked.

Else scanned over the gate, looking for wires, explosives, or other alarms and booby traps. Satisfied it was safe, she unlocked the gate. "Look where you are stepping," she warned, ushering the others through and closing the gate behind them.

On the inside of the fence the yard had been arranged with tables, chairs, and folded sun umbrellas. An unlit neon sign traced out the word OPEN.

Else tried the front door. The handle turned and it opened easily. "Hello?" she called into the church.

The piano stopped immediately. A few moments later the sound of singing cut off. Footsteps, too light for a man, Else realized, came walking towards the door. Light flared and they all blinked in the sudden pool of white, cast by halogen bulbs on stands. A set of double doors swung open and a figure with long white hair stepped into view. "Why hello!" she beamed at the group.

"Hi," Else grinned back.

The woman was thin and elderly. Her skin appeared as soft and wrinkled as a crushed tissue. "Well come on in, I've been waiting for you." The smiling woman stepped aside, holding the inner doors open. "Oh and be a dear and shut the door behind you," she called. "It lets the moths in you understand," she confided in Else.

Beyond the curtain a café decor had been set up in the church. Tables, chairs, and white linen with glassware and place settings awaited them on each table. A piano waited for the player to return. Only the pews were missing.

"Take a seat," the woman gestured to the room. She went to a table at the end and poured jugs of colored liquid into carafes; she set these on a tray and returned to the table where the salvagers stood in confusion.

"I'm Else, this is Rache and…"

"Uhh, Anchor," one of the scavengers said, looking surprised to be singled out.

"Pisty," said the first engineer.

"Johno," added the second.

"I'm Will."

"Crab," the last of the scavenger team said.

The old woman clasped her hands together. "What fine boys you have, Miss Else."

"They're not mine," Else said.

"I have drinks for everyone, on the house of course." She laid out the carafes and turned away, hesitating as if she had forgotten what to do next.

"What is your name?" Rache asked.

"Oh…I'm Mary Elizabeth Watson. My husband will be back soon."

"Where is he?" Else asked, looking around the church.

"He…he's at work of course. Always at work these days. So much do to you understand."

"I'm sure there is," Else said, slowly sinking into one of the seats at the nearest table.

The others followed Else's lead, Crab pouring the orange drink from the carafe into the glasses. Else sniffed it and took a sip. The others waited until she had taken a larger swallow and then followed suit.

Mary vanished behind the alter and then the church filled with the sound of voices raised in song. A hymn came from all four corners of the church. Everyone jumped slightly.

"It's a recording," Else said.

"It sounds…beautiful," Rache said, her face shining with awe.

"How is she powering the lights and the sound system?" Else asked, looking around.

"Solar, connected to batteries. I saw the panels on the roof," Pisty explained.

Mary reappeared, and ignoring her guests she went to the piano and started to play the same music as the recording, her piano synched with it perfectly and added a strange harmony to the singing. The scavengers drank their cordial and watched her play.

When Mary stopped playing, Else turned to Rache. "Search the building, see what you can find." She stood up and walked over to the piano. The old woman sat there, her eyes lost in a memory.

"Mary?" Else prompted. "Mary can you hear me?"

"Hmmm?" Mary's eyes refocused and she smiled at Else. "Hello, dear. Is Clive back yet?"

"No, not yet. Who is Clive?"

"Clive, is my husband, your father of course." Mary looked at Else as if she were playing some kind of game.

"Of course," Else nodded. "Did Clive do all this?"

"No, silly, Clive never had much to do with the café. That was always me. I loved to cook and see the people come and have a cup of tea. My scones, they're always a favorite."

"I know," Else said. "What did Clive do, for work I mean?"

"Oh it was something to do with bridges. He was always drawing pictures of bridges and going off to build them."

"Clive was an engineer? A civil engineer?" Else asked.

"I suppose. I never really understood his work. He was very proud of what he did. I just love him all the same."

Mary's awareness faded and she returned to the keyboard, joining the choir without missing a beat.

Else left her to it and went to find Rache. The salvage crew was leafing through piles of papers in a back room: blueprints, sketches, and graph-paper drawings of detailed plans.

"What's all this?" Else asked.

"It's the plans for the protection of this place. Whoever did it, they're gone now. Unless Mary went crazy after building the fence." Rache showed the drawings to Else. They were diagrams, technical layouts showing the flow of evols around the barrier system and out into an open area. The church had become an island with the evols flowing like a river's current around the barrier. The simplicity and the effectiveness of the system amazed Else. It reminded her of something and a moment later she said, "Temple Grandin. This is based on Dr. Temple Grandin's work with livestock."

"Huh?" Rache asked.

"Someone worked out how to manage the movement of evols. We build square fences, walls, and the dead come to them and push against them. They are stopped and then more come and they attract others. In the end the fence is overwhelmed. But this," Else traced a finger over the curving lines of the plan. "This makes them keep moving, they think they are going forward, when really they are being turned away, turned around and stopped from gathering. It's so simple…and so clever."

"Cool," Rache said.

Else rolled up the plan. She sorted through the other papers and selected some likely looking documents, which she added to her rolled-up bundle.

"Let's go," Else said.

"What about the old woman?" Rache asked.

"Leave her, she's no use to us."

Rache hesitated, and then followed Else and the others out into the church.

Mary was playing the piano again, keeping time with the choir as her fingers fluttered over the keys. Else walked past her without a glance, the salvage crew trailing after. Rache stopped at the front door of the church, looking back at the old woman, lost in her own world.

Else and her salvagers met up with the rest of the group at the gas station. They had brought the SUV up on the last of its fuel and were loading sloshing gas tanks into the back. Else called out to them, identifying herself from the darkness rather than risk startling someone and being shot. Her first priority was checking on her son; he stirred in his sleep and she watched him for a moment.

"We're getting enough fuel to get us to Mildura," Eric confirmed.

"Good," Else said without looking away from the baby. When they had finished refueling, she stowed the barricade plans in the glove box of the SUV and looked forward to the drive.

CHAPTER 9

Else never dreamed, even though everything she had read suggested that dreams were the brain's way of processing memories. It puzzled her because she remembered everything, from the warm floating haze of her first consciousness in Doctor Haumann's growth tanks to the time she spent with the Courier in their wild ride across the wasteland of the post-apocalyptic continent.

Everything was there in her mind, every detail, every word, heard, seen, or spoken. Mostly she ignored the memories, compartmentalizing them into a different part of her consciousness, like closing the door on a rowdy party so she could focus on what was happening now. When she slept she would walk the endless maze of rooms in her mind, reliving events, conversations, and things that, at the time, she didn't understand. This review was not a dream; it felt like analysis of memories, and they were legion.

They spent the night in Mary's café, Eric, Rache, and the others insisting that it seemed like a safe place to rest. Else agreed. The need she had to move south, to tread the ways she had come months earlier, gnawed at her and she could not determine why.

She slept, walking the halls of memory, turning over things and rereading old books. A presence startled her. Without waking, she turned in her mind and saw the ghostly figure of the Courier again.

She immediately went to the memory of what she had seen walking towards her in the rain.

"You are dead," she told the phantom in her subconscious.

"Dead doesn't mean what it used to," the vision replied.

"This is not a memory," Else insisted.

"No, it's not. This is me and you Else. Just like it was."

Else felt a surge of conflicting emotions surge through her. The colors around her flared angry in red and orange shades. "You went away!" It burst out of her in a howl of raw grief.

The Courier nodded. "You know I had to. We saved the world. At least, what's left of it."

"There are still evols," Else reminded him.

"No shit."

"Why am I seeing you? Why now?" Else restored her emotions and began to analyze the experience.

"Remember the connection you had with the dead? The way you could feel them?"

Else shivered. "Of course."

"Well, I died with a bloodstream full of your genetically engineered cells. I was the poisoned chalice that Adam drank, and it destroyed him. It left me like an evol, but like you as well. Dead, but not dead, my body buried under a blank grave marker, with my mind able to access the same necrotic network that the Adam virus created."

"You are the new Adam?" Else bristled.

"No. There are others, though. In other parts of the world. We won the battle, Else, but not the war."

"Why haven't you spoken to me before?" Else asked.

"I was laying low, thinking things through, working out what I can do. I've avoided making contact with evols; the last thing we need is for them to be organized again. But you are close enough now, within the range of my perception. When you sleep you are more open to transmission."

"We made a baby," Else said.

"Well, kinda. I'm pretty sure Doctor Preston and her fellow Frankensteins used my sperm sample to impregnate you while they were rejigging your DNA. Which is what I wanted to warn you about."

"What do you mean, warn me? My son is going to be okay, right?"

"Yeah, the kid is more you than me genetically. He's going to be around for a long time. You're heading towards the old convent, aren't ya?"

"Maybe," Else said.

"Well when you get there, look out for Donna-fucking-Preston. She sent an expedition back to Woomera, recovered a lot of data, computer systems, and fifteen frozen zygote clones of me."

"She can bring you back?" Else's voice was filled with hope.

"Hell no, just clones. You know, genetic copies. C'mon, Else, you're smart. Think about why she would want to start a new cloning program…"

"She wants to fulfill the original parameters of the project making super soldiers?"

"Bingo," the Courier's image said. "Arrogance is an ugly trait in anyone. But in a geneticist with access to advanced cloning technology and no one to tell her it's a stupid idea, it's fucking scary."

Else frowned, "The sisters, they will help us. They were building a new community. That is why I need to take these people there."

"You saw how that was changing, even when we came back through. Sister Mary was beating her plowshares into swords and shit. With Donna talking in her ear about a new master race, I'm not sure you are going to find what you are looking for."

"There is nowhere else to go," Else said.

The shape of the Courier looked down at the swirling floor.

"There really isn't. Fuck, Else. If you could have you shoulda stayed in the rainforest. With this lot hanging on you're screwed."

Else lifted her chin. "They are my responsibility. I brought them off the ship. The ones who have joined us since, they just don't want to be alone anymore. They believe in Rache's leadership."

"Just watch your back," the phantom said, fading into a memory of rain.

By the time the road turned west, a convoy of twelve vehicles rolled down the highway. Five of them were running on salvaged diesel, three on homemade methanol, and the remaining four were cut-down car chassis drawn by horse teams. The people going to Mildura now numbered over a hundred.

Food continued to be the biggest problem. Else wanted to keep moving, but the need to find sustenance for such a large group meant that days traveling were lost waiting for hunting parties to come back with enough meat, scrounged vegetables, and fruit for everyone.

Else wrote everyone's names in a book, along with what skills they had. Most were useless in the new world, office and shop workers. Some were real engineers, two were nurses, and the closest they had to a doctor was a woman who had been a third-year medical student when the Great Panic started.

Rache's reading improved and she took over the management of the group. Else wanted as little to do with the day-to-day organizing as possible. Her response to the endless questions was always the same: "Ask Rache."

Hob's wound healed and the girl Anna watched him constantly. He tried to ignore her, but anytime he swore or was too slow to follow an order from anyone, Anna would whack him across the back with a stick.

He tried complaining to Rache, who reminded Hob that he

belonged to Anna now and she could do whatever she wanted with him.

Else listened in on that conversation but didn't say anything. Slavery was not going to help their future survival, but the purpose of punishment was to create aversion to crime.

She noted that Anna never mistreated Hob. The girl let him ride in the back of a truck, usually sitting at her feet. He was allowed to sleep, eat, and squat when he needed to relieve himself. It was only when he started showing aggression that she would hit him. The training paid off. Hob stopped cursing everyone out and did what he was told, but only when Anna nodded her assent.

The final change with Hob came one rainy evening when the group was huddled under tarpaulins and in salvaged tents. A hunting party had been out since early morning and were yet to return. The two brothers, Michael and Sam, were proving their worth by bringing back butchered cows, sheep, and kangaroos. They had moved away from rifles and started hunting with bows. Now both of them could hit a fist-sized target at over a hundred paces with deadly accuracy.

Else was rocking the baby to sleep in a car seat. They used infant car seats for all the little ones now. Even when you were traveling at no more than ten miles an hour, it made her feel safer.

A shout came from the perimeter, where guards were on the constant lookout for evols. Leaving Cassie to watch the babies, Else stepped out of the tent, gun in one hand, blade in the other. Eric came splashing past, water streaming from his hair and beard.

"It's Sam, something's wrong with him," Eric said, running to fetch the nurses and the girl they called Doc.

Else found a crowd gathering around Sam and Michael. Michael had carried his brother in his arms for several hours to get back to camp. A quick examination showed no signs of evol bites on either of them.

"What happened?" Else asked.

"I dunno. He said his stomach was hurting, then he couldn't walk and he fell over. I couldn't get him to stand up again."

"Bring him to the big tent," Helen the nurse called through the rain. Else helped the others lift the stricken boy and they carried him in out of the weather.

Doc arrived. She was a petite Asian girl with a short haircut and scars on her arms that she kept covered with long sleeves. She examined Sam, looking concerned when she palpated his lower right abdomen and he moaned.

Only Else, Eric, Michael, and Rache remained in the tent. "I think it might be appendicitis," Doc said.

"You can fix him, right?" Rache asked.

Doc shook her head, "That would require surgery. I don't...have those skills." She looked close to tears. "I keep telling you, I'm not a doctor, I was just a medical student."

"What about the nurses?" Eric suggested.

Else shook her head, "They never worked in surgery either."

"Fuck," Eric muttered, casting a sideways glance at Michael, who stood shivering and dripping water in the tent.

"Is my brother going to die?" he asked.

"Yes," Doc said. "I'm sorry, but there is nothing we can do."

"Sam..." Michael said and moved to where his brother lay on the tent floor.

They left the two boys alone, everyone else moving out into the rain to talk about the case.

"It's not your fault," Else said to Doc. The girl nodded, rubbing her sleeves in an anxious gesture.

"Those dead things are just one of the many ways to die these days," Doc said. "Disease, injury, a simple infection. All of it will kill the strongest of us." She fell silent as Anna and Hob approached. Hob was on a thin rope leash, like a dog, and he didn't look at all happy about it. Anna tugged on the leash. "Sit," she said. Hob scowled but sank down to kneel in the mud.

"I heard that Sam was hurt. Is he okay?" Anna asked.

"He's sick, appendicitis Doc reckons," Eric said.

Anna looked around the grim faces. "You can help him though, right?"

"He's going to die," Else said.

"He can't..." Anna insisted.

"There's nothing we can do. He needs surgery and there's no way we can do that," Doc said.

"I can save him," Hob muttered.

Anna whipped him with the end of the rope leash. "Did I say you could speak?"

"Hang on," Else said. "What did you say, Hob?"

Hob scowled at the mud and remained silent.

"Make him answer," Rache demanded. Anna lifted the end of the rope.

"Alright, alright," Hob said. "I can save the kid."

"He probably has appendicitis. How are you going to save him?" Doc asked.

"Surgeon," Hob muttered.

"What?" Rache asked.

"I'm a veterinary surgeon," Hob said and then dropped his head to glare at the mud again, as if embarrassed by the admission.

"What does that mean?" Rache asked, looking at the others in confusion.

"It means he could, maybe, save Sam's life," Doc said.

"Yeah, maybe I could. But I'll only do it if you agree to my conditions."

"Like fuck," Rache snarled. Else waved her to silence. Stepping forward, she loosened the noose around Hob's neck and dropped it in the mud.

"Stand up, come inside and take a look at Sam. If you think you can save him, then we'll talk."

Hob wiped the water from his face and walked into the tent, a smirk darting around his lips.

Hob sat back on his haunches. "It's appendicitis. I can operate, but not here. We need to get him somewhere clean, with supplies and boiled water and shit like that."

"Okay," Else said. "We can move him, right? If we are careful."

"You'd better be quick, otherwise he'll die," Hob said.

"Eric! Rache!" Else called them in. "Get the SUV, empty it and make room for Sam. We need to get him to the nearest town or farm or somewhere."

Rache slipped outside, calling to people to come and help. Within five minutes Sam was being lifted into the back of the SUV. Eric got in behind the wheel, Doc took the passenger seat, and Hob sat in the back with the patient.

Else stood back while the vehicle turned out of the field they were camping in and headed back up the highway. Anna came and stood next to her, Hob's leash trailing on the wet ground.

"What did he make you do so he would save Sam?" Anna asked.

"He wants you to stay away from him. He said saving Sam will mean what he did to you should be forgotten."

Else felt Anna flinch. "What did you say?" she asked, her voice dropping to a whisper.

"I said, 'Sure, Hob, whatever you want. Just do what you can to make sure that Sam lives.'"

"I can't forget," Anna whispered.

Else turned and put her hand on the girl's shoulder. "Neither can I."

CHAPTER 10

E lse sent Michael out hunting at dawn the next day. The SUV hadn't returned and without his brother, Michael paced around the camp like a caged animal.

Anna spent the night with her mother in a tent with other women, emerging at sunrise to look around and see if the patient had returned.

Rache organized the people into work details, cooking food, tending babies, and maintaining perimeter security. She had three young kids working as her messengers; they ran to and fro across the camp, breathlessly reporting to Rache and then dashing off in a new direction with a new set of orders.

Else sat in the front of her tent, the baby cradled in her arms, waving his hands at the strands of hair that she dangled in his face. She looked up at the sound of a vehicle approaching, the SUV slowly turning into the campsite.

The survivors gathered around and waited while Eric climbed out. Doc and Hob slid out of the backseat. "Gizza hand," Hob called. Volunteers came forward, lifting a blanket stretcher out of the back, a pale and lifeless-looking Sam cradled in it.

"He did it," Doc said. "Sam is going to be sick for a while, but he's strong and Hob saved him." Sam was carried into a tent. Anna stood to one side, grim faced and slowly coiling the loops of Hob's leash in her hand.

Hob stood next to the SUV, the smirk on his face lifting some of the cowed expression he had worn for the last few weeks. "I saved the kid," Hob said, loud enough to be heard by those standing around watching. "She said if I saved the kid, I'd get my life back. None of you cunts can treat me like shit anymore. She said so," Hob nodded at Else.

The crowd turned to look at Else. She went over to Anna and took the rope from her hands. Walking over to Hob, she handed him the noose end of the leash.

"Put this on," she said.

Hob's eyes flashed. "You're fucking kidding me?"

Else widened the noose and flipped it over Hob's head, dropping it onto his shoulders and jerking it tight.

"What the fuck're you playing at?" Hob demanded.

Else roundhouse kicked him across the back of the knees, sending Hob crashing into the mud. She uncoiled the rope to where Anna stood, wide-eyed and trembling.

"Yours, I believe?" Else said putting the rope in Anna's hands.

"Thank you…" Anna said, the fear fading from her eyes.

"You can't do this!" Hob roared. "You said if I saved the kid it was finished!" Else ignored him and went back to her tent.

Anna coiled the slack in the rope and jerked on the taut line. "Hob!" she yelled. "Shut up!"

"You little fuckin' cunt!" Hob's eyes narrowed and he sprang up, charging towards Anna, his snarl promising murder.

The girl stood her ground, coiling the rope as he charged; then at the last minute, she stepped aside. Hob's lunge went wide and he overbalanced, slipping in the wet grass. Anna yanked hard on the rope, the noose tightened around Hob's neck, and he gagged, clawing at the rope that dug deep into his throat.

"You will not speak unless I say so. You will not swear or threaten anyone or Else will cut your tongue out. You will do what you are told, when you are told," Anna said, letting a little slack into the rope. Hob loosened the choking noose and took a shuddering breath. "Now get up. You're not a pig in the mud."

Hob remained on the ground and then slowly stood up, his eyes downcast. The people turned and went back to their chores. The show was over, everything was back to normal.

Sam died two days later. Doc did her best to treat the infection that burned through his surgical wound. Without antibiotics and only rudimentary antiseptics, his fever spiked and his organs began to shut down. Else watched over him in the final hour, Michael curled up on a blanket next to his brother, finally asleep after watching him for so long. When Sam took his final shuddering breath Else stood up. Laying her baby down, she rolled the emaciated boy on to his side. Drawing a heavy-bladed knife, she felt for the gap at the base of his skull and punched the knife deep into his brain. She let Michael sleep until she was quite sure that Sam wasn't coming back.

Else was curious to see the funeral arrangements. The people let Michael dictate the service. He said a few words, mumbled a prayer, and then they lowered the blanket-wrapped body into the hole dug to receive him.

"We should mark the grave with his name," Else said. They heated a knife in a cooking fire and carved his name in a split log. Michael watched impassively as the wooden post was hammered into the ground at the head of his brother's grave.

They left the campsite that afternoon, with less food than they had when they arrived and one less mouth to feed.

Ten days of slow travel followed. The vehicles ran out of fuel, and other than the occasional evol, which was quickly dispatched, they spent their days trudging. Children rode in the horse-drawn cars; everyone else walked. Hunters ranged ahead, the survivors stopping when they came across butchered meat, the exhausted hunters dozing in abandoned cars.

"We're low on food, water, and patience," Eric reported at the nightly council meeting. Else bit back her frustration; on her own, she could cover twice as many miles in a day as these people.

"We are close now." Else stroked a finger over the map. "Mildura is on the other side of the river. And we should reach the river by tomorrow."

"You sure that there's no one living there now?" Rache asked.

"I don't know. We pretty much killed every one last time I came this way."

Eric sighed and poked a stick into the fire. "That story of yours gets stranger every time you tell it," he said.

"It's exactly what happened," Else replied.

"I believe you, but it's crazy just the same."

Else shrugged. "It's my life story, so it's the only one I have to tell."

"Sam died," Rache said. "We could all die, get sick or something."

"It's no reason to quit," Eric replied.

"I'm never going to quit," Rache insisted. "I'm going to get my own ship, sail the world."

"I reckon you will too," Eric smiled.

Else called a halt when the bridge over the Murray River came into view. Standing on the running board of a wagon, she checked the land ahead with a pair of binoculars and frowned. The bridge was barricaded, but not like it had been the day she and the Courier came through, with roofing iron, a wooden frame, sandbags, and concrete blocks. Now the bridge was blockaded with a proper wall at least twelve feet high, constructed of cemented concrete blocks behind railway iron that had been cut and welded into giant caltrops, like the tank busters of the Normandy beaches in World War II.

The dead were gathered against the blockade, a seething sea of desiccated corpses, straining against the impenetrable wall. Else wondered why the dead didn't ford the river. The barrier only extended across the bridge, and the water on each side was clear. She stared at the wall, scanning every inch of it, pausing and going back when she saw a glint of sunlight reflecting on glass. A pair of binoculars staring back at her.

"How do we cross?" Eric asked.

"We need to clear the dead, then we can pass over the bridge."

"How? Is there a gate?" Eric shaded his eyes and stared into the distance.

"You don't barricade a bridge without having a gate. Otherwise you just destroy the bridge," Rache said.

"There is no gate," Else said. "They have a second bridge. It is submerged under the water just upstream from the main bridge."

"How can you tell?" Rache took the binoculars and peered at the distant scene.

"There are posts on each side of the river, and the water flow is different just up from the bridge."

"How are we going to clear the dead?" Eric asked.

"We'll draw them off. Arthur, get me a horse!" One of the wagon drivers climbed down and unhitched a horse. Leading it forward by the bridle, he stopped next to Else. She swung up onto the horse's back. Taking the rope reins, she nudged the beast with her heels and rode down the highway.

Rache watched through the binoculars as Else rode down the road, yelling and waving her arms. The dead turned, confused by the noise. Else's horse reared, alarmed by the smell and the moaning of the predators on the bridge. She held her steed in place until the first of the evols tore at its flanks. Only then did she turn and let the animal run. The mob of zombies poured after her. Else turned the horse downstream and led them away from the bridge.

"Is she okay?" Eric demanded.

"Yeah," Rache replied, turning slowly to follow Else's progress.

The horse plunged into the water, Else goading it on with her heels digging into its ribs. The dead followed, and Else slipped off its back and, trailing the reins behind her, she swam strongly across the wide, brown current. The evols surged into the stream, wading and then sinking underwater as they headed out over their heads. Else's horse suddenly screamed, its head rearing up and jerking the reins from Else's hand. She let go and swam for the far bank, where she climbed out and shook herself dry before vanishing into the trees up the riverbank.

In the center of the river the water seethed and rolled. Rache wondered if crocodiles were in the water, feasting on the dead and the horse whose screams could now be heard all the way back to the vehicles.

"The bridge is clear, let's go!" Rache urged her people forward. The wagon drivers whipped the horses and those on foot broke into a shambling run. The armed guards ran along the edges of the road, weapons clanking as they jogged.

The convoy reached the road before the bridge and ground to a halt. "Where do we go now?" people called from all sides.

"Upstream!" Rache turned and headed towards the posts buried deep in the mud. The ground trembled and smoke rose from beyond the trees on the other side of the river. With a rhythmic clanking sound, two thick cables rose up from the mud and water. Hanging from the cables, chains supported a wide bridge of railway sleepers.

Rache stepped on the dripping bridge first. Water still streamed over it, the heavy wood barely breaking the surface. The people followed, looking around fearfully for crocodiles or evols.

On the other side, Rache urged her people on. They hurried

across the bridge, the wagons emptying and mothers carrying children. Cassie had Lowanna and Else's baby in her arms, both of them howling.

Within twenty minutes the last of the people were across and moving beyond the trees. Men on horseback rode along the bank. One of them gave a shrill whistle and an answering whistle came from a steam engine further back. The bridge began to descend underwater again.

The water downstream still surged and rolled. Rache turned her back on the river and walked up the trail through the trees, wondering just what lay underneath the surface that could take a horse and all those evols.

The traction engine that ran the winch raising and lowering the steel cables of the suspension bridge fascinated Rache. The heavy boiler and firebox devouring split lengths of gum tree made her weak at the knees. Else stood talking excitedly with two women, wearing jeans and dark blue work shirts.

"This is fantastic!" Rache said, grinning at the engine.

"Kylie, Lilly, this is Rache. She's an engineer," Else made introductions.

"Welcome to Mildura," Lilly said.

"Is this a safe place?" Rache asked.

"Sure," Kylie replied. "We work hard but we are building a community here."

"We made it…" Rache felt an upwelling of grief and tears spilled down her face.

"I need to see Sister Mary and Donna," Else said.

"Let's get you all registered and checked over. You can see Donna soon enough," Kylie replied.

"Registered?" Eric asked, walking up to the conversation.

"All new arrivals need to be registered. You'll then be assigned a living space, job details, and have a medical."

The former convent remained as a center of operations, but now the community of Mildura was being rebuilt. Else saw at least three hundred people working fields, building houses, and driving stock. Women and children watched the new arrivals pass through into a fenced-off area, while armed guards discreetly took up positions herding the survivors into the pen.

"What's this for?" Rache stopped and stared at the high mesh fence and gate.

"Quarantine," Kylie replied. "You can stay here until you are checked for any illness and cleared."

"My people need food and water, not to be put in a cage," Rache replied.

"They will get all that. Everyone goes through the same process."

Rache looked around. Else would stop this and make the women listen. Except Else had vanished. Cassie cradled Lowanna and shrugged when Rache's gaze fell on her.

"How long does this process take?" Rache asked.

"Two, maybe three days," Lilly replied.

"It better not take any longer," Rache warned and followed the survivors into the pen.

CHAPTER 11

Else followed the road north towards the convent. The land around Mildura had once been farmed and now it was again. People looked up from their toil as she walked past, smiled, waved, and went back to weeding and tending the crops.

The white dome of the convent still glowed in the late afternoon sun. The fences were still up around the compound, but the gates were open, allowing a steady stream of riders to pass under the open doorway where once Else had practiced her archery on the advancing dead.

A guard with a rifle took aim from atop the wall. "Who are you!" he called down.

"I'm Else. I'm here to talk to Sister Mary and Donna Preston."

"Wait there," the sentry said, then vanished. Else stood in the sun, shading her baby from the light with the edge of a blanket and fanning him gently.

A woman appeared at the gate. "Else?" she called. Else looked up and grinned.

"Hey, Sister Mary!" Else hurried forward, the elder nun opened her arms and embraced her. The baby squalled and Mary stepped back, a shocked look on her face.

"A child?"

"My son," Else confirmed.

Sister Mary's lips thinned. "Born out of holy matrimony I'm sure."

"Nope," Else said with an innocent expression. "We were married, and shortly after I found out I was pregnant, I was widowed."

"I will pray for this child and the soul of his departed father."

"Thank you, Sister. The place is really thriving now."

"Yes, through God's mercy and our efforts to attract new settlers, the land of Mildura has been taken back from the unholy dead. We now have over four hundred people in our community."

"The place is looking good," Else said.

"We have people with skills: farmers, mechanics, a doctor, and two midwives. We have people spreading out in all directions, gathering supplies and technology."

"Technology?" Else asked.

"Doctor Preston's program requires a great deal of technology. I don't pretend to understand the details. But let's get you inside, out of the heat."

Else followed Sister Mary through the crushed limestone courtyard and into the convent. When the doors were closed the air was cool and moist, the hum of air-conditioning whirring in the background. Thick bundles of electric and data cables ran along the walls and disappeared through a duct in the wall to the chapel interior.

"I need to talk to Doctor Preston," Else said, following the cables with her eye.

"I'm sure she will be delighted to update you on her work." Sister Mary's voice took on a stern tone. Else subsided a little.

"I want to thank you for everything you did for me. Without you I would have never survived."

"You are God's creature, my child," Mary said. "That you live is due to his mercy and his hand alone."

Else had learned the value of silence and kept her smile in place instead of responding to Sister Mary's assumptions.

Given everything she had seen and experienced in the year she had been alive, nothing suggested to her that any kind of God existed. She found expressions of faith to be the most alien thing that separated her from most people, even though sometimes she wished she could place all her trust in an invisible god.

The entrance to the chapel opened with the heavy rustling of plastic curtains behind the door and Donna Preston emerged. She looked tired, Else thought, and thin. But other than that it was Donna. She pushed a pair of glasses up onto her head and regarded Else with an analytical expression.

"Why are you here?" she asked by way of greeting.

"I brought some people to join the community," Else replied.

Donna's interest seemed piqued. "Genetically diverse?" she asked.

"Yes. Men, women, children."

"They are being processed?" Donna asked.

"I think so," Else replied.

Donna nodded. "Come into the lab." She ignored Sister Mary entirely. The nun's lips went thinner.

"Well I have work to do. Else, I will see you at our evening meal." She turned on her heel and marched off.

"Is she mad at me?" Else asked Donna, following the scientist into the chapel.

"No, she's just upset that I'm running things here now. She knows that my ways are better, but she thinks I'm a godless heathen and that really rubs her up the wrong way." Donna seemed pleased that she irritated Sister Mary.

The chapel had been converted into a functional laboratory. Else stopped inside the door, the plastic sheeting draping over her shoulders, a sense of panic tightening around her chest. Her breathing became a whispered hiss as she regarded the tubes, winking computers, swirling glass, and plastic tanks of viscous pink fluid.

"You okay?" Donna asked, with a detached curiosity.

"It reminds me of...where I was born."

"Well it should. I've spent months recovering what I could from the Opera House and Woomera facilities."

"Woomera was dark…" Else said, a fresh wave of panic washing over her.

"Yes. We went back in. There were no survivors. They had crawled out when the lights didn't come back on and the evols got them. Fortunately the equipment and computers were salvageable."

Else shuddered. The idea of going into the underground facility at Woomera, into that oppressive darkness, so thick it felt like heavy cloth wrapped around her head, made her dizzy and nauseous.

"I have been able to continue my work, regardless of Sister Mary's objections."

"You recovered clone embryos. You have the Courier's viable clones," Else whispered, the dream replaying in her mind with startling clarity.

"Yes I did." Donna regarded Else with new interest. "How did you know?"

"He told me," Else said.

"Where is he? I could use another sample of his sperm."

"He died. Is he the father of my baby?" Else lifted the infant sleeping in her arms.

Donna came forward and peered at the child. "Fascinating," she said. "I'd need to do a full DNA analysis, but he does bear a resemblance."

"I haven't had sex with anyone else," Else said.

"Did you notice the patch under your arm?" Donna asked.

"He found it, when we were together the first time."

"What color was it?" Donna asked.

"Purple," Else replied. "Why? What does that mean?"

"It means he is the father of your child. We took his fresh sperm sample and impregnated you while the work was being done on your telomere terminator sequencing."

"Will my son be alright?"

"A child with 50 percent of your DNA?" Donna gave a sour chuckle. "The kid will grow up to be a god."

"I hope I'll be around to see him grow," Else said, stroking the soft hair on the baby's head.

"You do understand what we did to you? At Woomera I mean."

"You made me into the evol-killing bomb that was meant to infect the Adam organism. Which is what happened. The Courier infected himself with my antibodies and gave his life so that I could have my baby."

"We also made you immortal. Removing the terminator sequences from your DNA. You will never suffer the same level of cell death as humans. You will never die of old age. The only thing that should kill you would be a lethal infection or serious injury."

"My son had a head cold," Else explained.

"And he looks like he recovered completely," Donna replied.

"Why are you making new Tankbread?" Else asked.

"Tankbread? This isn't Tankbread. We aren't producing clones here to feed evols. No, this is about the original purpose of the project. Creating an improved human being. An entity without any of our weaknesses, the perfect soldier."

"Wasn't that what led to the evols in the first place?" Else asked.

"And I have learned from their mistakes. We aren't looking at genetically engineering viruses anymore. This is about genetic manipulation. The antibodies in your blood will inoculate our soldiers. Then once field trials prove successful, I intend to start a vaccination program. Every living survivor will become poisonous to the virus."

"How many do you have now? Clones of him, I mean," Else asked.

Donna frowned. "Of the viable embryos I recovered, only two have survived through the adult development phase."

"Why not make clones of other people?" Else asked.

"The Courier—what was his name?" Else shrugged and Donna continued. "Never mind. He had a particular survival talent. He was resourceful, a good fighter. How much of that was genetic and how much of it was environmental, we may never know. The key thing is that he had good survival genes. Cloning him is a good start for the new race of Australians."

"You shouldn't do this," Else said. "He died to destroy the Adam. You shouldn't bring him back, not like this."

"I thought you of all people would want someone like you to spend the rest of your life with," Donna replied.

"He is with me, always. I can feel him. My memories of every moment with him are clear and I can visit them whenever I want."

Donna pressed on. "Wouldn't you like new memories?"

"They wouldn't be the same. He was the product of his life experience, a particular person. The clones will just look like him. They won't have his smile, or his personality. They will just look like him."

"And soon they will number in the hundreds, then the thousands. I'm working up a mix of zygote implantation into surrogate mothers and direct cloning in the Tankbread growth system."

"It's a bad idea, Donna. You should stop now. Use your talents to save the living, not create new monsters."

"You're only saying that because you haven't met them." Donna beckoned Else to follow and went to the back of the former chapel. Unlocking a door, she ushered Else through.

She went in. The room beyond was dark and before she could voice her concern, an electric spark crackled and a jolt shot through Else, sending her tumbling to the floor. Her baby screaming was the last sound she heard before passing out.

Else crawled back to consciousness. Her mouth and throat felt like she had swallowed desert sand. Everything ached, from her bound wrists and ankles to a sharper pain from deep inside her lower abdomen.

The room was dark and silent. She lay on a carpeted floor, naked and thirsty. Senses straining into the darkness, she whispered, "Baby?" A flood of panic washed through her. Not again. Never again would anyone take her son away from her. She had promised him that. Else flexed her arms and legs, forcing the cord binding her to bite into her skin.

"If you have hurt my baby, you are all going to die," Else muttered. She couldn't stand; the rope ran from her ankles up the back of her legs to loop around her wrists. Her legs were bent backwards at the knees, preventing her standing up. Instead she rolled across the room, feeling for anything other than the dust on the floor and the smooth paneling of the walls. Growling in frustration, Else wiggled into the corner of the room. Pushing herself up, she ignored the swirling pain of pins and needles that erupted through her legs. Standing now, hunched and supported by the wall, she doubled over, feeling her arms strain against the cord as she lowered her head and flexed her knees apart. The rope pulled tighter with each movement. Exhaling, Else pushed her head between her knees, curling herself up until she could barely breathe and the rope between her ankles and her wrists brushed against her nose. Wiggling her face, she snagged the cord with her teeth and began chewing on it.

Else came to, her head pounding and the stars on her retina spinning in a nauseating cycle. She remembered being doubled over, chewing on a rope, the pressure building in her head until she fainted. That, she decided, would explain the headache and disorientation. Gritting her teeth she straightened her legs, feeling the cord strain and then at the edge of her endurance the rope snapped. Else shuffled backwards on her rear, working her body through the circle of her arms, feeling her shoulder joints pop until she had her hands in front. She attacked the knots at her wrists with renewed enthusiasm. Once they were undone she started working on her ankle bindings.

Five minutes later Else stood up, rubbing her wrists before feeling her way along the wall till she found the door. It wasn't even locked.

Opening it carefully and peering out into the chapel, she froze as Donna's voice came to her across the room.

"Initial analysis of samples taken from subject indicates that her ova are a key source of the missing genetic material. When fertilized with the clone spermatozoa the resulting zygote has the genetic markers that indicate immunity to the Adam virus. The question remains, why is it not possible to simply clone Else's cells and re-create the savior units in her image? Testing of Else's infant child indicate that he has extremely high levels of effective antibodies. Whether this immunity will fade as he develops his own immune system or whether this will be a permanent feature of his blood serum remains to be seen. Harvesting of sufficient stem cells to begin a new line of clones is scheduled. This will be followed by an autopsy to determine differential organ structure."

Donna stopped talking and clicked a handheld tape recorder off.

Else picked up the Taser gun that Donna had stunned her with and pressed it against the back of the woman's neck. "You have one sentence to tell me why I shouldn't kill you. Think very carefully about what you choose to say."

"Kill me and you will never see your baby again," Donna responded promptly.

The Taser crackled against Donna's skin. She convulsed and crumpled to the floor. Else dragged Donna's limp body over to a gurney, lifted her onto it, and strapped her down. Flexing one hand, she slapped the bound woman across the face. Donna mumbled and her eyes snapped open.

"Where is my son?" Else asked.

"In the nursery." Donna moved and then realized she was restrained. "Hey! Untie me!"

"Where is the nursery?"

"In the first dorm room upstairs."

Else turned to walk away and then stopped. "Your clone work. It's dangerous. Don't you understand? The Adam virus, it is in everything. You can do so much to rebuild the world; don't fuck it up by making new monsters to hunt us to extinction." Still naked, she walked out of the lab, closing the door behind her, shutting off Donna's angry shouts.

The dormitory was easy enough to find. Else remembered it from when she had stayed at the convent of Saint Peter's Grace previously. The dorm was like a hospital ward, with a row of beds on each side. A room at the end closest to the stairs now contained cots, baskets, and incubators. When Else looked in, most of the baby stations were empty. Her baby was asleep in the middle of a cot. Else left him there and went to the nearest cupboard. Opening it, she took out clothes and dressed quickly, searching two more closets to find boots that fit her comfortably.

Gathering up her baby and securing him in a blanket sling around her chest, Else headed to the top of the stairs and then froze. Voices raised in anger erupted from the level below. From the sounds of it, Donna had been rescued.

Else headed along the dorm. The window at the end led to an outside staircase, a fire escape. She opened the window and hurried down the creaking metal stairs.

The sun was setting in the west, leaving Else unsure of how long she had been unconscious and tied up. Had it only been a couple of hours? Or had an entire night and day passed?

Armed women were coming out of the convent building, spreading out in a search pattern. Else started running, getting to the compound wall and then moving along in its shadow. The gate had closed, so Else jumped on the back of a parked wagon and with the baby heavy against her front she jumped. Her hands caught the edge of the top ledge. Her knees slammed into the white stone blocks, shielding the baby from the impact.

Pulling herself up, Else stood on the top of the wall. From up here, the ground looked a long way down. There were no convenient wagons to jump down onto. She took a deep breath and turned to face the convent buildings. Jumping backwards, she slapped her hands and booted toes against the sheer surface of the wall. In the three seconds it took her to reach the ground she left a smeared trail of bloody handprints on the wall.

"Fuck," Else muttered as she hobbled away into the rising darkness.

CHAPTER 12

Mildura lay in near darkness, campfires providing the only light source. Else slipped past the sentries, men and women armed with rifles and bows. It didn't take her long to find the quarantine zone where her people were being kept behind a mesh fence, under armed guard.

Moving carefully, Else took up a position where she could watch the two perimeter guards from cover. They followed a casual pattern that made it hard to establish a routine to their patrol. They stopped and chatted with each other before meandering off along the fence line.

Else went to the darkest corner of the quarantine zone and hissed to get the prisoner's attention.

"Where's Rache?" she whispered.

The girl came forward, her mouth set in a furious line.

"The fuck is going on here, Else? You said we would be safe here. This was a place where we would be welcomed. Instead we're penned up like...like we're still on the ship."

"I'll get you out. You're safe in there. It's only for a few days, until they process you."

"What the fuck does that mean? Process?"

"I think they want to make sure you are healthy and they want to write down who you are and what you can do to help around here."

"That sounds like bullshit," Eric said, pushing his way through the watchful crowd that had gathered at the fence.

Else looked both ways; the guards would appearing any moment now. "Keep quiet, do what they tell you. I will be back." The baby started to grizzle in his sling. Else slipped away into the darkness without another word.

She toured the town. Women and babies seemed common enough, so when she sat down to nurse the baby, very few people took notice. Those who did smiled at the scene.

It became clear that there were two groups within the Mildura community. The first were the women and men that Sister Mary and her followers had gathered in the first weeks after Donna Preston's arrival. They were marked with crosses, some painted on their foreheads or across the bridge of the nose. The others were what Else considered civilians, regular people. Men, women, and children of all races and creeds. They were building and surviving, accepting whatever laws and rules Sister Mary placed on them in return for some kind of security and maybe even a little bit of hope.

Else found a building with a large room filled with beds. No one complained when she took an empty one and closed her eyes. Baby cuddled against her.

She slept until dawn, waking up to feed the baby only once during the night. In the morning she found a communal bathroom where she could wash the baby and herself. Food was also communal, people gathering at trestle tables to help themselves to a breakfast of cooked eggs, large loaves of sliced bread, and fresh fruit.

The quarantine people had food taken to them, which they ate without question or complaint. Else couldn't shake the nagging sense of unease. Donna's plans were dangerous, and Else was never going to let her touch the baby again.

After exploring the town, Else concluded that no matter what was happening here, the clone research and whatever projects Donna was working on, the people of the new Mildura knew nothing about it. They spent the day farming, building houses, and taking care of children.

In the afternoon, two new survivors arrived. A man and a woman, both gaunt and looking half-starved. They shuffled into the quarantine zone and didn't show any sign of life until they were offered food and water. They fell on the sustenance, cramming food into their mouths and drinking water till they almost choked. Else wondered how they had survived as long as they did.

When darkness eventually fell, she made her way back to the quarantine pen. The gates were opened and the survivors from the ship were being guided out. They were all given a tag to wear around their necks. It had their name, blood type, and a barcode on it.

"Just until everyone gets to know you and we have some kind of medical record for each of you," was the explanation.

"So what now? We can go where we want?" Rache asked.

"Absolutely. We recommend you stay within the community area. Wandering outside of the fences can be dangerous."

"We have survived all kinds of shit," Rache said. "This place is like paradise by comparison."

"There are spare beds in the communal dorms. We're building new houses at a rate of about one a week. They're not much but it's a start." The survivors were escorted to the same long building that Else had spent the night in. She kept in the shadows, alert for any sign of the convent operatives. The people of Mildura didn't seem to be looking for her or even know who she was.

"Eric," Else said, drawing him aside as the people filed past. "I've seen some things around here that might be useful for making stuff. Like what we used on the ship."

Eric did a double take. "Are you fucking kidding me? Why would we want to blow shit up around here?"

"There's more going on here than you think," Else replied.

"I know, stuff like hot showers, fresh food, a bed to sleep in."

"It's more than that. Get Rache. Meet me over there, by the kitchen place." Else slipped away, leaving Eric shaking his head and moving after the others.

The temporary accommodation of the communal room was filled with the survivors. Most settled on beds with their children cuddled against them. Some simply sat on the floor with their backs against the wall and slept.

Rache and Eric wandered around the community encampment; they found Else leaning against the back wall of a building used as a communal kitchen.

"I need you to make something that will burn. Something that will burn really well," Else said to Eric.

"Anything else?" Eric asked.

"Can you do it?" Else responded.

"Make you some kind of Molotovs? Sure I can do that. Let me just wander down to the local gas station and pick up some kitchen supplies."

Else slammed Eric against the wall. "Smarten the fuck up, Eric," she snarled into his startled expression as the baby started to cry at the sudden movement.

"Okay…It's okay. I'll see what I can find." Eric pushed her hands away.

"What the fuck is going on, Else?" Rache demanded.

"Donna Preston, she's making new clones. She wants to repeat the experiments that created the evols in the first place." Else shushed the baby and cuddled him against her shoulder.

"The fuck?" Rache asked.

"I don't know what she is doing exactly, or how far she has come. But I need to burn everything she has going on up there at the convent."

"Jesus…" Eric swept his hands through his long greying hair.

"What the fuck is wrong with these people? Ending the world once wasn't enough?"

"I'm not giving them a chance to find out," Else said. "I need enough flammable stuff to burn the convent down by morning."

"I'm on it." Eric started to walk away and then turned back. "There's no one else out there doing this shit, is there? If we end this it stops, right? No more crazy fuckers trying to play God?"

"I don't know," Else said. "But if this is the end, then it starts now."

Eric proved that he could make explosives or flammable gels out of almost anything. Five hours later he had six plastic bottles containing an oily looking sludge. Each top had a fuse protruding through a putty seal.

"It's quite simple," he said. "Light the fuse and get the fuck away from it. This stuff will stick to anything and it will keep burning. Water will just piss it off. If you get any on you, smother the burn."

"Is this enough?" Else eyed the bottles.

"Try it and see." Eric gave the grin that always made Else wonder about his sanity. "But make sure you are a long way away when it goes up. Do you have anything to light it with?" he added.

"I'll find something. Take my baby to Cassie. Tell her to look after him and I will be back soon."

Eric nodded and held the baby gingerly. He was wet and smelled like he'd taken a dump. "Burn, baby, burn," Eric whispered. Giggling, he held the child at arm's length and went to find Cassie.

Cassie took Else's baby without a word. "Keep him safe. His mother'll be back soon," Eric told her. The idea of leaving Else's son with anyone, even someone she trusted like Cassie, made him uneasy. "He needs cleaning," he added, as if the smell wasn't enough.

CHAPTER 13

Leaving town and jogging along the edge of the road to the convent, Else could see the compound was running on solar power. The white stone of the high walls glowed in the aura of halogen lights powered by batteries. The fence at the end of the road might be an issue. If they had closed the gates by now, Else had a plan for that too.

There were no guards on the road that Else could see. The sentries were further out, beyond the fields, along the haphazard fence line that marked the border of civilization. From what she remembered of the convent, they had a lot of extra space. Donna had taken over the chapel, but there were other rooms, plenty of places for the geneticist to be keeping clones and other secrets.

The bottles of goo banged against her hips as she ran. A cord wrapped around the neck of each bottle held them in bandolier fashion. As she ran, Else wondered if the Courier could touch her mind at this distance. According to the road maps, they had been closest to Sydney, and his grave, when he came to her in the dream.

The darkness between the convent and the community of Mildura glowed with moonlight and the smear of the Milky Way. Else had spent weeks counting the stars, plotting each one in her head and noticing when they moved. Books on astronomy and constellations had given her a new context to place these mesmerizing spots of light against. Now she could navigate with ease, knowing the Southern Cross, the constellation shown on the Australian flag, and the twin stars called the Pointers. Using them as a reference she could orient herself and know which way to travel to get home. As long as the sky was clear.

An eerie noise reached her from the east. A vibrant, rumbling buzz. It was a tonal sound, low enough to make her body feel like it was quivering in harmonic response. At the same time the sound progressed up a scale, becoming a ghostly, birdlike cry.

Else turned east, the sound drawing her as surely as a marked path. Evols did not make music; they moaned and sometimes snarled. But now, they never used tools or had any remaining sentience. Her feet slapped on the hard ground as the light breeze whispered through the low foliage of the crops growing in the field. Maybe it was some rusting pipe that was catching the breeze?

A flickering light came into view as Else ran, a small campfire, silhouettes arrayed around it and the dirge-like moan of the music growing stronger as she approached.

Else sank into a crouch at the farthest edge of the firelight, unsure whether she should approach and taken aback by the display of painted dancers and the coiling rhythms of the music coming from the long wooden pipes that the men played by blowing air down from their bulging cheeks.

A steady beat rang out from two sticks clapped together, a sharper harmony to the eerie wail of the long pipes. An old woman rose from the fireside, her wrinkled face and drooping skin painted with white ash. She kept the beat of the clapping sticks in her hands, taking a shuffling step with each sharp report, kicking up dust and making her way to where Else rose to her feet.

The woman beckoned Else forward with a toss of her head. Else shyly followed her closer to the fire and sank down into a cross-legged position between a man playing the long pipe and the old woman keeping time with her clapping sticks.

Else watched as the people danced. A young man, his chest marked with raised welts, caked in ash and fresh blood, stomped and pranced around the fire, his eyes seeing some other place or some other time.

Else listened to the voices singing and chanting in a language she could not understand. The performance continued until the fire burned down to white ashes and red embers while the darkness slipped closer to their backs.

Finally the circle fell quiet and a man with a white painted face and wearing a simple red cloth wrapped around his waist came over and crouched down in front of Else.

"Hey you," he said and grinned.

"Joel?" Else said and beamed. "Where the fuck have you been?" Else rolled to her knees and hugged her friend.

"Oh you know, on walkabout," Joel replied. "You know Jirra's people, aye?" he added.

"Yes. I'm sorry. Jirra died," Else said to the old woman next to her. The woman just nodded, her face a mask of sadness.

"But he lives on through his baby girl, Lowanna," Joel reminded them.

The group nodded. They were a mix of old men and women, with a few young people and two babies. No more than twelve people in all.

"Where is she?" Lowanna's grandmother, Sally, asked.

"She is safe. She is with someone who has been taking care of her. They are in Mildura, the town over there."

"Will she come back to us?" Billy asked.

"Of course," Else said. "Cassie is just helping out."

"What you doin' out here, girl?" Joel asked.

Else took a deep breath and then started talking. She explained the journey from Queensland and the horror she had discovered at the convent. How her hope for a safe future in the Mildura community had been dashed by Donna's plans to use her son's body as source material for a new series of clone experiments. The kind of experiments that brought the world to its knees a decade ago.

No one interrupted her monologue. They listened in respectful silence and then Sally put some more wood on the fire, sending sparks twirling into the night sky.

"You could use a hand, aye?" Joel asked.

"Sure…I guess." Else laid the line of six bottles out in front of her. "This is what I'm going to use to burn the convent down."

"That gonna work?" Joel asked, eyeing the bottles skeptically.

"It has to," Else said. She stood up, brushing the dust from the knees of her jeans.

"Reckon you could use a hand, aye?" Joel said, rising to stand in front of her.

"Reckon I could," Else replied.

Joel stooped to gather his weapons before they left the family scene that had been a common site on this land for forty millennia, and headed off towards the distant glow of the convent of Saint Peter's Grace.

Joel moved silently through the sun-parched grass, making Else feel like a lumbering cow beside him. She followed his lead, slipping behind him and stepping where he did, trying to match his effortless stride in the dark.

The perimeter fence stood as it always had, but strengthened with more mesh and now a palisade of wooden stakes, pointing outwards at a forty-five degree angle on the outside.

She sank to a crouch when Joel stopped and ducked in front of her. A handheld spotlight swept over the ground just ahead. A guard on the convent wall was checking for any evols that might have made it through the fence.

"You got a way in?" Joel whispered.

"Yeah," Else pulled a pair of pliers from her jeans pocket. "We cut the wire with this."

"How you gonna cut through the concrete block wall with that, aye?" Joel's eyes twinkled in the starlight.

"I was going to have a look around the back," Else replied.

With careful maneuvering they climbed over the sharpened stakes and crouched at the wire fence.

Else cut a slit in the mesh and pushed the ends apart, creating a hole for her to slip through. Joel followed and then they pressed the wire back into shape.

"Quite a bit of clear ground for us to cover," Joel warned.

"Four hundred meters," Else replied, her gaze fixed on the distant wall.

"You hear that?" Joel cocked his head. Else listened. On the air came the sound of distant groans and shouts of alarm.

"Evols. They must have gotten through the barricades somewhere and are in town."

Else and Joel waited, crouched in the dark, for a few long minutes. The sound of gunfire from the direction of Mildura tightened the tension on Else's every nerve to near breaking point.

"Please be okay. Keep him safe," she whispered to Cassie and her baby.

"You wanna go back to town?" Joel asked.

"No, we have to keep going." Else stood up and started running towards the corner of the convent wall.

The gates in the wall opened and a truck with people standing on the back roared down the driveway towards the fence. Else and Joel threw themselves flat as the truck thundered past. The fence gate opened automatically and the truck rolled out and headed towards Mildura.

"Come on, while the gate's still open." Else sprang up and ran, her eyes watching the wall, looking for the silhouettes of guards with spotlights.

A beam of light played over the ground behind them as they slid to a halt at the base of the wall. Else gestured towards the open doors and drew her blades. Above her she heard a woman say, "I'm sure I saw something moving out there. It was moving fast, though."

Another light came on and swept over the open ground between the wall and the fence.

"Could have been a 'roo," another woman's voice suggested.

"Maybe." The first woman did not sound convinced. Else and Joel moved quietly along the base of the wall.

Peering around the edge of the open gate, she saw the courtyard was empty and dimly lit all the way to the main entrance of the convent building.

"Watch out for sharp stones," Else whispered to Joel, noting his bare feet.

Joel grinned and wriggled his dusty toes. "I've walked on worse."

"Let's go." Else darted out into the courtyard, her feet scraping lightly on the hard-packed limestone gravel. Joel followed close behind. They paused when they reached the doors, pressing themselves against them and waiting for a shout of alarm from one of the guards on the wall.

The door was unlocked, so Else and Joel slipped inside, Joel looking around at the high vaulted ceilings with some interest.

"Nice place," he whispered.

"We start there," Else indicated the chapel. "That's the lab."

Else led the way, staying close to the wall, listening intently for any approaching nuns. The chapel door was locked. Else frowned at it.

"Else?" Sister Mary's voice sounded surprised. Else started a little and turned to face the woman who approached them down the wide corridor.

"Sister Mary," Else said, nodding to the floor in a faint reflection of a bow.

"Doctor Preston is quite displeased with you," Sister Mary said. Else lifted her gaze. "And as ungodly of me as it is, I do take some small pleasure in seeing her put out."

"Sorry," Else said, not knowing what else to say.

"Never mind, I'm sure the good doctor will get over it. Who is this you have brought into God's house?"

"Joel, missus," Joel said.

"And what may we do for you, Joel?"

"I'm here for some salvation, missus. I went to a Catholic school when I was a kid. Reckon it's time to meet Him again and pray."

"Bless you, child," Sister Mary said and made the sign of the cross.

"Thank you, missus," Joel said.

"The chapel is unavailable. We have a newly consecrated space at the rear of the building. You may pray there." Sister Mary indicated the way. Else and Joel remained where they were, looking like guilty schoolchildren.

"Thank you, Sister, we'll make our way there presently," Else said using her best words.

Sister Mary regarded the two of them for a moment and then swept away down the corridor.

"Can you open that door?" Joel asked.

"I don't have a key," Else replied.

"No kidding. I mean can you like, pick the lock or something?"

"We'll have a look around and see if we can find someone who can get it open for us."

Else stopped skulking in the shadows. If Sister Mary knew they were there and didn't raise the alarm, she figured maybe they would be safe.

"You wanna light this place on fire, aye?" Joel asked.

"Yeah," Else replied, listening hard for anyone else approaching.

"Well, maybe we should start with the basement. Lots of old places have basements. They keep old paint and rags down there. Fires start in places like that all the time. At least they used to. On TV and stuff."

"I don't know if the convent has a basement." Else looked up and down the corridor. "How do we find it?"

"Stairs going down? Maybe a door?" Joel started walking down the corridor, in the opposite direction that Sister Mary had left in.

"Maybe off the kitchen or something?" he asked as he went.

"Kitchen is this way." Else turned her back on Joel and headed for the kitchen. Joel came loping after her.

The kitchen was empty and quiet. Else wrinkled her nose. "What is that smell?"

Joel inhaled deeply and sighed, "Homemade bread. That's the smell of yeast rising."

They slipped into the kitchen, with its worn countertops and polished pans hanging from hooks. The first doors they tried opened on pantries stocked with hundreds of tins, jars, and packets of salvaged or harvested food.

"Man, they could feed an army on this lot," Joel said, taken aback by the quantity of food on display.

"I think that is exactly what Donna is trying to do," Else said, helping herself to a box of matches and closing the doors.

The next door was sealed with a padlock. Else ran her fingers over the hasp and then went back to search the kitchen drawers. She returned with a honing steel for sharpening knives. In shape it looked like a half-formed screwdriver, without the flat or crossed tip. Else jammed it into the wood under the hasp and levered the entire latch out of the wall.

"I thought you said you didn't have a key?" Joel teased.

Else ignored him and peered into the darkness beyond the door.

A series of stone steps went down into darkness, and the smell wafting up was more familiar to her than home baking.

"This is where we start," she whispered. "This is what we need to burn."

The way ahead was lit by caged bulbs hanging from hooks in the ceiling. The bulbs in them were dull and flickered as Joel followed Else down the stairs.

Else drew her blades and carefully separated the hanging sheets of heavy plastic at the bottom of the stairs. The chapel above was a laboratory and this chamber was a mix of charnel house and butchery.

"Jesus, what the fuck is this?" Joel's wide eyes glowed white against his dark skin.

Else stepped further into the room, passing the bins of hacked-up body parts, some covered in a pink slime, the blood spilt on the stone floor, until she reached a still form draped in plastic and laid out on an operating table.

Using the tip of her blade she lifted the plastic and peeled it back from the body on the table. The chest cavity had been dissected, the skin peeled back and clamped with clothespins. Straps at the ankles, wrists, and neck held the body to the table.

"Ohh..." Else's breath slipped out in a sigh. The face and body were her own.

She reached out and stroked the blood-spattered hair. It wasn't her. It couldn't be her. It wasn't even a perfect copy. The hair was shorter and soft like a baby's. This Else's skin was pale, missing the tan from months spent under the harsh Australian sun. The limbs were twisted, deformed, and underdeveloped. Some slight but essential genetic coding had failed during the development process. This clone was a failure.

"I'm sorry..." Else whispered, the nauseous horror looming inside her threatening to swamp everything in a tsunami of tears and vomit.

The creature's eyes opened. Her head twisted as the mouth opened slightly. The organs in the chest cavity had not been eviscerated; they pulsed with a soft squishing sound as some form of life surged through the vessels of the flayed figure that would not die.

"Maa…thaagghh…" the thing on the table gurgled.

"Shhh," Else whispered, stroking the smooth skin of her own face. "Sleep now," she said softly and straightened up. The blade in her hand came swooping down, piercing the skull through the forehead and splitting the bone. The thing on the table shuddered and then let out a long sigh as it died.

"Fucking Frankenstein shit…" Joel muttered, wiping his feet on a clear patch of stone floor.

"She's fucking them up…she's making them…monsters and then cutting them open to find out what went wrong," Else shuddered.

"Else…" Joel hissed from the other side of the room. She walked away from the dead body and pulled another plastic curtain aside to see what Joel had found.

The five incubator tanks were arranged against the far wall. Standing vertically, and over six feet tall, each tank had barely enough room to hold an adult human being. Their cylindrical glass walls and polished stainless steel gleamed in the dim light. Two of the tanks were empty; the remaining three were filled with a thick pink liquid that swirled and bubbled. Dim shapes could be seen floating in those tanks, each shape curled in a fetal position and all connected to umbilical tubes attached to their chests.

Each of the floating bodies was an insane parody of the human form. One had a head swollen with intracranial fluid until it took on an alien proportion, the limbs withered and weak by comparison. The second had grown to fill the tank, but had not developed past an early embryonic phase. It floated there like an enlarged photo of the early development of some kind of animal, unrecognizable as human or any other species.

The final failed experiment had long waving tentacles in place of arms and legs. Its face pressed against the glass. When they peered in at it, Else felt another pang of disgust and aching grief as she recognized the features of the Courier, father of her baby and savior of the world.

"Half man, half octopus…" Joel muttered, his face screwing up with disgust.

The thing in the narrow cylindrical tank retreated and then slammed its head against the glass, the toothless mouth wide open as it screamed through the swirling liquid.

Else's face was pale with shock. "This is where I came from. A tank like this, in Sydney. Hundreds of us, grown and then fed to the dead."

"That's really fucked up," Joel said.

"It ended. He saved me. The Courier. We saved the world."

"Which is exactly what I am trying to do," Donna's voice echoed around the chamber.

CHAPTER 14

E lse spun around, forcing Joel to duck under the sweep of her blade. Donna stood in the middle of the dissection room, her white coat stained with splashes of blood.

"You just don't understand the work I am doing here," Donna continued.

"I understand enough. I'm going to destroy it all. You will have to find some other way to create monsters."

Donna flicked the accusation away like an annoying fly. "Mistakes in the gene sequencing. I lack the computer power of either Woomera or the Sydney facility. What I wouldn't do for access to their supercomputers and a nuclear reactor to power the hundreds of incubation tanks it would require to perfect the process."

"You can't keep making these things from our cells. They...they don't need to live like that."

"Humanity needs to live. A stronger, purer humanity. One resistant to the virus, one with your strength, your longevity, and your antiviral blood. The Courier and you have something in your genetics, something that made the solution possible."

"I'll give you some blood. You can make your vaccine from that," Else insisted.

"I've tried that!" Donna snapped. "Christ I have fucking tried that in over a thousand experiments. Your blood is the carrier for the antiviral. I need to understand what it is about you that makes you toxic to the evols."

"*You* made me like this. Why don't you know?" Else demanded.

"We finished the work that took Haumann ten years to develop through hundreds and thousands of generations of Tankbread. If he had lived, he would have sacrificed you to the Adam and destroyed everything himself. Instead he died, taking his secrets to the grave with him."

"So, go to Sydney, go to the Opera House. Find his notes, his files, and all his research."

Donna put a hand to her head as if feeling a migraine coming on. "The small, experimental, and highly effective fission reactor they had installed as a power source under the Opera House had something of a meltdown after you passed through. The damage was slight and the radiation was mostly contained, but the lab area is completely irradiated."

"I'm going to burn all of this," Else said, sliding one of her homemade incendiaries from the rope bandolier.

"You can't!" Donna rushed forward and skidded to a halt as one of Joel's spears jabbed at her.

"I have to. You can decide if you want to burn with it or not."

"Please!" Donna tried to step around Joel's spear. He moved with her, keeping her back.

"You have no idea what you are doing!" Donna pleaded.

"I have no idea?" Else blinked. "I have…? Fuck! Joel, kill the bitch."

"What?" Joel hesitated and Donna took the opportunity to scramble for the stairs. Else put her hand on Joel's shoulder, holding him back.

"We don't have much time. Help me with these."

They found drums of chemicals and put the bottles at the base of the ones labeled "*Flammable*." Once the incendiary bombs were in place, Else sent Joel to the top of the stairs. "Make sure that door is open," she said.

When Joel called the all clear, she punched a hole in the nearest drum, lit a match, and set it to the fuses. With one last look around the room, she ran for the stairs.

With Else on his heels, Joel dashed out into the kitchen. They could hear Donna shouting, and a bell started ringing somewhere in the convent.

"How long do we have?" Joel said as they ran for the exit.

"Dunno, not lo—"

A dull *whumph* sounded deep in the belly of the convent. The floor shook and dust drifted down from the ceiling. The air rushed past them as the explosion took a deep breath. Else and Joel crashed against the outside door, tumbling into the courtyard as the basement exploded upwards, tearing through the kitchen and sending a rolling wall of flame down the corridor.

The blast washed over them and Else cringed, feeling her hair singe and the wash of heat sear her skin. The memory of the pain from the burning ship was as fresh as all her memories.

"Fuck me..." Joel said hoarsely. "I think ya used a bit much."

They stood up. The interior of the convent was flickering with an eerie orange glow. Nuns and other people started running out of the building. Some were coughing and spitting in the thick smoke, others shouting instructions and calling for water to fight the inferno engulfing the building.

As a second explosion rocked the convent, Else pulled Joel by the arm and they ran for the gate in the wall.

"Now what?" Joel shouted as they ran.

"I guess we get the others and get the fuck out of here!"

Joel nodded and kept pace with Else as they dashed through the gate and headed down the trail towards the mesh fence and the road to Mildura that lay beyond.

By the time they reached the outskirts of the town, it seemed clear that a major evol incursion was underway. The dead stood out among the ruins, the half-built structures and a few that were now on fire. The people of Mildura had survived in different communities and encampments across Australia for ten years. They knew about fighting the dead, and the shambling invasion met heavy resistance.

"Find Eric and Rache. Tell them to get our people ready to move out!" Else yelled at Joel, who nodded in response. They split up, each readying weapons to fight the zombies as they plunged into the fight. Else let her rage flow. The nauseating memory of seeing herself on Donna's dissection table, the tanks with the failed clones—these images drove her into a frenzy of killing. Howling, she cleaved the skulls of the dead who reached out to tear and bite. The dead never ceased in their mindless quest for meat, the virus in their cells driving the craving for stem cells sucked from the pure tissue of the living.

A zombie stumbled too close to the disorientating rage of a burning shed and came tottering towards Else, his ragged clothes and hair erupting in a pillar of flame. Else swung her blades, crossing them and severing the dead man's neck in two places. With a kick she knocked his body back and moved on.

Smoke clouded Else's vision as shapes loomed in the fog. Weapons ready she lunged forward, striking out and catching her swing just short of a young man's eye that went wide with terror as he saw her snarling face appear so close to his.

"Get a weapon and fight them or get the fuck out of here!» Else shouted at him. The boy nodded and scrambled away into the smoke and darkness.

Running through the streets, the screams of women caught Else's attention. A wooden building was under siege, maybe a hundred feral dead. Clawing at the doors and smashing the windows. From the inside a legion of spears, furniture, and crude weapons fought back. Else hacked her way to the front door, cutting through dead flesh, crushing skulls, ending unlives one at a time. Most of the women inside were fighting, saving their breath for the battle.

"Who's screaming?" Else yelled through a broken window.

"My sister, she's having a baby," one of the defenders called back.

"Well tell her to bite down on something. That noise is bringing the dead right to you!" Else spun away from the window as a ragged hand with broken nails tore into the back of her shirt.

"Fuckers," she hissed and buried a blade in the zombie's head. Kicking the body off the blade, she ducked under a swinging arm, rising to sever it at the shoulder, then with an upwards swing she punched her other blade through the side of the evol's head.

"Is Cassie in there?" Else yelled through the window as she fought to keep the dead away.

"I'm here!" Cassie shouted from inside.

"Keep my baby safe!" Else reminded her as the dead mob seethed and rolled down the streets of Mildura.

The buildings funneled them into one long parade that bore down on the defenders. Else stepped out into the street, people gathering behind her. They were armed with blades, machetes, axes, clubs, sticks, shovels, and a few guns. Rache stepped up beside Else. "We kill them all, right?"

Else nodded. "Kill them all." She raised her weapons high over her head and struck the steel blades together, making sparks fly against the night sky. "Kill them all!" Else yelled.

With a wordless battle cry, Rache charged towards the approaching mob. The people rushed forward, raising weapons, their shouts joining Rache's. The two groups came together in the smoke and flying cinders of a burning house that drifted over the street.

People screamed, and the evols howled. Blood sprayed, black under the dim light of the moon and stars. The survivors clubbed evols, cutting them down and fighting for their lives. The dead synapses of the evols sparked and flared, the stimulus of the noise, the fire, and the blood driving them into a frenzy. Bared teeth and clawed hands ripped at blood-filled skin as fangs met steel and the street became slick with black slime and spilt guts.

Eric appeared at the side of the advancing dead. With a calm deliberation he crouched and set an armload of duct tape–wrapped balls in a pile at his feet. Retrieving a burning stick from the nearest fire, he touched it to the wick of a softball-sized package in his hand. The fuse fizzed and sparked and he lobbed the ball into the center of the dead crowd before retrieving the next one and repeating the process.

He had just tossed his third grenade when the first one exploded: a loud bang, a flash of light, and a zipping sound cut the air as nails, screws, glass shards, and stones exploded outwards in a deadly cloud of hot shrapnel.

The bombs tore evols apart. The ones nearest the explosions disintegrated; others had limbs torn off and body parts catapulted over a wide area. The noise confused the dead, turning them from the attraction of living flesh within reach and sending them shuffling into each other as they started to mill about, disorientated by the overwhelming stimulus.

Eric bowled his last bomb underarm, sending it into the forest of zombie legs before backing away and disappearing into the smoke.

The explosives wrought destruction and chaos on the ranks of the dead. The tide of battle turned and the survivors rallied. With renewed strength and a glimpse of hope, they charged into the fray once again.

Else saw Hob wielding two axes, the rope leash he wore coiled around his neck like a necklace of shame. He slashed and killed the dead who rose up around him. The handles of both axes were black with gore, and chunks of hair and bone flew from the heads of the axes with each swing. The look on Hob's face as he destroyed the dead was a bestial grimace of uncontrolled rage and loathing. Else wondered where Anna was and hoped she was still safe.

When the sun breached the horizon, the smoke was breaking up. A bucket brigade was dousing smoldering buildings next to the bonfires of lost houses. Another group, with cloth tied across their faces, were heaving withered corpses onto the flames.

Rache and Else sat on the steps of the building where the women had sheltered. From inside came the cries of babies being cuddled and comforted by mothers and wet nurses. Else's son fussed and cried in her arms, the smoke in the air getting in his eyes and making them tear up. He had been fed and washed and was now wrapped in a clean blanket, but he remained unsettled.

"This place isn't safe either," Rache said and spat phlegm flecked with black into the dust.

"It's no safer or more dangerous than any other place," Else replied, moving the baby to her shoulder and rubbing his back.

"It's not our place. It's too far from the ocean. I need to be close to the sea. How can I be the captain of my own ship if we are in the middle of onland?" Rache frowned at the carnage and destruction.

"If I was going to have a place, I would do it differently," she continued.

"I'd like to try setting up the zombie control barriers, like on the plans we found in the church," Else said.

"Exactly, and have better food and resources and not be so far from the sea," Rache replied.

The cleanup crews on the street scattered as horses came thundering down the road. They reined in, nearly a dozen riders in all, armed with rifles, faces marked with the painted crosses of the convent disciples.

"We're looking for the woman called Else," the lead rider said.

Else stayed where she was. "I'm Else, what do you want?" she said.

"You have to come with us, you're under arrest."

"What does that mean?" Rache asked, half-rising, with a machete gripped in her hand, to defend Else.

"It means I have to go with them." Else stood up and gently handed her baby over to Rache. "I'll be back soon. Don't worry."

Stepping out into the street, she approached the lead rider. "Let's go."

A rider slid off his horse and approached her, open handcuffs cradled in his hands. "Touch me and I will kill you," Else said in a friendly, conversational tone.

The rider hesitated and looked to his leader. "You'll come quietly?" the lead rider asked.

"Yes," Else nodded.

The lead rider urged his horse forward and extended an arm down to Else. She gripped it and he swung her up into the saddle behind him. The riders turned and galloped out of Mildura, heading up the dusty road past the dying lake towards the convent of Saint Peter's Grace.

The fire set by Else and Joel had gutted the main building of the convent. Work crews were busy piling up rubbish, and others tended the injured that lay under a tarpaulin shade at one side of the courtyard.

The rider in front of Else helped her slide down before dismounting himself. With a firm grip on Else's arm and the other riders standing behind them, she was led into the shade of the tarp.

"She's here," the rider said.

Most of the wounded were burned. Some rasped and wheezed with smoke inhalation; others had suffered fractures from falling debris. It took Else a moment to recognize Donna under her bandages;

she reclined in a padded chair, one side of her face swathed in white cloth, her remaining eye glaring at Else with pure hatred.

"You fucking cunt," Donna hissed, her burnt lips making it hard to form proper words. "You have destroyed my work. You have set the program back an incalculable number of years."

"I did what I had to do," Else replied.

"That's what you think. Well I have news for you, freak. I'm going to rebuild, and I'm going to slice your skin off one sliver at a time. I'm going to dissect you and keep you alive so you can watch me do the same thing to your fucking offspring." Donna slumped back in the chair, her energy spent.

Else tensed. "You come near my son and I will kill you. Then I'll let you come back and I'll keep you on a leash and let you endure eternity as a mindless evol."

Donna laughed, a harsh sound that seemed to rip her burnt throat. "Take her away, lock her up. I'm going to enjoy hearing her scream," she croaked.

Else lashed out as the riders grabbed her arms. She felt the satisfying crunch of bone as her fist connected with someone's nose. More hands grabbed her and she snarled and kicked, grappling with her attackers and ignoring the blows that rained down on her.

Fighting for her life was all Else had ever known—against the dead, against a world that went from terrifying and confusing to senseless with each passing season. She struck out with her boots, hearing the screams of someone whose knee dislocated under her kick. More riders piled on, punching her belly, face, and head. They held her down and someone kicked her hard across the face. Blood gushed from her nose and the taste of hot copper almost choked her.

Struggling against the vicious melee, even as her body was pinned down, Else screamed as a blade passed through the tangle of arms and pressed into her side. The white-hot pain flared through her body.

"Stop!" a woman's voice rang out. The riders hesitated and slowly withdrew into a circle around Else, who clutched her wounded side and made it to her knees before vomiting blood on the ground.

"What is the meaning of this?" Sister Mary strode through the ring of people. She stopped in front of Else, gently sinking down on one knee and pressing her hand against the spreading bloodstain on the woman's shirt.

"Stay out of this, Sister," Donna rasped from her seat.

"I asked, what is the meaning of this?" Sister Mary repeated.

"She burned the convent, she destroyed my research. She's going to pay," Donna rasped.

"Your abominable work was destroyed because it was God's will that it be destroyed. You shall not raise a hand against his will." Sister Mary helped Else to her feet. Her left eye was swelling shut, and blood dripped from cuts and abrasions on her face.

"His will?" Donna crawled out of the chair, standing and brushing aside the hands that tried to help her. "Your fucking ideas are insane. You would all die without me."

"No, we would survive because God wills it," Sister Mary said. "Your meddling with the Lord's creation is what has brought his wrath down upon this place. There will be no more experiments. No more monstrosities in God's house."

"You have got to be fucking kidding me," Donna snarled. Else could see months of friction and growing tension between the scientist and the devout leader of the convent reaching an explosive point.

"You are forgiven, for that is God's mercy," Sister Mary declared. "You should use your God-given talents to help shape and guide us to a successful future. You shall not do the devil's work with your foul experiments!"

Donna screamed in rage and ripped the bandages off her face. Her right eye had burned away, along with a good chunk of her scalp that now oozed yellow plasma.

"You think your God did this to me!?" the scientist screamed. "This cunt, right here! She did this!"

"Else is God's child; his rod and his staff. She has achieved so much in her short life. All of it with the Lord's blessing and you shall not harm her." Sister Mary's voice remained level, but her tone was stone cold.

"You can't take her away from me!" Donna screamed as Sister Mary supported Else and helped her limp towards the gate. "I'm going to use her to save the fucking world!"

Else stopped and twisted in Sister Mary's arms. "No," she said through a split lip and bloody teeth. "You're never going to see me again. You will have to find some other way to make your soldiers. I'm going to leave and find a place to live and raise my son. We may have to fight and maybe we'll suffer. But we sure as hell won't let anyone like you use us as a fucking science experiment. Never again."

Else started hobbling away again. The crowd parted and let Sister Mary help her through. Outside the walls two women came forward and helped Else climb into the back of a horse-drawn wagon.

"Take her back to Mildura, see she is given medical aid, and no one harms her," Sister Mary instructed the women who climbed up and took the reins.

Else squeezed Sister Mary's hand. "Sister, I'm sorry I said your beliefs were stupid. I don't believe like you do, but I can see how your faith makes you strong."

"God watches over all his children," Sister Mary said, a smile crinkling the corners of her mouth, "even the ones who deny his existence."

Else sank back on the wagon floor, her skin already starting to burn and itch as her cells repaired the damage.

CHAPTER 15

Water trickled into Else's mouth, waking her with a start, her hand snapping out to grab at the half-seen shape nearby.

"Whoa!" Eric said, tumbling off his chair. "You must've been fuckin' hard on alarm clocks."

Else blinked. Rache was rising from a mattress on the floor and stretching sleepily. Hob was crouched near the door, and he gently reached out and shook a blanket-draped Anna, who lay sleeping next to him, the cord of his leash gripped in her hand.

Cassie came forward, Lowanna and Else's baby filling her arms and sleeping soundly in spite of the sudden noise.

"How long did I sleep for?" Else asked, her hand scratching at the dressing under her shirt where the skin itched.

"All day and all night," Rache said. "We were worried about you, thought you might have gone into an unconscious or something."

"You mean a coma. But I told you she was just sleeping," Hob muttered, his gaze set on the floor.

"You did good," Anna said, without any tone of praise or warmth in her voice.

"Baby," Else said, sitting up and extending her arms. Cassie transferred him and moved Lowanna to a more comfortable position.

"He's getting so big," Cassie said. "Going to be a strong man, that one."

Else nodded, reacquainting herself with every curve and pore of the baby's face.

"People are leaving," Eric said. "They reckon it's not safe here. Dead are turning up, following the stink of the others or something, some reckon."

"We are leaving too," Else said, looking up and meeting the gaze of everyone except Hob in turn.

"We're going west? Towards the ocean?" Rache said hopefully.

"No, back the way we came, north and east. Up the coast, in Queensland, we can build ourselves a community there in the bush. Plenty of trees for building, lots of food for hunting, and it's close to the ocean, so people can fish and Rache can find a boat to be the captain of."

"I dunno about these buggers, but I've followed you this far and it ain't killed me yet," Eric said. "Reckon I can follow you a bit further."

The others nodded in agreement. "Right you lot, we've got some organizing to do," Rache said. "Get the word out we're going to a safer place. Any who want to come with us can do it. Get vehicles, weapons, horses, anything you can to help ship supplies and kids."

"I'll go and tell our people you are okay," Cassie said. "They will come with us, and I reckon most of them living here might want to start somewhere new too."

Else sat in the shaded gloom of the shelter, her baby sleeping in her arms, only looking up when a shadow fell over her.

"Hey missus," Joel said, one foot resting against his knees in a figure 4 stance. "I hear you lot are going on a walkabout?"

"Hey Joel. Yeah, we're going back to Queensland. It's a long way, but everyone agrees that we might have a better chance up there."

Joel nodded. "Reckon I could show you lot a faster way, avoid them roads and shit and get there a bit quicker, aye?"

"And Billy and Sally and your people?" Else asked. "They will come too?"

"Sure, they're keen to keep moving. We'll see you safe back to your house in the bush."

In the end, less than half the Mildura residents chose to join the convoy, swelling their numbers to nearly five hundred. They crossed the river, with an armed party fighting the few remaining evols and clearing a path along the dusty highway for them to take their first steps on the long journey towards a place that finally they could call home.

The sun rose in a fire of orange and red that turned the sea to gold and painted the sky in broad strokes of color, from the dark purple of a bruise to the healthy pink of a laughing baby's cheeks as the sun rose through an oncoming front of heavy rain cloud.

Else sat in the sand and cradled her son as he nursed at her breast. Behind her the people were preparing for the last leg of the journey to a new place they would call home. She thought she might not see the ocean again for a while. Although, she thought, maybe, just maybe, she could live long enough to see the lands across the oceans. Those painted places of the maps and atlases she had studied.

Did the dead rule over the living in the Americas, Europe, Africa, or Asia? Else watched the waves and hissing against the golden sand of the beach and decided there would be plenty of time to find out. For now, she had work to do.

Her son grizzled and twisted against the warmth of her skin. Lifting him free of the sling, she held him up to the last rays of sunlight and told him his name.

ABOUT THE AUTHOR

Paul Mannering is an award-winning writer living in Wellington, New Zealand. Paul has published dozens of short stories and radio plays in a range of genres across many different international markets. In 2007 he co-founded BrokenSea Audio Productions, which podcasts free audio drama each week to an audience of millions. Paul lives with his wife Damaris and their two cats.

KING ARTHUR AND THE KNIGHTS OF THE ROUND TABLE HAVE BEEN REBORN TO SAVE THE WORLD FROM THE CLUTCHES OF MORGANA WHILE SHE PROPELS OUR MODERN WORLD INTO THE MIDDLE AGES.

EAN 9781618685018 $15.99   EAN 9781682611562 $15.99

Morgana's first attack came in a red fog that wiped out all modern technology. The entire planet was pushed back into the middle ages. The world descended into chaos.

But hope is not yet lost— King Arthur, Merlin, and the Knights of the Round Table have been reborn.

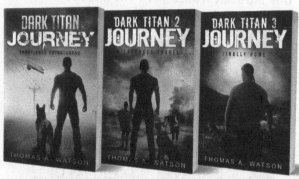

THE MORNINGSTAR STRAIN HAS BEEN LET LOOSE—IS THERE ANY WAY TO STOP IT?

EAN 9781618686497 $16.00

An industrial accident unleashes some of the Morningstar Strain. The doctor who discovered the strain and her assistant will have to fight their way through Sprinters and Shamblers to save themselves, the vaccine, and the base. Then they discover that it wasn't an accident at all—somebody inside the facility did it on purpose. The war with the RSA and the infected is far from over.

This is the fourth book in Z.A. Recht's The Morningstar Strain series, written by Brad Munson.

PERMUTED
PRESS